‖‖‖ ‖‖‖‖‖ ‖‖ ‖ ‖‖‖‖‖‖ ‖‖‖‖ ‖‖‖‖‖‖‖‖ ‖‖‖ ‖‖‖

W9-ASW-496

"Do you know what caused your uncle's death, Janice?"

Lance's voice seemed troubled, and she glanced quickly toward him. "No."

Taking a deep breath, Lance said, "He committed suicide at Mountjoy. There was some talk that he was murdered, but it looked more like suicide. The police department searched around a while, but they couldn't prove anything."

Janice's optimism about her inheritance crashed. "My dad didn't talk much about his family, but I've heard him say that someone in each generation of Reids died a tragic death."

"Yes, that story goes around." He hesitated, but Janice had to be warned. "It isn't just *any* Reid, but the owner of this house."

Her eyes widened. "If that's the case, then I might be the next victim."

Books by Irene Brand

Love Inspired

Child of Her Heart #19
Heiress #37
To Love and Honor #49
*A Groom To Come
   Home To* #70
Tender Love #95
The Test of Love #114

Autumn's Awakening #129
Summer's Promise #148
*Love at Last #190
*Song of Her Heart #200
*The Christmas Children #234
*Second Chance at Love #244
*Listen to Your Heart #280

Love Inspired Suspense

Yuletide Peril #12

*The Mellow Years

IRENE BRAND

Writing has been a lifelong interest of this author, who says that she started her first novel when she was eleven years old and hasn't finished it yet. However, since 1984 she's published thirty-two contemporary and historical novels and three nonfiction titles. She started writing professionally in 1977 after she completed her master's degree in history at Marshall University. Irene taught in secondary public schools for twenty-three years, but retired in 1989 to devote herself to writing.

Consistent involvement in the activities of her local church has been a source of inspiration for Irene's work. Traveling with her husband, Rod, to all fifty states, and to thirty-two foreign countries has also inspired her writing. Irene is grateful to the many readers who have written to say that her inspiring stories and compelling portrayals of characters with strong faith have made a positive impression on their lives. You can write to her at P.O. Box 2770, Southside, WV 25187 or visit her Web site at www.irenebrand.com.

YULETIDE PERIL

IRENE BRAND

Steeple
Hill®

Published by Steeple Hill Books™

If you purchased this book without a cover you should be aware
that this book is stolen property. It was reported as "unsold and
destroyed" to the publisher, and neither the author nor the
publisher has received any payment for this "stripped book."

STEEPLE HILL BOOKS

Steeple
Hill®

ISBN 0-373-44228-9

YULETIDE PERIL

Copyright © 2005 by Irene B. Brand

All rights reserved. Except for use in any review, the reproduction
or utilization of this work in whole or in part in any form by any
electronic, mechanical or other means, now known or hereafter
invented, including xerography, photocopying and recording, or in
any information storage or retrieval system, is forbidden without
the written permission of the editorial office, Steeple Hill Books,
233 Broadway, New York, NY 10279 U.S.A.

All characters in this book have no existence outside the imagination of
the author and have no relation whatsoever to anyone bearing the same
name or names. They are not even distantly inspired by any individual
known or unknown to the author, and all incidents are pure invention.

This edition published by arrangement with Steeple Hill Books.

® and TM are trademarks of Steeple Hill Books, used under license.
Trademarks indicated with ® are registered in the United States Patent
and Trademark Office, the Canadian Trade Marks Office and in other
countries.

www.SteepleHill.com

Printed in U.S.A.

For God did not give us a spirit of timidity, but a spirit of power, of love and of self-discipline.
—*II Timothy* 1:7

Thanks to Lieutenant Carl Peterson, Mason County Sheriff's Office, for providing information about meth labs and other illegal drugs.

Prologue

The summer storm reached the old house as the fourth member of the gang stepped up on the porch. A clap of thunder, as loud as a mortar blast, rumbled across the metal roof. A bolt of lightning sliced the skies and struck a spruce tree, toppling half of the tree on the roof of the house. The man jumped as if he'd been shot and scuttled inside like a scared rabbit.

Another streak of lightning revealed three other men lounging on the dilapidated furniture. One of them laughed uproariously. "I believe the old house is getting to you, boss. We'd better can some of this noise—it's better than what we've been using to scare people away."

Rain blew in the broken windows soaking the ragged carpet, and the intermittent lightning revealed a room that at one time had been elegantly furnished. But time and the elements had taken a toll on the old house—its grandeur was a thing of the past.

Ignoring the comment, the newcomer took off his hat and shook the water from it. "We'll have to suspend operations for a few days. The big heiress is coming to town. I don't think she'll visit the house, but just in case, be sure that everything is hidden. We don't want any evidence that we've been using the house in case she gets nosy."

"You say she ain't apt to be around long," the man who'd first spoken commented.

"Chances are she'll pocket her money and leave without causing any trouble," the leader of the group said.

"Don't give me that baloney, man. I've been shadowing her for a month, and she strikes me as a stubborn woman who won't be easy to scare. You'd better let me get rid of her."

"No," the leader said in a tone that brooked no argument. "We've got a good thing going here, and I won't ruin it. If we kill the woman, we'll have cops all over the place. Murder is not an option, for now, at least."

Chapter One

Stanton was a step above her hometown of Willow Creek, but that still didn't say much for the town where Janice Reid intended to make her home. Her primary reason for coming to Stanton was to meet with the lawyer who'd handled her uncle's estate. As she braked at the town limits and drove slowly into Stanton, Janice focused her attention on the street in front of her, because she'd only had her driver's license four weeks.

Brooke, her eleven-year-old sister, perched on the edge of the seat and watched for the office of Loren Santrock. Brooke located all of the fast-food restaurants, but she didn't spot the lawyer's office as they drove through the town.

Glancing at the fuel gauge of the car, Janice said, "Let's stop for gas, then we'll look for Mr. Santrock's office again." She pulled off the street, stopped by the pumps of a convenience store and took a deep breath, thankful that they'd made a safe journey. She didn't have much confidence in her driving ability.

"What do you think of the town?" Janice asked Brooke. With a pensive glance at her sister, she added, "Does it look like a good place to live?"

"Oh, it's okay. I don't care where we live as long as we can finally be together."

Janice's throat tightened and tears stung her eyes. Brooke was only ten years younger than Janice, but she felt almost like her mother. She'd had the primary care of her sister until their parents were sent to prison when Janice was fourteen. Brooke was placed in a foster home and Janice had been sent to the Valley of Hope, a residential facility for children with a variety of problems. Janice had been allowed weekly visits with her sister, but the years before Janice could be Brooke's legal guardian had passed slowly for both of them.

Janice leaned over and kissed Brooke's cheek before she got out of the car. "We'll be together from now on—that's a promise."

She took a credit card from her purse, stepped out of the car and flexed her muscles. Unaccustomed to buying gas, Janice carefully read the instructions on the pump before she inserted the credit card and punched the appropriate tabs.

While the tank filled, Brooke tried to make friends with a scrawny black Labrador that was standing on its hind legs, eating food from a trash can beside the store.

"Hey, Brooke! Don't bother the dog. He might bite you."

"He looks hungry. Is it okay if I give him one of our peanut butter and jelly sandwiches?"

"As long as you put it on the ground and let him pick it up. Don't try to feed him. You don't know if he has any diseases or fleas."

Janice watched her sister while she waited for the receipt to print. Brooke took a sandwich from a plastic bag, unwrapped it and laid it a couple of feet from the dog. He seized the food, ran across the street and disappeared behind a residence.

"Look at him run!" Brooke said, laughing. "He must be awful hungry."

"Wait in the car for me," Janice called as she glanced over her shoulder at Brooke and started into the store. "I'll ask for directions to the lawyer's office."

Brooke's brown eyes widened. "Look out!"

Janice swung quickly toward the store just as a tall tawny-haired man opened the door and bumped into her. Janice staggered backward. The man's strong arm suddenly wrapped around her waist and kept her from falling.

"That was a close call," he said sternly. As if reprimanding a child, he added, "You should look where you're going."

Janice's face flamed. Although she knew the man was right, she motioned toward her sister and quipped, "I preferred looking at what was behind me, rather than what was in front of me."

Realizing that she was still in his embrace, Janice squirmed free, as with a pleasing grin, the man said, "Touché. Thanks for reminding me *I* wasn't being careful, either."

Janice lowered her gaze, deeply humiliated and irritated that she'd given way to one of her failings—a tendency to lash out at people when they criticized her. That wasn't the way to start life in a new town.

"That was rude of me. Thanks for saving me from a fall. I should have been more alert." Taking a deep unsteady breath, she stepped away from him.

The man's short, wavy hair flowed backward from his high forehead, and his warm dark blue eyes clung to her heavily lashed green ones for a moment. His face reddened slightly, and he said, "No problem." He strode purposely toward a black van parked at one of the pumps.

It took a lot to fluster Janice, but she realized that her pulse was racing. Surely it must be from the near fall, rather than the thrill she'd experienced when the man had embraced her. She hurried back to the car, slid behind the wheel and started the engine.

"Did you learn where to find the lawyer?" Brooke asked.

With a start, Janice remembered her reason for going into the store. "Oh, after I almost fell, I forgot about it. But Stanton is a small town. We'll find his office."

Traffic wasn't heavy, and Janice drove slowly along Main Street, hoping to spot Santrock's office. When they didn't locate it, she said, "Let's get out and walk. Since Stanton's downtown area covers only a few blocks, it should be easy to find."

She pulled into a diagonal parking space and fed the meter. They went into a drugstore and the clerk gave them directions to the lawyer's office.

Brooke took Janice's hand as they walked to his office, one block west of Main Street. Janice squeezed her sister's hand, wondering how apprehensive Brooke was about their move. But if they didn't like Stanton, she could sell the property she'd inherited from her uncle and return to Willow Creek. Despite their sordid family background, they'd been accepted there. People in Stanton might not be as understanding.

Janice hadn't doubted her decision to move to Stanton until a few weeks ago when she'd read a letter from the uncle who'd willed his estate to her. A few of his words had seared her memory and they were foremost in her mind today.

I've recently become aware of some mysterious happenings at Mountjoy, but I intend to find out what's going on. I pray that I haven't saddled you with more trouble than you needed.

Santrock's office was on the second floor of an old, two-story brick building, but his reception room was impressive. When her feet sunk into the thick gray carpet, Janice had the sensation of walking on a bed of woodland moss. The windows were dressed with long, heavy maroon draperies. A semicircular arrangement of wood veneer furniture, finished in cherry, dominated the room. The desktop held the very latest in computer equipment, including extralarge flat-screen monitors.

The middle-aged receptionist turned from her computer to welcome Janice and Brooke with a smile. The woman's black suit obviously hadn't come off the bargain racks where Janice bought her clothes. She felt ill at ease in such affluence.

"I'm Dot Banner," the receptionist said. "What can I do for you today?"

"I'm Janice Reid. I have an appointment with Mr. Santrock."

A somber look replaced the woman's smile. "Mr. Santrock couldn't be in the office today, and we didn't know how to reach you. Did you come far?"

Irritated at this turn of events, Janice said bluntly, "Yes, I did. It's a four-hour drive from Willow Creek, and I have to return in time for work tomorrow morning. This really puts me in a bind."

Gesturing helplessly with her hand, the receptionist said, "I'm sorry."

"I'm sorry, too," Janice replied, her irritation evident in the tone of her voice. "I made this appointment two weeks ago to discuss my inheritance. Now that I'm twenty-one, Mr. Santrock said he'd have the papers ready to transfer the property and bank accounts to me today."

"The papers *are* ready, but you'll have to see Mr. Santrock to finalize everything."

Discouraged at this delay, Janice sat down uninvited in one of the upholstered guest chairs and motioned Brooke to another one. "I have to return to Willow Creek tonight, so I'll call in a few days to make another appointment. I would like to see the house though. If you'll give me the key, I'll take a look at it."

"I have no authority to give a key to you. You'll have to see Mr. Santrock. He's a stickler on seeing that everything is done legally."

Janice had the feeling that she was being given the run-around and she couldn't imagine why. Her uncle had died three years ago. Santrock had had ample time to know when she'd take control of the property. If he couldn't be in his office today, he should have contacted her.

"I don't suppose I'll break any law if I *look* at the property," Janice said tersely. "Surely your boss won't mind if you tell me where to find the house."

"Oh, you won't have any trouble finding the Reid property," the receptionist said smoothly, apparently choosing to ignore Janice's sarcasm. "It's the last house on the right side of the highway as you leave the city limits. If you see a sign that says, 'Leaving Stanton,' you've gone too far."

As they left Santrock's office, Janice reasoned that with the setbacks she'd had in her life she shouldn't be surprised that this venture had fizzled out. When they reached the street, the scent of food from a nearby restaurant reminded Janice that she was hungry.

"How about some lunch?" she asked.

"Yeah!" Brooke gave Janice a thumbs-up, and her brown eyes shone with merriment. They walked across the street to Brooke's favorite chain restaurant.

Brooke ordered her usual hamburger, fries and glass of milk. Janice chose an Oriental fruit and vegetable salad and iced tea.

As they ate, Brooke talked excitedly about having their own home. "Wonder if we can have a big, big Christmas tree? And outside decorations, too?" she added hopefully.

"Since it will be the first time in our own home, I think we can afford to celebrate," Janice agreed, before she added cautiously, "but I can't promise until I know exactly how much money I've inherited. Our uncle was very cautious—he left matters in the hands of his lawyers until he assumed I'd be old enough to handle money."

Since Christmas seemed to be a high priority with Brooke, Janice intended to have a good holiday season to make up for all the ones they'd both missed as children.

After living from hand to mouth most of her childhood, Janice had dreamed of having a home of her own. Since she'd heard that John Reid had remembered her in his will, Janice had been anticipating living under her own roof. She'd nightly thanked God that her bachelor uncle had chosen her to inherit his estate. The legacy included the Reid family home and several thousand dollars, but she didn't know the exact amount. Any amount would seem like a fortune to Janice, who'd always had to save up for everything she'd had. She thought that her life had taken a turn for the better when she inherited her uncle's property.

Following Dot Banner's directions, Janice rounded a curve in the road and had the first look at her house, situated on a hill about a quarter of a mile from the highway. Although stunned into disbelief, she was alert enough to glance in the rearview mirror before she slammed on the brakes and pulled off the highway. Her dream had suddenly turned into a nightmare.

"Is this it?" Brooke asked, blinking with disappointment.

"I'm afraid so," Janice said. "There's the sign Miss Banner mentioned, and this is the last house on the right. Besides, I've seen a picture of the place. This is it."

The Reid home, Mountjoy, the same name as the family's ancestral home in England, was a two-story frame house with an upstairs balcony on the front of the building. Untrimmed rhododendron and laurel bushes, as well as a tall evergreen hedge, obscured the first floor.

At one time the weatherboarding had been white, but the paint had peeled off, leaving it a dingy gray. Some of the windows were broken and strips of curtains dangled through the holes. Weather-beaten green shutters hung askew. Janice assumed that the first floor looked as bad as the rest of the house.

"Can we live here?" Brooke asked in a frightened voice.

"Not right away. I can see why the receptionist was amused when I asked for a key. It will take a bulldozer to clear a path through that wilderness so we can reach the house."

Janice's great-grandfather had built this house in the late nineteenth century with money earned from the coal industry. He had accumulated vast wealth, and his sons and grandsons had squandered most of his fortune, but Janice had no idea that the family home had fallen into such disrepair. John Reid, their uncle, had lived in a house in Stanton for several years prior to his death. From the looks of things, nothing had been done to the property since he'd moved to town.

Not only was Janice disappointed in her legacy, but as she glanced around the property, a flutter of apprehension played a staccato rhythm up and down her spine. She'd experienced plenty of fear when she'd lived in her parents' home, but after she'd landed in the sheltering arms of VOH, she'd had no reason to be afraid. So what had caused her sudden jolt of terror? A shock so powerful that Janice wondered if she should forget about moving to Stanton and return to Willow Creek where she still had a job, as well as friends and acquaintances. Cutting ties with the past might not be the sensible thing to do. Should she ask Mr. Santrock to sell this property and transfer all the assets to her banking account in Willow Creek?

But during the uncertain years of her childhood, Janice had developed a hardness of spirit and self-reliance that had kept her going when most girls her age would have given up. After she'd survived long days and nights alone as Brooke's only caregiver, to preserve her own sanity, Janice had learned to overcome her fear.

She put the car in gear and moved forward until she found a place to turn around. Brooke huddled beside her, a fearful expression on her face. Janice had thought that relocation would be good for Brooke, as well as for herself, but now she was uncertain about her decision.

Trying to put on a cheerful face for her sister, Janice said enthusiastically, "Let's stop by the school and see if you can register today. You'll enjoy coming to a new school."

"But if we don't have a house to live in, how can we move here?" Brooke asked in a voice barely above a whisper.

"I don't have an answer to your question now. But I've been planning for months to start a new life in this town, and I *will not* willingly give up my plans."

Eventually, she might have to return to Willow Creek, but not without checking her options. Janice wondered if her alternative idea of selling Mountjoy and buying another house in Stanton would be feasible. She doubted that the property would bring a good price in its present condition. Janice slowed the car to take another look as they drove past her legacy on the way into town.

"Looks like a haunted house to me," Brooke observed.

A chill tingled along Janice's spine again, for the same

thought had occurred to her. She sensed that Mountjoy spelled trouble for her. Did danger lurk behind the thick undergrowth?

Her father's visits to the family home had been infrequent, and after he became an adult, he never spent a night in the house. He avoided the place because, in every generation, a Reid had died a tragic death at Mountjoy. Would she be the Reid to die in the present generation? Annoyed at the thought, Janice questioned what had happened to her common sense. Again she remembered her uncle's letter and his comment about mysterious happenings at Mountjoy.

During the four years she'd spent at the Valley of Hope, Janice had learned a lot about the Bible. Miss Caroline Renault, the director of the facility, had emphasized the necessity of memorizing Scripture verses. When she was especially troubled, Janice always reached into her storehouse of Scripture verses for a spiritual truth that encouraged her to carry on.

Glancing at Brooke's woebegone face, fear again threatened to overwhelm Janice. Searching frantically for an antidote to combat this fear, Janice dipped into her memory bank.

"Brooke, Miss Caroline always said that the Bible can help us work out our problems. Let's think of some Bible verses to encourage us to face the future with hope."

Brooke sniffled and blew her nose with a pink tissue that she took from the pocket of her brown shorts. "I don't know many verses 'cept the Lord's Prayer and the Twenty-third psalm."

"That psalm has a lot of encouraging words. Can you think of one verse to say over and over when you're scared?"

"'The Lord is my shepherd, I shall not want.'"

"That's a good one," Janice said. "The one I'm thinking about is from the New Testament. The apostle Paul encouraged his young friend, Timothy, by saying, 'God has not given us the spirit of fear; but of power; and of love, and of a sound mind.' We won't let that old dilapidated house scare us. Let's think about how it looked a hundred years ago."

"In that picture you have?"

"Yes. Maybe we can make it that way again."

With a wistful sigh, Brooke said, "I *do* want a home of our own. I'm always afraid I'll have to live with Dad and Mom again."

Janice winced when Brooke expressed the fear that had worried her until she turned eighteen. "I'm your legal guardian now, and wherever I am, you're going to be with me," she said firmly.

"I don't suppose they'd want me anyway."

Hatred, so acute it almost choked her, surged through Janice. Her feelings about her parents had been one barrier she couldn't overcome to maintain a satisfying Christian outlook. She couldn't forgive her parents for the way they'd neglected Brooke and her. Leroy and Florence Reid were addicted to drugs and alcohol, and they spent most of their time in bars. Even when they were at home, they lolled around in drunken stupors. Most of their money was spent on alcohol, not food for their children.

She could have stood it for herself, but when it became clear even to her young eyes that Brooke was in danger of becoming malnourished, Janice had started hoarding away money taken from her parents' wallets for food. She'd been successful in keeping them alive for six months before her parents were arrested and convicted of robbing a convenience store. They'd been sent to prison for ten years, with the possibility of parole after seven. Brooke had become a ward of the Department of Health and Human Services when Janice had been sent to the Valley of Hope.

Suddenly it dawned on Janice that it was almost time for her parents to be paroled. Even if they hadn't contacted their daughters while they were in prison, if her father found out that she'd inherited his brother's estate, he'd try to take the money away from her. She wished now that she'd been more secretive about where she was moving.

The compassion of Miss Caroline and the other staff members at VOH had compensated somewhat for the physical misery of Janice's first fourteen years. But her parents' neglect gnawed at Janice's spirit every day, and she didn't think she could ever forgive them. Even when she'd prayed the Lord's Prayer in chapel services, she had always remained silent when they came to the phrase, "Forgive us our debts as we forgive our debtors."

Her unwillingness to forgive had always stood between Janice and a satisfactory relationship with God. She believed that Jesus had died for her sins and she'd accepted Him as her Savior. But could she ever claim Him as Lord of her life until she humbled herself and forgave her parents?

Chapter Two

The one-story, rambling elementary school, with a redbrick and stone exterior, was a relatively new structure. Janice halted the car beside a man who was sweeping the sidewalk in front of the school, and rolled down the car's window.

"Are any of the school officials in today?" she asked.

"Yes, ma'am," he said. "The principal and the guidance counselor are here, and a secretary."

"Good. Where should I park?"

He motioned to the front of the building. "Right here beside the school is okay," he said. "There ain't much traffic today." With a chuckle, he added, "But wait 'til school starts—we'll have plenty of cars around here then."

"Thanks."

The man waved a friendly hand and continued sweeping as she and Brooke got out of the car and entered the building through a set of double doors. They faced a long hallway with other corridors to the left and right. An arrow on the wall, labeled "Office," pointed to the right.

"I'm scared," Brooke said, her steps lagging.

Janice was uneasy about their situation, too, and she muttered, "'God has not given us the spirit of fear; but of power.'"

She straightened her back, took Brooke's hand and headed resolutely toward the office. Her shaky self-assurance suffered an immediate setback when she turned the corner and narrowly missed colliding with the same man she'd bumped into at the convenience store earlier in the day.

Lance Gordon couldn't believe his eyes. He couldn't be encountering this young woman twice in the same day! Normally, he wouldn't have given the previous incident a second thought, but this woman's long-lashed green eyes and stubborn chin had flashed frequently into his mind as he'd continued his daily schedule. Assuming that she was just a stranger passing through town, he was surprised at his low spirits when he thought he wouldn't see her again.

"So we meet again," he said, a wide grin spreading across his face.

"But at least this meeting wasn't as dramatic as the one this morning," Janice said, trying to match his light tone.

Lance glanced from Janice to Brooke, noticing the resemblance in their features.

"What can I do for you?" he asked.

"I want to enroll my sister in school."

Lance's heart skipped a beat and he sensed a rush of pleasure to know that meeting this woman hadn't been transitory. His eagerness to get acquainted with her surprised him.

"The guidance counselor is the one to see, but she's busy with another family right now," he said. "Come into my office. I'll take down some of your personal information, and she'll schedule your classes later on in the week."

He motioned them to the door tagged with a principal's sign.

"You're the principal?" Janice asked as she walked through

the door he held open for them. He seemed very young to be the administrator of a school.

"Yes. I'm Lance Gordon."

"My name is Janice Reid, and this is my sister, Brooke. She'll be entering the sixth grade."

Janice apparently wasn't married since she had the same name as her sister, Lance thought as he pulled out two chairs from a conference table in his office. And what difference does that make? he demanded of his inner self, looking surreptitiously at her left hand, which didn't have a ring of any kind. After Brooke and Janice were seated, he took a chair opposite them and picked up a yellow pad that was on the table.

"Are you living in Stanton or in the rural area of the county?"

"Does it matter?"

He looked at her questioningly. "Not at all, as far as attending school here. We serve the whole county, but I wanted to know if she'd travel by bus."

"I don't know. When I bumped into you this morning, literally speaking, that was the first time I'd ever set foot in Stanton. I don't know anything about the area."

"Where are you going to live?"

"I don't know that, either," she said, with a glance at Brooke.

Momentarily, Lance wondered if he had a homeless family on his hands. But, with the spirit of independence that hovered around Janice Reid like an aura, she didn't resemble any homeless person he'd ever known. Besides, both Janice and her sister were well-dressed, and if he remembered correctly, the sedan she'd been driving this morning was only two or three years old.

A slight tap on the door interrupted them, and a child

peeped into the room. "I wanted to see if you were busy, Uncle Lance. I guess you are."

"Come on in, Taylor," he said, "and meet a new student, who'll be in your grade this term."

The sandy-haired girl with blue eyes stepped to her uncle's side.

"Brooke, this is my niece, Taylor Mallory. She's entering the sixth grade, too. Brooke Reid and her sister Janice are moving to Stanton. How about giving Brooke a tour of the building while her sister and I complete her enrollment?"

Taylor clapped her hands, and it was evident that she was an enthusiastic child, a perfect foil for Brooke's quiet, meek nature. "That will be big fun. Come on, Brooke. This is a great school, but we're going to have a tough teacher."

Taylor's chattering continued as the two children left. Janice was pleased to have the opportunity to talk without Brooke in the room.

"Why are you reluctant to tell me where you're living?" Lance asked, interrupting her musings.

"I don't know where I'll live," she said. "And if I tell you where I *thought* I'd be living, you'll laugh."

"Try me," he said, a compelling expression in his piercing blue eyes.

"I've inherited the Reid property on the outskirts of town. I'd intended to live there until I saw it for the first time today."

Instead of being amused, Lance was momentarily appalled that Janice was related to the local—and infamous—Reid family. He could understand why Janice was disappointed about the house's condition, because after John Reid's death, the house had deteriorated rapidly. It seemed strange that no one had informed Janice about the condition of her property.

"So you're John Reid's niece?"

"Yes, but it was a surprise when he remembered me in his will. My father is the black sheep of the family, and he's had nothing to do with the Reids for years. I haven't seen any of them since I was a child."

John Reid was a respectable member of the community, but most of the Reid family did have a poor reputation. John had prospered, but Lance supposed that his long illness had depleted his finances. Janice's inheritance probably wasn't a large one.

"I couldn't inherit until I was twenty-one," Janice continued. "I've only had a car for a few weeks, so I hadn't looked over my legacy until an hour ago. As you can imagine, I had quite a surprise."

"When I was a child, it was a nice house, but I don't suppose it's fit to live in now."

"I'm not giving up on that idea until I see the inside of the place. I had an appointment to see Mr. Santrock, the lawyer, this morning, but he won't be in his office today. His secretary wouldn't let me have the key to the house."

"But I…" Lance started and paused. On his way to work this morning, he'd seen Santrock walking along Main Street. But perhaps he shouldn't tell Janice—the lawyer may have had a good reason for not keeping the appointment. Maybe something unexpected had come up after he'd seen him.

Janice looked at him curiously, but when he didn't continue, she said, "I've quit my job, and I intend to live somewhere in Stanton. What do you need to know about Brooke? I'll have her school records transferred as soon as we go back home."

"Her age?" Lance asked

"Eleven."

"Where has she attended school?"

"The elementary school in Willow Creek. I'm Brooke's guardian."

Janice seemed young to be the guardian of her sister. Lance wondered if their parents were dead.

"We can probably find everything we need to know from her records when they arrive."

"I'll have them transferred right away. When does school start?"

"August twenty-fifth."

"That will give me more than a week to finish my work and move. I noticed there's a motel where we can stay for a few days until I settle on something."

Glancing through the window behind Lance, Janice saw Brooke and Taylor shooting baskets on the playground, and she felt compelled to confide in him. She wouldn't start a new life by concealing the ugly things in her past.

"Thanks for not asking questions, but there are things about us that you should know, things you won't find in Brooke's records."

Janice's mouth was tight and grim and her long-lashed green eyes smoldered with bitterness. Still staring out the window, she explained. "The reason I'm Brooke's guardian is because our parents are in prison. They've been alcoholics and drug addicts as long as I can remember. They illegally traded their welfare benefits for money whenever they could. When their welfare payments stopped because they wouldn't work, they started stealing to support their addictions."

Janice paused and closed her eyes. Those days were a nightmare she wished she could forget.

"They were caught robbing a convenience store and sent to prison. Brooke was placed in a foster home and I was sent to the Valley of Hope." She looked directly at him. "Do you know what kind of place that is?"

Lance had heard of the Valley of Hope, a reputable institution that ministered to at-risk children and teenagers. He couldn't envision Janice Reid as an at-risk teenager. At a loss to know how to comment, Lance said, "Yes."

"I was fourteen and Brooke was four when that happened. I left VOH when I graduated from high school, got a job and saved enough money to prove I can support my sister. Uncle John's legacy also helped to convince the Department of Health and Human Services that I'm a fit guardian."

Janice's hands moved restlessly and she clenched them in her lap.

"I've prayed that this inheritance was the end of our troubles and that Brooke and I could have a home together here." She looked at Lance quickly, hopefully. "How will people in Stanton react to us when they learn that our parents are in prison?"

Lance leaned forward in his chair and placed his elbows on the table. The compassion in his dark blue eyes lessened the tension Janice experienced when she talked about her parents.

"Stanton residents are no different from people the world over. Most of them will accept you, believing you shouldn't be blamed for your parents' actions. Others will mistrust you."

"It doesn't matter for me, but Brooke is a timid, trusting child. I don't want her hurt."

"I can understand that all too well," he said. "Taylor's father served three years in prison, and it's been rough for her. Dale was sent to prison because he'd embezzled funds from the local bank, although he's always asserted his innocence. Linda, my sister, had divorced Dale before this happened, and she and Taylor moved in with me."

"Then Brooke and Taylor should get along all right."

"I'm sure of it. Taylor seems happy-go-lucky, but she loves her father, and she feels sorry for him."

"When I inherited this house, and a fair amount of money, I thought it would be good for Brooke and me to start a new life. I intended to go to college while Brooke was in school. Now I'm not so sure, but since I've put my plans in motion, I'll give it a try. I've been working at SuperMart in Willow Creek, and since they have a store here, I can work part-time if I have to. If the house isn't worth renovating, I'm sure I can sell the property. Considering that it's within the city limits, it should bring enough so I can buy another house."

"Actually, the city limits run through your property, so it's hard to tell what part is within the city. But it should sell if you put the property in the hands of a reputable real estate agent, and I can recommend one to you. Or Loren Santrock can advise you. He's the town's leading attorney."

Janice heard Brooke's voice in the hallway, and she took a small notebook from her purse and wrote down her cell phone number. Standing, she said, "We'll have to leave now, because I want to get back to Willow Creek before dark."

She tore the sheet from her notebook and handed it to Lance. "I don't have a phone in my apartment, but you can reach me on my cell if you need to contact me."

Lance walked to the car with Janice and Brooke, and he stood on the sidewalk and waved goodbye. He had observed many things about Janice during their meeting, but he was struck by the fact that she hadn't once smiled. Had her miserable childhood and the responsibilities she'd had to assume for her sister taken all the gaiety from her life? Janice would be a beautiful woman if laughter erased the grimness around her mouth and pleasure brightened her eyes. Fleetingly he wondered what could bring about such a transformation.

* * *

As they left Stanton behind, Brooke immediately voiced her excitement about the school and her new friend.

"I like Taylor," she said at once. "Her parents are divorced, and Taylor and her mother live with their uncle. Taylor wants her uncle to get married. She thinks if he has a wife, her mother will move out, and they can go back to live with Taylor's dad. I told her that you weren't married, either."

Janice slanted a curious glance at her sister. "Is there a connection between those two statements?"

"Well, it *would* be neat if you'd get married, Janice. We could have a dad in the house like other people. And Taylor said her uncle is a really nice man."

"I'm sure he is, but I doubt he'd appreciate having his niece find a wife for him."

"Did you like him?" Brooke persisted.

Janice felt her face get warm, and she said, "Oh, let Lance Gordon find his own wife. Marriage isn't in my plans for the future. Tell me about the school."

"It's awesome. There's a great big computer lab, a gym and neat classrooms. The school takes two or three field trips every year. The sixth graders usually go to Washington, D.C. I love it already."

Janice chatted with her customer and automatically scanned the items the woman placed on the counter. She'd already turned on the closed sign at her SuperMart checkout station. Janice had long ago convinced herself that she could stand anything for *five* more minutes. She tried to send that message to her back and feet, so they'd hold her erect until she received the customer's money and sacked her purchases.

"We're going to miss you, Janice," the woman said sincerely. "You're my favorite clerk."

"Thank you," Janice murmured with a catch in her voice. She'd made many friends at the store during the past three years. She would miss them, and she hoped she wouldn't regret her decision to move.

Somewhat apprehensive of the big change a move to Stanton would make in her life, Janice walked quickly to the office to clock out of the store for the last time. She wanted to avoid any last-minute goodbyes to delay her because she still had a few things to do before she could leave Stanton.

Her co-workers had surprised her with a farewell party the night before and had given her a television, complete with DVD and VCR. She appreciated this evidence of their friendship, but the gift meant that she must rent a small U-Haul trailer to move her belongings, because there wasn't room in her car for a television. She was pleased with the gift though, for it would be enjoyable for Brooke to have a new television to watch.

Her intention to slip out of the store without notice was thwarted, however, when her supervisor called, "Here's a letter for you—came in today's mail."

Janice took the letter, thinking it must be a card from one of the employees who'd missed last night's party. She stuck the envelope in the pocket of her jeans and waved a general goodbye to her co-workers as she hurried out of the store.

Janice made her first stop at a garage, and she sat in the car while the mechanic attached a trailer hitch to her car. Fidgeting over this inactivity, Janice remembered the letter in her pocket.

The wrinkled envelope had no return address, and the postmark was smudged. Letters containing hazardous materials came to mind. She'd heard warnings on television about opening an envelope or package if it looked suspicious. She discounted the idea that an insignificant person like herself would be targeted for a terrorist's attack, but she decided to be cautious. She stepped outside the car, held the envelope at arm's length, and opened it with a nail file. No white substance was evident, and she concluded that the message was harmless.

Unfolding the single sheet of paper, she read it and stared in horror at the words.

If you know what's good for you, stay away from Stanton.

Stunned by the message, Janice staggered to the car, her rapid pulse thudding in her forehead. Slumping in the seat, fearful images built in her mind and her stomach quivered with terror. What kind of prank was this? What difference could it make to anyone if she moved to Stanton?

After the first wave of fear, anger replaced Janice's distress and she rationalized the situation. This letter had probably been sent by her father's relatives still living in the Stanton area. Was this their way of telling her they were angry because the Reid property had passed to her?

Janice's stubborn streak was stronger than her fear. She set her jaw and muttered, "They can like it or lump it! I'm moving to Stanton."

Her face flushed when the man working on her car said, "What did you say, ma'am?"

She admitted she was talking to herself, but her embarrassment passed when the mechanic said, "My old daddy talked to himself, too—said he liked to talk to a smart man once in a while."

The man's remark amused her and eased the tension, but the note was unsettling. She fretted about it as she drove toward the Valley of Hope to say goodbye to Miss Caroline. When she turned the curve, and had a bird's-eye view of the place that had once been her home, Janice paused briefly to survey the area with nostalgia. She had found the first security she'd ever known at VOH, and it was wrenching to leave it all behind. She couldn't use Miss Caroline as her security blanket forever, but she would always be grateful for the care she'd received at VOH.

After she'd lost her fiancé in a coal mine accident, Caroline Renault had established the facility forty years ago in northeastern West Virginia. In anticipation of their marriage, her fiancé had named Miss Caroline the beneficiary of his life insurance. She'd added the insurance money to her own fortune and had started VOH with two buildings and a few children. Gas wells on the property provided an income that had helped VOH become self-supporting. Several of Miss Caroline's family and friends had also contributed liberally to the growth of the facility.

Through the years VOH had increased to twenty brick buildings, comprising well-equipped elementary and secondary schools. Residents lived in a family atmosphere in several dormitories with adult supervisors. The majority of the teachers lived off-campus.

Janice had enjoyed the independence she'd had during the three years she'd been away from VOH. But as she slowly approached the buildings, she thought of the time she'd come here as a scared and rebellious teenager. She shuddered to think where she might be today if she hadn't been sent to VOH.

Although her mentor had just turned seventy, Janice always considered Miss Caroline an ageless woman. Yet now Janice saw a myriad of fine lines etched on Miss Caroline's pearl-like complexion. Her hair was totally white, although when Janice had arrived at VOH, her dark hair had only been streaked with gray. But her generous and tender smile hadn't changed. Janice thought she'd remember the smile longer than anything else about this woman.

The hand Miss Caroline held out to Janice trembled slightly. "And how did you like Stanton?" she asked, her eyes alight with interest.

Janice explained about the condition of the property, and added, "Since the house is in such bad shape, maybe I should put it on the market and stay in Willow Creek. At least I have friends here, and I don't know anyone in Stanton. Am I doing the right thing?"

"I don't know," Miss Caroline said, the interest in her eyes changing to concern. "I believe this is something you *have* to do. I was aware that you chafed at the restraints we put on you at VOH."

Janice stared at her in surprise. "Oh, no, Miss Caroline. You'll never know how much I appreciate what you've done for me."

"I know that, but still you didn't like being under obligation to me."

"That's true. I *don't* want to be obligated to anyone, and I considered it a godsend when I heard my uncle had remembered me in his will. I have a picture of Mountjoy taken years ago, and it was a fine-looking place. I didn't doubt that I could move in there, take a part-time job to pay living expenses and use the money I inherited for college expenses for Brooke and myself. Now, I don't know what to do. I'm excited and hesitant at the same time—if that makes any sense. Actually, I suppose I'm afraid to cut my ties with the past."

Miss Caroline smiled. "But you'll only be two hundred miles away, and I'm always as near as the telephone."

"I know. I suppose I'm being foolish. And in spite of all you've done for me in the past, I want to ask your advice once again. I assume that you don't know the contents of the letter my uncle entrusted to your care, which you gave to me when I turned twenty-one."

A surprised look came into Miss Caroline's eyes. "No. When he sent your letter, he enclosed a message to me asking me to be the guardian of the letter until you came of age."

Janice took the letter from her purse and handed it across the table. "Read it, please."

Adjusting her glasses, Miss Caroline read aloud.

"'Dear Janice, when you read this letter, I will be gone. I'm sorry I haven't stayed in touch with you and your sister. My brother and I have been at odds for years, and I'd lost track of you. However, my investigations have proven that you've overcome the problems of a difficult childhood and have grown into a fine woman. I hope my legacy will make the rest of your life easier.'"

Caroline read the last paragraph silently. Her eyes expressed alarm, and she glanced quickly at Janice before reading the final words of the letter.

"'I've recently become aware of some mysterious happenings at Mountjoy, but I intend to find out what's going on. I pray that I haven't saddled you with more trouble than you needed.'"

Miss Caroline glanced at the date of the letter before she folded the page, put it in the envelope and gave it back to Janice. "Wasn't this written a few days before his death?"

"Yes. I'm wondering if he solved the problem before he died, or if it's something I'll have to contend with."

Miss Caroline shook her head. "A lot can happen in three

years. I wish I could help you, but I don't know enough about the situation. I'll pray that when you move to Stanton, God will provide someone to advise you."

Janice bent forward to kiss Miss Caroline's cheek. She wanted to cry, but that was a luxury she'd denied herself years ago.

"Thank you. As you know, I have a lot of confidence in your prayers."

Miss Caroline stood and hugged Janice tightly. "You will never be so far away that my prayers won't go with you. Be assured that anytime you're in distress, I've talked to God about you that day."

During her dysfunctional childhood, Janice had become hardened to saying goodbye, so once she left VOH, she didn't look back. She drove to the home of Brooke's foster parents to pick up her sister.

The Smiths had given Brooke security and love. They'd grown fond of Brooke, and losing her was heartbreaking for them. Now that the couple was in their mid-sixties, they'd decided to turn their responsibilities over to younger people. Brooke was the last resident they would invite into their home. Brooke cried and clung to the Smiths when they said goodbye. She was still sobbing when they drove into downtown Willow Creek.

"I have all of my dishes and pans packed," Janice said. "Let's stop for Chinese food and take it to the apartment to eat."

"That's okay," Brooke said, smothering a sob. "I feel sad because I don't have a home anymore. You're giving up your apartment, I'm leaving the Smith home, and that house in Stanton is terrible. Where are we gonna live?"

Was it a mistake to take Brooke away from the only security she'd ever had? Janice hadn't slept the night before, won-

dering if she'd made the right choice. She drove into the White
Dragon lot, went inside with Brooke and placed their order.

While she waited for the food, Janice said, "I don't know
where we'll live, little sister, but trust me. If you're unhappy in
Stanton, we'll come back to Willow Creek. I feel this move is
the right one, so let's put the past behind us. Think about the
new school you'll attend and your new friend, Taylor. And don't
forget I'm planning to turn Mountjoy into a nice home for us."

"Okay. I'll try."

By the time they reached the apartment and started eating
sweet and sour chicken, vegetables, rice and fruit, Brooke's
sunny nature had resurfaced. Janice surveyed the efficiency
apartment that had been her home for three years. Having
lived four years at VOH, where she had no privacy at all, Janice had enjoyed the quietness of the apartment. She'd rented
a furnished apartment because she'd had nothing when she'd
moved in except two boxes of clothes. Stripped of the knick-
knacks and pictures Janice had bought at garage sales and the
bargain shelves at SuperMart, the apartment looked as vacant
now as it had the first week she'd lived there.

All of the possessions she'd accumulated were packed in
medium-sized cartons, the contents listed on each box with a
permanent black marker. The boxes were stacked near the
door ready to be packed in the trailer.

Knowing that tomorrow would be a long, traumatic day,
soon after nine o'clock, Janice encouraged Brooke to take a
shower in the pint-sized bathroom and get ready for bed.
While Janice waited her turn for a shower, she hummed a song
she used to sing with Madison, her best friend.

Madison, who liked to be called Maddie, was a sophomore
at West Virginia University. They hadn't see each other often
after Maddie had left VOH, but they talked by phone several

times each month. She hadn't heard from Maddie for several days, and when her cell phone rang, Janice figured Maddie was calling.

She was totally surprised when she answered the phone.

"Miss Reid, this is Lance Gordon. We received Brooke's papers today. Everything was in order. Her grades are excellent."

"Yes, I'm proud of her," Janice said. "She's always been a good student."

"Are you about ready to leave?"

"Bright and early tomorrow morning. The manager of the apartment building is going to help us load our things. My car is small and it won't have much speed crossing the mountains, pulling a trailer. But I intend to arrive in Stanton by midafternoon."

"I took the liberty of checking the Montrose Apartments, and they have a vacancy."

The warmth and concern in his voice surprised and pleased Janice.

"Thanks for telling me. That will save me the trouble of looking for an apartment if I need one. I've made reservations at the motel for a couple of nights. I don't want to rent an apartment if Mountjoy is livable at all."

"I'm afraid it would be primitive living."

"Believe me, Mr. Gordon, I've lived in primitive conditions."

"If there's anything I can do to help you settle in, let me know."

"I sure will. Thanks for calling."

A smile had spread across Janice's face while they talked, and it refused to leave. She smiled so rarely that she marvelled at the soft creases in her normally sober face visible in the mirror. Was Lance Gordon interested in her as more than a student's guardian?

Janice didn't know much about the opposite sex. Her father certainly hadn't been a role model, and at VOH, the girls had outnumbered boys. Besides, Miss Caroline had discouraged anything beyond casual friendship between the girls and boys at the facility, urging schoolwork over dating.

After Janice had started working, she hadn't had time to date anyone. She was so desperate to make money that she worked forty hours each week, and all the overtime she was allowed to have. Although Lance Gordon seemed like the answer to any woman's dream, Janice couldn't allow herself to consider dating him, even if he was interested in her. She had a house to renovate, a sister to care for and a mystery to solve. Would that leave her any time for romance?

Chapter Three

Lance sat with his hand on the phone, staring into space, unaware of the beautiful bed of dahlias blooming outside his bedroom window. He had many female friends, but he hadn't dated a woman since college. His profession and his church commitments filled all of his time. What had prompted him to telephone Janice? He was happy as a bachelor, and he had no desire to change that status, yet Janice had hardly been out of his mind since he'd met her. What was there about Janice Reid that had stirred his imagination as no other woman ever had?

Perhaps it was her rigid back and purposeful posture that had first alerted him to the fact that, despite her young age, she was a woman with a strong personality. Her facial features had impressed him so much that, if he were an artist, he believed he could paint her portrait from memory.

Janice possessed a small delicate nose and long-lashed green eyes set in a smooth ivory skin with a hint of roses in her cheeks. Her chestnut-brown hair was short and straight. She was of average height, about five feet, six inches tall, and she had a well-proportioned body. She could be considered a beauty, except for her stubborn chin and a grim expression that spoiled the loveliness of her full, curved mouth.

As soon as Lance had dialed her number, he'd suddenly hoped that Janice wouldn't answer, or that she'd tell him she wasn't coming to Stanton. Still, his heart had lurched with excitement when, in her husky voice, she'd said she would arrive in Stanton tomorrow. Why did it matter to him?

Was it because he was worried about Janice's reception in Stanton? The Reids in the area were known as shiftless and dishonest, usually staying a few steps ahead of law. Would the local residents welcome two more Reids? He prayed that people wouldn't condemn Janice and Brooke because of their relatives.

The next morning before he went to work, with Janice's interests in mind, Lance drove to her property. He put on heavy leather boots and carried a sturdy walking stick to push aside brush that blocked the pathways, and for protection in case any poisonous snakes had infested the vacant property. It had rained the night before and fog drifted down from the mountain peaks.

Stepping from the car, he surveyed Janice's inheritance anxiously. As the house peeked in and out of the wispy fog, he was reminded of the illustration on the cover of a mystery novel he'd read recently. He couldn't imagine Janice and Brooke living here. He wasn't sure that *he* would contemplate living in such an isolated area. But it wasn't his concern.

Knowing that he should back off and let Janice Reid make her own decisions, Lance approached the metal gate blocking the entrance to the property. The hasp on the gate had rusted shut and Lance went back to his car to get a screwdriver out of the toolbox he carried in the trunk.

The hasp shattered and fell to the ground when he pried

on it with the screwdriver. He pushed the gate open and stepped into a jungle of shrubbery that had once neatly lined the driveway but had spread into a wilderness during recent years. An untrimmed yew hedge partially concealed the house from the highway. In his effort to get close enough to judge the house's condition, Lance blundered into a thicket of multiflora rosebushes. A sharp thorn tore his shirt and pricked his shoulder. Disgusted with himself for sticking his nose into Janice's business, Lance knew he'd have to go back home and change before he went to the school. And how was he going to explain the torn shirt to his sister, who watched his activities like a hawk?

Veering to the left and climbing the hill, he saw a corner of the house several yards beyond him. He turned in that direction. Several hardwood trees and a couple of spruces marked the border of what must have been the lawn. If the tall hedge along the foundation was trimmed and the underbrush cleared away, the house wouldn't seem so depressing.

Experiencing the strange feeling that he was being watched, Lance stopped abruptly and looked carefully around him. He had a good view of the house and the hill beyond it from this point. It would be easy enough for someone to hide behind any of the big trees or behind the outbuilding to the right of the house. Determined that the disturbing stories he'd heard about the house wouldn't affect his common sense, Lance strode forward purposefully. He heard a sound to his left and jumped behind a tree. Slightly amused at himself when a rabbit ran under a large bush, he walked on and paused before the three steps that led to the front porch.

The steps looked sturdy enough, but he put one foot cautiously on the first step to be sure it wouldn't collapse under his weight. Suddenly, Lance heard someone groan beside him, and he stumbled to the floor of the porch. Goose bumps popped out on his arms as sounds of thunder and the roar of hurricane-force winds swept around him. Did he hear bells ringing or had the stories he'd heard about Mountjoy caused him to imagine these sounds? Lance hadn't watched a horror movie for years, but this sudden assault on his senses reminded him of the movies he'd watched when he was a teenager.

For a moment he was stunned, unable to move. His flesh crawled and his palms moistened with sweat as the sounds faded into the distance. Lance jumped off the porch and ran for cover in the dense shrubbery beside the porch. His heart thudded in his chest and he gasped for breath.

What, or who, had made those sounds? Not for a moment did he believe that ghosts inhabited the house, but he knew now that the stories he'd heard about people being scared away from the area had been true. Something was wrong at Mountjoy. It was no place for Janice Reid to live.

When his pulse steadied, Lance returned to his car. If he reported this incident to the police, he'd be ridiculed like other people who believed the house was haunted. But as he drove into Stanton, he questioned if he should tell Janice what had happened. Or was it time for him to stop involving himself in Janice Reid's life?

When they left Willow Creek early Friday morning, Janice learned that cutting her ties with the Valley of Hope was more difficult than she'd anticipated.

During her childhood, Janice's parents had moved so often that she hadn't gotten attached to any one place, and she'd made few friends. She had since realized that her parents lived in one house until they couldn't pay the rent, then moved to a new area and rented another house. She hadn't attended any school long enough to get a basic education and she was behind her peers when she'd gone to VOH. With special tutoring, she'd soon caught up with her classmates and had graduated from high school with average grades.

All of the residents at VOH had come with problems of some kind, so she hadn't felt inferior there as she had in the other schools she'd attended. At the Valley of Hope, Janice had the assurance of a warm bed at night, all the food she needed and no fear of what the next day would bring.

Janice's car pulled the heavily loaded trailer better than she expected, and they arrived in Stanton about two o'clock. When they passed the convenience store where they'd bought gas on their previous visit to Stanton, Brooke shouted, "Look, Janice, there's that dog I fed last time."

Slowing for a red light, Janice glanced in the direction Brooke pointed and saw the dog standing beside the road. He looked worse than he had the last time.

"Poor doggie," Brooke said. "He's still hungry." The light turned green, and Janice moved forward slowly. Brooke rolled down the window and tossed the hamburger she'd been eating toward the dog. He snatched the sandwich in midair and disappeared from sight.

"He must not have a home, either," Brooke said, and the pathos of her words stabbed Janice's heart.

She started to say that Brooke *had* a home now. But not knowing the condition of the Reid house, she remained silent.

The motel was located several blocks from the convenience store, and when Janice checked in, she received permission to park the trailer until she could make further plans. While Brooke was in school on Monday, Janice would find a place for them to live.

Hoping to make some decision about the property over the weekend, Janice took Brooke with her and went to Loren Santrock's office. She was fortunate that she not only found the man in his office, but that he was willing to talk to her.

Mr. Santrock was a fatherly man, whom Janice liked at once. Miss Banner was talking on the phone, and he personally escorted Janice and Brooke into his office, which looked as if it hadn't changed for twenty years. His old, comfortable furniture was a stark contrast to the reception area.

Perhaps interpreting Janice's appraising glance, he said with a smile, "Miss Banner persuaded me to update her equipment and office furniture. She insisted that I should make a better impression on prospective clients. She's been my right arm for over fifteen years, so I let her have full sway in the outer office, but I balked when she tried to change *my* office." His eyes twinkled like a mischievous child when he added, "I'm too set in my ways to want a lot of new furniture."

From a small refrigerator concealed behind a screen, Mr. Santrock brought a pitcher of tea and some glasses. He poured a glass each for Janice and Brooke, then one for himself. He placed a tray of cookies within their reach, saying, "This is Miss Banner's little touch. Help yourself."

After he'd seen to their immediate comfort, the lawyer said, "I'm sorry I wasn't on hand to meet you last week, but it was one of those uncontrollable situations. I'm at your service today. I have all the papers ready for your signature to turn John Reid's assets over to you. The local bank will help you transfer the money to a banking institution of your choice."

"I intend to leave everything in the local bank."

"Wouldn't it be more convenient for you to have the money in Willow Creek?"

"Not when I intend to live in Stanton."

The lawyer stared at her, a look of horror evident on his face. Suddenly, he was speechless, although he'd been quite talkative before.

"Besides the house, how much cash is there?" Janice asked. "I don't mean to sound mercenary, but I need to know where I stand before I start renovating the house."

Concern replaced incredulity on Mr. Santrock's face, and his heavy eyebrows lifted. In a fatherly tone, he said, "My dear child, you can't live at Mountjoy."

Flushing, Janice said, "That's been my intention since I learned I'd inherited the property, though I'll admit I was discouraged when I took a quick look at the house from a distance. It may be beyond repair, but if it is, I'll sell it and use the money to buy a house in town."

"I haven't been in the house for a long time, but I'm sure it's a wreck."

"You're probably right, but I won't know until I look over the place. Will you give me the key so I can check it out?"

"I don't have a key, and I doubt you'd need one anyway. I don't suppose the house has been locked for years. Most people hereabouts never lock their doors. If there is a key, Henrietta Cunningham might have it."

"Who's Henrietta Cunningham?"

"Your uncle's housekeeper. She took care of him for several years. In exchange for her services, he gave her the house he owned in Stanton."

"If you think the house is unlocked, I won't bother Mrs. Cunningham."

"But you shouldn't go to the property alone. I don't know how stable the floors are, and you might fall and hurt yourself. It will be several days before I'm free to go with you."

"I don't want to wait that long."

Shrugging his shoulders, Mr. Santrock said, "Well, don't say I didn't warn you."

Remembering the letter she'd received telling her to stay away from Stanton, a cold chill tingled down Janice's spine. She wondered if there *was* some danger at the house, and the lawyer was trying to protect her. She had the distinct feeling that he didn't want her moving to Mountjoy, although he'd seemed glad to see her today. But was that because he thought she'd be leaving Stanton? When he hadn't kept his appointment with her before, she'd questioned if he was deliberately avoiding her. But Mr. Santrock seemed helpful enough now, and Janice knew she had to curb her suspicious nature. He was probably only concerned with her safety. Remembering that Miss Caroline was praying for someone to advise her, she thought Loren Santrock might be that person, when he continued in a kindly tone.

"Now about the rest of your inheritance—your uncle had some government bonds, as well as several accounts in the local bank worth about fifty thousand dollars. Add the property to that, and you've come into a tidy fortune. Of course, the house and land aren't worth a great deal."

"I thought the land might be valuable even if the house isn't much good."

He shook his head. "Except for the spot where the house stands, the rest of your property consists of a few acres of hilly land that isn't fit for development. At one time the Reids owned several hundred acres in this county, but most of it was sold years ago. I'll be glad to help you find a real estate agent if you decide to sell, but don't expect it to bring a high price."

"I'll appreciate any help you can give me," Janice said.

"Let's call Miss Banner in to notarize your signature on

some documents and I'll send copies to the local bank. I'm chairman of the bank's board of directors, so come to my office either Monday or Tuesday, and I'll take you to the bank and introduce you. Is there anything else I can do for you?"

"No, thank you," Janice said as she stood. "I'll see you Monday morning."

"I'll have Miss Banner put you on my appointment list for ten o'clock. It's my pleasure to serve you as I did your uncle."

Frustrated at the delay in exploring her inheritance, Janice wondered when she *could* go to Mountjoy. She didn't intend to wait a week to see her property even if she had to go alone. But she didn't want to take Brooke to the property until she'd checked out the place, so she'd have to wait until Monday when Brooke was in school.

As they went down the stairs from the lawyer's office, Janice said, "Let's walk to the school now, and see if there's anything you need before Monday. I'll find out from the guidance counselor if there are any rules about clothing, and then we'll go to the mall outside of town and buy some clothes for you."

A smile brightened Brooke's small features, and she said, "I have enough clothes, but it would be great to have one or two new outfits."

Janice's pulse quickened as they entered the school. Would Lance be in his office? The secretary in the reception room took them to the guidance counselor's office. Janice was pleased with the efficiency of the school staff. The counselor was sensitive to Brooke's position as a new student and when they left the building, Brooke had no fear of starting to school on Monday. Janice wished she was as confident of the future.

After dinner they went to the motel and carried their suitcases to their spacious room. Brooke was fascinated by the large pictures, the spacious bathroom, the two phones, the entertainment center and the advertising brochures on the desk. She hadn't stayed in a motel, although Janice had been in motels a few times when she was a child before her father had squandered all of his inheritance. Brooke was intrigued by the many channels available on the cable station and she quickly scanned all of the available programs.

The past two weeks had been traumatic for Janice, and she felt as if she'd reached the end of her tether. The responsibility of making decisions about her sister's future weighed heavily on her mind. While Brooke watched the Disney Channel, Janice stretched out on the bed and dozed until the ringing phone awakened her.

Startled, she reached for the phone receiver.

"Turn the volume down, Brooke." Hoping Mr. Santrock was calling to say he'd take her on a tour of Mountjoy, she said, "Hello."

"Miss Reid, this is Lance Gordon. I'm sorry I missed you at school today. Did the staff take care of you?"

She sat up in bed and shoved a couple of pillows behind her back. Pleased by his call, Janice said, "Yes, very well. Brooke is excited about starting school."

"What time did you get to Stanton?"

"About two o'clock."

"So you've cut the ties with your former home."

"Yes. For better or for worse, I've moved to Stanton. I saw Mr. Santrock today and signed the papers to transfer the ownership of my uncle's property to me. He didn't have a key to Mountjoy and questioned whether there was one. I'm going to explore the place as soon as I can."

Lance hesitated before he asked, "Alone?"

"Yes. Mr. Santrock couldn't go with me for several days,

and I don't want to wait that long. I won't take Brooke with me until I see what the place is like, so I'll have to wait until Monday."

He didn't say anything for a minute or two, and Janice asked, "Mr. Gordon, are you still on the line?"

"Yes. I shouldn't give you unsolicited advice," he said hesitantly, "but you shouldn't go out there at all—especially alone."

Why was Lance Gordon so determined that she shouldn't see her property? She didn't want to suspect him of trying to keep her away from Stanton, but it did seem strange that he was taking such an interest in her affairs. Was he the one who'd sent the warning note to stay away from Stanton?

"I don't have much choice. My sister and I are homeless until I see the condition of the house."

"Then I'll go with you."

It crossed Janice's mind that she didn't know much about Lance Gordon, even if he was a school principal. But she did dread exploring the place by herself. And though she couldn't understand why he was befriending her, she thought she'd have to accept his help.

Perhaps Lance sensed that she was considering his offer for he remained silent.

"I *am* afraid to go alone," she admitted. "I'd like to have your company."

"Good! And let me make a suggestion about Brooke. My sister is taking Taylor to the movies tomorrow afternoon, and Brooke can go with them. If she's with Linda, we can go to Mountjoy and take all the time we need to look at your property. I'll come by the motel about one o'clock to get you and Brooke."

"That's all right with me, but maybe you'd better check it out with Taylor and your sister."

"Taylor has talked about Brooke most of the time since she met her. She'll be excited to have her along." He gave Janice his phone number, saying, "Call if you need to, but if not, I'll see you tomorrow."

Janice replaced the phone and a warm tenderness caressed a place in her heart that had been cold for years. She was accustomed to standing on her own two feet, not relying on anyone else. She'd thought she preferred it that way, but she suddenly realized how much simpler a problem seemed when someone shared it with her.

She bounded off the bed, saying, "You're in for a fun day tomorrow, Brooke."

When she explained about the planned visit with the Mallorys, Brooke grinned widely. "It's nice to have friends."

"Sure is," Janice said, and she picked up a brush and started combing Brooke's long silken brown hair, a bedtime ritual they'd started when Brooke was a toddler.

Lance wasn't coming until one o'clock, and Janice had anticipated a leisurely morning, but the telephone beside her bed rang before seven. She pushed aside the covers and swung her feet to the floor when the motel clerk answered her hello.

"Miss Reid, something terrible happened last night. I just arrived for work, and when I walked across the parking lot, I noticed that the tires are flat on your car. Looks like they've been slashed. Since the damage occurred on our property, I've called the police."

Janice's hand shook as she replaced the phone. Stunned for a moment, she fell backward on the bed. This had to be another deliberate effort to drive her away from Stanton. Was it worth all of this drama to move to this town? She was tempted to return to Willow Creek as soon as her tires were repaired. Rallying, she hurried out of bed.

The ringing phone hadn't awakened Brooke, but after Janice hurried into jeans and a T-shirt and strapped on a pair of sandals, she shook Brooke's shoulder gently. When she thought her sister was awake, Janice said, "I'm going downstairs for a while. Stay in bed until I come back. I'll bring breakfast."

A police cruiser was parked behind her blue car when Janice rushed through the double doors of the motel and ran across the parking lot. The tires had been new when she'd bought the vehicle, but long punctures, presumably made with a knife, had destroyed them. As she viewed the vandalism, a myriad of emotions coursed through Janice's mind.

At first she was incredulous that such a thing had happened. Disbelief faded into fury. Fear replaced anger when she considered the ramifications of what had happened to her car. Would her enemies attempt physical attacks on Brooke or her now that she had moved to Stanton?

Janice became aware that the chief of police stood beside her and she transferred her gaze to him.

He tipped the brim of his gray felt hat. "Bill Goodman at your service, ma'am. The hotel clerk says this is your car."

She nodded, without speaking. Her throat was numb, and she swallowed with effort.

"Who are you, ma'am?"

"Janice Reid," she stammered.

The chief of police's brows shot up in surprise. "Any relation to the Reids in this county?"

"John Reid was my uncle."

"Aha!" he said, and his brown eyes brightened with sudden comprehension. "So you're the one who inherited his estate?"

"Yes. My father is his youngest brother. Although," Janice added in a contemptuous tone, "I don't go around bragging about it."

"Do you know any of your relatives in these parts?"

She shook her head. "I don't remember ever being here until I came last week."

"Where's your pa?"

"In prison somewhere. I haven't heard from him for years."

The officer fingered his mustache as he walked around her car. A few inches shorter than Janice, Chief Goodman was probably in his late fifties, and there was a slight stoop to his shoulders. His neat brown uniform failed to provide him with an impressive appearance.

"I'll have to inspect the car before you can have the tires replaced," he said. "Do you need the car today?"

"No. Can you recommend a garage to repair the damage?"

"There's a tire store in town that will give you a good price if you can wait until Monday. They're closed on Saturday afternoons and Sunday."

"I can wait until then, I guess. I'll be taking my little sister to school on Monday, but we can walk there."

"You're planning to live in Stanton?"

"Yes," and motioning to her car, she added, "but it seems I'm being warned to leave."

The cop's eyes twinkled with admiration. "You're a sharp lady!"

"What else can I think? I've looked around and no other cars in the lot have been touched. I don't think it's a random act of violence. This was deliberate and planned."

"I'm sorry it happened to you."

The chief got in the cruiser and drove away. Janice walked slowly into the motel and picked up some rolls and juice in the lobby. Unwilling to ruin Brooke's pleasure in the day, she didn't mention the vandalism.

Lance Gordon lived in a two-story stone house in a subdivision located on a plateau north of Stanton, about five miles from the center of town. Driving from the motel to his home, he explained, "I'd just built this house five years ago when Linda got her divorce and she moved in with me. I turned over the running of the house to her. I wanted Linda and Brooke to be free to entertain their friends, but I like my privacy. I reserved two rooms for my bedroom and office, and except for meals, that's where I spend my time."

Linda Mallory was a quiet, blond, sad-faced woman, but she was obviously pleased to look after Brooke for a few hours. Janice had no qualms about trusting Brooke to Linda's care for the afternoon.

"One of my major worries about moving to Stanton has lessened now that Brooke has found a friend," Janice said as Lance drove away from his house. "She's always made friends quicker than I have."

"Kids do seem to make friends easier than adults. For the most part, people in Stanton are easy to know. I believe both of you will find friends here."

He wanted to assure her that she'd already found one in him, but Lance was puzzled by the air of defeat Janice exhibited today. Her shoulders slumped, and her slender hands unconsciously twisted together in her lap as if her composure was hanging by a single thread.

To avoid thinking about the new crisis, Janice focused on Lance. The other times she had seen him, he'd been dressed in a suit, dress shirt and tie. Today, he wore heavy leather boots, jeans and a casual long-sleeved shirt. A ball cap covered his light hair.

Janice had dressed in jeans, too, and she wore a sweatshirt and lightweight boots with thick soles.

After he parked by the entrance to Mountjoy, Lance took a machete and a large flashlight from the back of his van. He passed the flashlight to Janice.

At the gate, he paused with his hand on the latch. "I've hesitated to tell you," he said, "but yesterday, I decided to check out your property. I got in sight of the house, and if I was superstitious, I'd say your property is haunted."

Conscious of the sudden gray pallor that spread across her face and the apprehension in her eyes, he quickly explained what he'd heard the day before.

"Judging from similar experiences others have had when they've trespassed on the property," he concluded, "this must be an effort to scare intruders away. I don't know if it's safe for you to go any farther."

Lance's words coming on the heels of the slashed tires alarmed Janice as nothing had ever done. She staggered against the gate, and Lance reached out a hand to steady her. She shook her head.

"I'm all right," she struggled to say. Through tight lips, she told him about the written message she'd received warning her to stay away from Stanton.

"Maybe I should have heeded the warning. I don't mind risking my own life to claim what belongs to me, but if anything happened to me, Brooke would be all alone!" Swallowing with difficulty, she continued, "And last night, the tires on my car were slashed. Chief Goodman is investigating."

Lance frowned and his blue eyes darkened with anger.

"Every time I decide I can make a home in Stanton," Janice continued, "something else happens. I don't know what to do."

"What do you want to do?" Lance asked.

"Forget I've ever heard of this place, take Brooke and move so far away that no one has ever heard of my family."

A gleam of interest in his eyes, Lance persisted, "But what are you *going* to do?"

Janice forced herself to remember the biblical promise, "God has not given us the spirit of fear, but of power." If anything happened to her, surely God would take care of Brooke.

"Stay here, claim my property and find out who's trying to drive me out of town."

Smiling, Lance opened the gate and stepped aside for her to enter. "Then be my guest," he said. Swiftly, he stepped in front of her. "On second thought, perhaps I'll not be a gentleman today. I'll walk in front—you stay behind me." He handed his car keys to Janice. "If anything happens to me, run as fast as you can and bring the chief of police."

Janice laid her hand on his arm. "This is *my* problem. I should take the risk, not you. Why are you going to all this trouble for me?"

A look of bewilderment in his eyes, Lance shook his head slowly. "I really don't know."

Chapter Four

Janice's face flushed. "I appreciate what you're doing, but I'm practically a stranger to you. I don't know why you'd put your life on the line for me."

"I don't understand it, either," he said, a hint of wonder in his voice. "Let's just say it's because you need help, and it's my Christian duty to help you."

"Except for the years I spent at VOH, I've taken care of myself and Brooke without any help. I'd like to think I can still do it, but I'm in over my head now. I can't manage alone anymore."

"Then let's check out your property and go from there. Be careful."

With the machete, Lance cleared a narrow path for them to follow until they came to the copse of evergreens. Dried needles matted the ground and walking was easier. Janice enjoyed a sense of pride to know that this property actually belonged to her. The grounds had been badly neglected and it was almost like walking through a wilderness, but she believed the lawn could be restored to its original splendor.

It was hot and stuffy under the trees, and Lance stopped to

wipe his face with a handkerchief. Some of the underbrush consisted of sturdy brier vines that were difficult to cut. Janice felt guilty when she noticed several scratches on his arms. He breathed deeply and took a swig of water from the bottle he carried. Looking around, he asked, "Who's been responsible for looking after this property?"

"Nobody, apparently. Mr. Santrock was administrator of Uncle John's estate, but he said he hasn't been here for years. Perhaps he thought the house was too far gone to need checking, and he may be right," she added, when Lance hacked down a large multiflora rosebush and she had a sweeping view of the house.

Paint had peeled from the structure, vines grew all over the front porch, and several windows on the second floor were shattered. Branches from a tall spruce tree lay on the porch roof.

"We had a bad storm a week or so ago. Looks like the lightning struck that spruce tree. It will have to be cut down."

The overall effect was disheartening. Janice wanted to turn tail and run, and authorize Mr. Santrock to sell Mountjoy before she went any farther.

Noting the dismay in her eyes, Lance said, "We're here, so we might as well look inside. Don't forget, I didn't hear anything until I started up the steps. I'll go first."

Lance tested his weight on the steps and the top one buckled under him. He leaped on the porch to keep from falling. The porch floor itself seemed sturdy enough, probably because it was protected from the elements by a rusty roof. He half expected a repetition of the raucous noise he'd heard the other time he'd visited this house, but all was silent except for a mockingbird singing from one of the bushes.

He held out his hand to Janice. "Watch your step."

Janice expelled the breath that she hadn't realized she'd

been holding and accepted Lance's help. In spite of the fear clutching at her heart, as Janice stepped on the front porch of her ancestral home, she had the unfamiliar sense of belonging.

Four windows fronting on the porch were placed symmetrically between a massive, oak door with an oval, leaded frosted-glass window. She put her face close to the cracked window panes, but they were too dirty for her to see the interior of the house. The sun shone brightly, but the towering spruce trees surrounding the house shut out the sunlight, and Janice shivered slightly. Lance tried the door but it was locked. He moved to a window, which lifted easily at his touch.

Taking the flashlight from Janice, Lance stuck his head cautiously through the window and flashed the light around the room. No danger seemed to lurk in the dim interior, so he stepped into the room. He reached a hand to Janice and steadied her as she climbed over the window sill.

Janice's eyes adjusted slowly to the dark room.

"The house is still furnished!" she said.

Lance's steps were loud as he walked around the room, the floorboards squeaking under his weight. He stopped beside a dark wooden divan upholstered in red velvet, noting two matching chairs.

"I've always heard that this house was luxurious. This was elegant furniture at one time."

"Everything is dusty, and look at the floor—we didn't make all of these tracks."

"I'd noticed that," Lance said, wishing that Janice hadn't. "The house hasn't been as vacant as it looked. Stay close to me and we'll look around."

The tracks had been made recently, Lance thought, and that there had been no effort to conceal them disturbed him.

Janice took hold of Lance's shirttail and, grinning, she said, "Try to get rid of me. I'll stick to you like a burr."

They walked slowly through four large downstairs rooms, separated by a wide entrance hall that ran the length of the house. They'd entered the room to the right of the hallway. Behind it was a bedroom, and across the hall was a kitchen and a dining room. The rooms were of equal size except the bedroom, where part of the room had been partitioned into a bathroom accessed from the rear hall.

Although the living room and the bedroom looked as they must have a hundred years ago, the kitchen held modern appliances. There were cabinets below and over the sink and Janice opened one of the doors.

"There's still some dishes and pans here," she said, and stepped backward as a mouse jumped out of the cabinet. "Looks like I've inherited some livestock," she said with a grimace.

Lance grinned, surprised that she'd wasn't scared. His sister shrieked and headed for higher ground when she saw a mouse.

He turned one of the faucets on the sink. "No water, of course," he said. "I suppose the plumbing was drained when John moved out of the house."

As Janice's eyes acclimated to the dark interior, a sense of discouragement swept over her. The carpets on the hardwood floors were threadbare. The upholstered furniture in the living room had been gnawed by vermin. Several layers of tattered wallpaper drooped from the ceiling and fluttered around the walls. Ragged curtains hung over the windows. Stimulated by a strong breeze wafting through a broken window, long strings of cobwebs swayed rhythmically, reminding Janice of puppets on a string.

Lance watched as Janice's expressions changed from gloom to optimism as she passed from one room to another.

"If this isn't a sorry mess," she said once.

After they'd scanned the downstairs rooms, they paused beside a walnut garment tree in the front center hall.

Forcing herself to overlook the bad and recognize the positive, Janice touched the hall tree and said, "I've heard of these," she said. "The hooks were for gentleman to hang their hats, and the mirror helped ladies take a last look at their appearance before they left the house." She lifted the lid of a narrow bench and a film of dust flew into her face. "This box was used to hold outdoors shoes. Except for dust, it seems in good condition."

"And it also served as a place to sit on while changing shoes," Lance said.

"The house itself seems sturdy enough and the furniture is beautiful. I'd like to live here."

"It will take a lot of hard work," Lance said.

"I know. But I think it's worth fixing up. Do you?"

Lance took his handkerchief and dusted a long deacon's bench in the hallway. He motioned Janice to sit down and he sat beside her.

"Most of this furniture has an antique value, and with time, money and hard work, the house could be turned into a showplace," he said slowly.

"I don't know much about antiques, but I'm sure you're right. When this house has been vacant and isolated for several years, why hasn't someone stolen this stuff?"

"I told you that a lot of people around here think the house is haunted."

Eyeing him to see if he was kidding her, she was surprised that he wore a serious expression. Since this was the first amusing thing she'd heard in days, she exploded into a deep, warm laugh. "That's ridiculous! You don't believe that, do you?"

Laughter erased some of the tension from Janice's face, and her green eyes glowed like sunlight shining on ocean waves. Lance was delighted to see her face alive with merriment.

His lips twisted humorously. "If I did, I wouldn't be sitting here. I didn't say I *believed* the house was haunted, but it has that reputation. That may have kept people from stealing everything."

"That's my good fortune, I suppose." Janice looked at her watch. "Let's look upstairs so we can go back to town. I don't want to impose on your sister to keep Brooke any longer."

"She won't mind," Lance said, then stood and walked toward a door in the rear hall that must lead to the upstairs. The door was locked.

Disappointed, Janice said, "I'd hoped to see the whole place while we were here."

"I could break down the door, but you'll have enough repairs to make without me adding to the list. We can bring a skeleton key and go upstairs next time."

Next time! Janice glanced at him curiously. Apparently, Lance's interest in her home wasn't to be a one-time event. He peered into the kitchen as they walked down the hall. "Let's see where that leads," he said, motioning to a small door to the right of the stove.

"It's a pantry," Janice said. "A lot of older houses have them."

A few jars of green beans and some containers of jelly were on the shelves. Mutilated cartons of rice and flour had been riddled by mice or rats and the contents spilled on the floor. Lance opened another door that led to a side porch, where a door in the floor opened into a cellar. A damp, moldy scent met their nostrils when Lance lifted the door on squeaky hinges.

"I'll check it out," Lance said. He walked down a few steps

and flashed the light around a small, dirt-floored room. "There's a gas furnace down here," he reported, "and a water pump. County water is available now so you won't need the pump, but you will need a plumber to check the water lines."

Although he didn't want to overly encourage Janice, Lance was optimistic that this house could be turned into a comfortable home. It would take determination as well as money, but Janice seemed to have an ample supply of both. If the menace hanging over the property could be dispelled, she *could* live at Mountjoy.

Janice must have had similar thoughts, for she took another look in all the rooms and said, "I'll give this a lot of thought over the weekend before I make a decision."

He closed the window behind them. The fog had lifted and they stepped out into the sunlight, which made the property seem much less threatening. Noting the optimism mirrored on Janice's face when she turned to take a final look at the house, Lance hesitated to burst her bubble. But Janice needed to know something else before she made a decision to live at Mountjoy, and he wondered if he should tell her. Santrock may have told her, but he doubted it. Before they stepped through the gate, he said, "Do you know what caused your uncle's death?"

His voice seemed troubled, and she glanced quickly toward him. "No."

Taking a deep breath, Lance said, "He committed suicide at Mountjoy."

"What!"

"There was some talk that he was murdered, but it looked more like suicide. The police department searched around a while, but they couldn't prove anything."

Janice's optimism about her inheritance crashed. She felt

as if the bottom had dropped out of her world. "My dad didn't talk much about his family," she said in a strained voice, "but I've heard him say that someone in each generation of Reids died a tragic death."

"Yes, that story goes around." He hesitated, but she had to be warned. "It just isn't *any* Reid, but the owner of the house."

Her eyes widened. "If that's the case, then I might be the next victim."

"I don't want to scare you because I personally think it's just a superstition. But that's one of the reasons the place has gained a bad reputation."

Janice had been somewhat animated as they'd left the house, but her hand pulled at the neck of her shirt and panic shadowed her eyes.

Lance placed his hand on her shoulder. "Are you all right?"

She nodded and swallowed with difficulty. "Don't worry, I'm not the fainting kind. But why didn't Mr. Santrock tell me how he died?"

Lance shook his head. "Maybe he thought you already knew. Would it have made any difference in your plans to live at Mountjoy?"

"I don't know."

He opened the gate and closed it behind them. Taking her arm, he steered Janice toward the car. When she was seated, he walked around the car to the driver's door and sat beside her.

"I didn't want to tell you," he said, "but I thought you should know before you made a definite decision."

"And I do thank you," she said gratefully, but Lance noted the despair in her voice. She clenched her hands together until her knuckles were white. He leaned toward her and took her hands. Gently, he unwound her fingers until they relaxed in his grasp.

"Janice," he said softly, "you've carried a heavy load by yourself for too long. I'll help you over the rough places as much as I can. I'd like to be your friend."

She withdrew her hands from his grasp, and her slender, delicate throat worked nervously. Lance waited anxiously for her response. He'd already determined that Janice, of necessity, had become an independent person. Would she readily accept a stranger into her life? And why did her answer mean so much to him?

Sunlight slanted through the car windows and momentarily blinded Janice as she exchanged a troubled glance with Lance. She turned her head quickly, so he wouldn't detect the joy that must be revealed in her eyes. What had happened to her? She'd always shouldered her own responsibilities. Now that Lance had offered his friendship, her heart spun giddily at the prospects of having someone share the despair that threatened to crush her. Momentarily her independence surfaced. Would it lead to more heartbreak if she trusted Lance and he disappointed her?

She faced him again and gazed with deep concentration into his face. Lance held his breath, fearful that she'd reject him. But a yearning look came into Janice's eyes, and she said softly, "I've only had two *really* close friends in my whole life. I left Miss Caroline behind at VOH. My friend Maddie is busy with college, and I don't see her often. I've never felt so alone in my whole life." She held out her hand. "I desperately need a friend, Lance."

The tension in the car was suffocating as thoughts they couldn't express bounced from one to the other.

Janice's eyes were luminous with unshed tears. He took her

proffered hand, squeezed it and lifted it to his cheek. "I'll be your friend."

Further words seemed unnecessary, so Lance reluctantly released her hand and started the car. They were silent during the short drive into Stanton.

Brooke had enjoyed her trip to the movies with Taylor and her mother. She chatted about it as Lance drove them back to the motel, so Janice and Lance didn't have any time for private conversation.

When they got out of the car and Brooke ran into the motel, Janice said, "I appreciate your offer of friendship, but being my friend doesn't mean you have to worry about my problems all the time. I'll try to stay out of trouble for a few weeks—you'll have your hands busy with getting the school year underway. You must have a large student body."

Lance felt as if he'd been dismissed, and he wondered if he had been too forward in pushing his friendship on Janice. But she'd seemed receptive to the idea.

Trying to match her mood, he said, "There are about four hundred kids. We have kindergarten through the sixth grade."

"Which is going to be a big adjustment for Brooke," Janice said. "Please send me word if she needs any special help."

"I will be busy," he said, "but not too busy to help you. Please let me know if you need *anything*."

She nodded agreement as she went into the motel. He watched her purposeful stride and ramrod-straight back, wondering why her attitude had changed so abruptly. He had intended to ask the Reids to attend his church tomorrow, but he didn't want to push Janice too far. He'd only asked for her friendship, and he didn't want their relationship to continue beyond that point. He'd lived thirty years without any serious involvement with women. He liked living his own life. So why start up a relationship now?

Chapter Five

Sitting in their motel room, as she partially listened to Brooke chatter about the movie, Janice wondered why she'd been so abrupt with Lance. The man had been a wonderful help today, and she'd enjoyed his company immensely.

The more she thought about it, she realized that she was afraid of Lance Gordon—afraid she'd become too dependent on him. The years before she'd been sent to VOH, she had to depend on herself. She'd allowed herself to be dependent on Miss Caroline, but at eighteen she left all of that behind. For the past three years she'd been on her own. Wasn't it less traumatic that way? If you didn't rely on anyone else, then you wouldn't be disappointed if they failed you.

Miss Caroline had told her often enough that God was a friend who would help her through any circumstances. After she'd moved to Willow Creek and gotten a job, when she wasn't working on Sunday morning, she'd sometimes gone back to VOH for worship services. But she'd gone mostly to see Miss Caroline, rather than to worship.

But now that she was responsible for Brooke, she should

take her to church. She moved to the window and looked at the church across the street from the motel. The date carved in the stone lintel above the door indicated that the gray stone building had been built in the early part of the twentieth century. A tall spire and columns graced the front of the church that was reached by six wide stone steps. Stained-glass windows added to the magnificence of the structure.

Squinting to read the worship hours on the lighted sign, Janice said, "Maybe we'd better go to church tomorrow. Sunday school starts at ten o'clock, but we can still sleep late, go downstairs to the breakfast bar and get to the church on time. Okay?"

"I guess so," Brooke said with some hesitation, "but I won't know anybody."

"You'll make friends easily enough, but we can skip Sunday school tomorrow and go to the worship service at eleven."

"I'd like that better, and we can even sleep later."

"That might be a good idea. You can't sleep in Monday morning because school starts at eight."

Brooke groaned, but it was a half-hearted response, for she was a good student and liked school. Going to school had never been a pleasure for Janice. About the time she'd gotten settled in one school, her parents would move. At VOH, because of her poor scholastic background, it had been an effort to keep up with her classmates. Janice longed for a college education, but she sometimes questioned whether she had the educational skills to get a college degree.

Long after Brooke was asleep, Janice lay awake contemplating her future. It would be weeks, maybe months, before she could have Mountjoy ready for occupancy. Her inheritance seemed like a fortune to Janice, but she knew it wouldn't last long when she started renovating the house. If she used all the money to give the house a face-lift, she would have nothing left for the upkeep of the house and living expenses.

How could she work to support them, go to school and be a mother to Brooke? Even if she took only part-time classes, she couldn't do it at night or on Saturday because she'd have to look after Brooke. Perhaps she should have left Brooke with her foster parents until she had a home ready for them.

The longer she thought about it, the more desperate she became. Janice finally got out of bed and sat in a chair to sort out her options.

The chain store she'd worked for in Willow Creek had a store in Stanton, too. With her three years of experience, she could probably get a job any time. SuperMart provided health benefits and she had to consider that. Her insurance from the store would expire in three months, and without an income, she couldn't pay for health insurance for the two of them. Even if she made Mountjoy livable, it would be two or three months before she could move there. She couldn't afford to live in a motel and eat in restaurants during that time. Would she have to take an apartment after all?

And what about the mystery surrounding Mountjoy? Had her uncle been murdered? Would she ever feel safe living there?

Because of her lack of sleep, the last thing Janice wanted to do was go to church, especially with a new congregation where she wouldn't know anyone. But she roused herself from the chair where she'd spent the night, showered and dressed. She woke Brooke, and while she took a shower, Janice went downstairs to the breakfast room and brought hot chocolate and rolls up to their room.

They arrived at the church just as the Sunday school classes were dismissed. An usher greeted them, handed each of them a bulletin and motioned for them to follow him down the center aisle.

"Hey, Brooke."

Taylor Mallory appeared behind them. "Hi, Miss Reid. I'm glad to see you. Mama told me I should have asked Brooke to come to Sunday school." She took Brooke by the hand. "Both of you come sit with Mama and me."

Brooke glanced at Janice—a question in her eyes. Janice nodded and smiled at the usher. "Guess we have a young guide this morning."

"That's fine," he said and patted Taylor on the shoulder. "The Mallorys will look after you."

As she followed the two children halfway down another aisle, Janice wondered if Lance would be sitting with his family. Linda Mallory was alone, but her smile of welcome was genuine.

"Thanks for choosing our church," she said to Janice, and she moved over in the pew to make room for the two girls to sit between them.

The organ prelude had started and Janice said quietly, "We're at the motel across the street and this seemed the likely place to attend."

"I thought Lance would invite you to church. I guess in the excitement of looking over Mountjoy, he forgot it. He has mixed emotions about your property," Linda said.

Janice grimaced slightly. "So do I."

The organ music increased in volume as the choir moved into place. Lance followed the pastor into the sanctuary.

"Lance is the lay-leader for this month," Linda explained quietly.

Lance's eyes roamed across the congregation, and when he made eye contact with Janice, he looked surprised. Surely he wouldn't think she was taking advantage of his offer of friendship when she didn't even know his family attended this church.

But he smiled in her direction, and when he welcomed visitors, he said, "Janice Reid and her sister, Brooke, have moved to Stanton. They're sitting with my family this morning. Brooke will be starting school tomorrow."

Janice sensed curious stares toward them, and she figured the congregation was linking them with the infamous local Reid family. To dismiss this dismal thought, she focused on the stained-glass window behind the choir loft that depicted the artist's concept of Jesus and His disciples crossing the Sea of Galilee. The expressions on the faces of the disciples showed their fear of the storm, and Janice identified with their terror. Most of her life had been stormy and her fears had already etched faint lines on her face. She transferred her gaze to Jesus, noting the serenity on His face. The artist had depicted His concern for His disciples, when he lifted His hand and commanded the storm to cease.

Janice bowed her head and prayed that Jesus would calm the storms in her life. Her prayer was partially answered when she listened to the pastor's message on friendship.

The pastor's text was taken from the eighteenth chapter of Proverbs. "'A man that has friends must show himself friendly; and there is a friend that sticks closer than a brother.'" The minister extolled the virtues of close friendships stating that Jesus was called the Friend of sinners. Janice knew that she was fortunate to have Lance's friendship, especially when he expected nothing in return. That was the unselfish kind of friendliness Jesus expected of His followers.

She wished she wasn't so hesitant to accept friendship, but Janice wasn't at her best when meeting new people. After the benediction, in spite of the pastor's message, she quickly said goodbye to the Mallorys and left the church as soon as possible. She and Brooke had crossed the street, ready to enter the motel when a woman called, "Just a minute, Miss Reid."

Janice turned to see a large woman, probably in her midsixties, bearing down on them like a battleship going into action. Her knees were bowed with arthritis and she favored her right knee as she hurried toward them. Because of her haste to intercept Janice, the woman was breathing heavily when she reached them.

"I'm Henrietta Cunningham," she said, and apparently realizing that the name meant nothing to Janice, she explained, "I was your uncle's housekeeper."

"Oh, yes. Mr. Santrock mentioned that you'd worked for him during the last years of his life."

"Your uncle was very good to me, and I want to help you any way I can. Let me take you and your sister out to lunch."

For a moment Janice was horrified, thinking she was going to cry. She instantaneously had the feeling that Henrietta was another Miss Caroline. She was brusque where Miss Caroline was quiet; she was huge where Miss Caroline was small; she was dark where Miss Caroline had been fair. But like Miss Caroline, she was reaching out a helping hand.

"Do you really mean that?"

"Of course, I do," Henrietta said, her brown eyes sparkling. "Wouldn't have said so if I hadn't meant it. Let's have lunch and then we'll see what I can do for you."

"I need advice more than anything else. Lance Gordon and his family have been helpful, but I'd like to talk to someone who knew the Reid family well."

Henrietta steered her to the church parking lot adjacent to the motel. "On second thought, let's go to my house to eat.

Restaurants are always crowded on Sunday. I often take some-one home with me for lunch, so I'm ready for company."

She stopped beside an old car that had a battered front fender. "Hop in," she said. "I don't live far from the church, but with my bad knees, I can't walk any distance."

Janice pulled forward the passenger's seat of the two-door car, and Brooke scooted into the back seat. Janice sat beside Henrietta, who started the car, shifted the standard gears, roared the engine and shot out of the parking lot with a speed that jerked Janice's head backward.

When Henrietta slammed on the brakes and crawled past the church, Janice saw Lance standing on the steps. She waved, wondering if he was looking for her.

Henrietta was a tall, stocky, mannishly built woman. Her hair, which had once been auburn but was now mostly iron-gray, was braided into a long pigtail and wound around her head like a halo. Her brown eyes were keen and penetrating.

She chatted about the morning service until they reached her home, a one-story brick house, located on a spacious lot two blocks east of the main street. Flower beds dotted the rich, green turf of her lawn. Baskets of blooming red geraniums hung from the porch ceiling. With scraping gears, Henrietta maneuvered her small car into the garage, then guided Janice and Brooke into the kitchen of her home.

"This is the first house I've ever owned. My husband and I lived in rented houses. And after he died, I took care of in-valids. I'd move into their houses, sometimes for a year or two at a time, so I didn't need a home. I was in demand all the time, for I gave good service, if I do say so myself that shouldn't."

Henrietta continued to talk as she put her purse and Bible on a dresser in the bedroom and shrugged into a large apron that hung on the back of the kitchen door.

"After the mansion got too much for your uncle to keep up, he bought this house and moved to town. I took care of him for about five years. Several weeks before he died, he deeded the house to me."

With a glance at Brooke, she said, "Some people made nasty comments about it. But I'm a God-fearin' woman, and I was John's housekeeper and nurse—nothing more."

The inside of the house was immaculate and Henrietta rustled around getting their lunch on the table. She removed a hamburger-and-rice casserole from the oven and gelatin salad from the fridge. She took a coconut cream pie from a kitchen cabinet and cut it into six pieces.

"Wow! And you didn't even know you'd have company!" Brooke said, her eyes widening as she watched the speed with which the meal appeared on the table.

Henrietta laughed heartily. "Well, I like to eat, too," she said, patting her ample stomach. "And never knowing when the notion might strike me to ask somebody to Sunday dinner, I always fix a little extra."

After asking their preference of beverages, Henrietta poured a cola for Brooke, and made iced tea for Janice and herself.

Although Janice was eager to hear what Henrietta could tell her about her relatives, she listened quietly as their hostess chatted about the town of Stanton.

"Coal and oil money built this town, but the industries ain't as thriving as they used to be. Business just about dried up during the Great Depression, then everything perked up during World War Two. Many of our businesses have closed now because they can't compete with the big shopping centers. I can see why—I like to shop at malls, too."

"The town of Willow Creek, where we used to live, has the same problems. I guess all small towns do."

"Stanton is still a great place to live though. Our churches and schools are good, and we don't have much crime."

Apparently Henrietta hadn't heard about the vandalism to Janice's car.

"No drug problems among the teens?" Janice asked, with a quick glance at Brooke.

"Well, we hear rumors about drugs being bought and sold around here, but nobody's been arrested."

When they finished eating, Henrietta said to Brooke, "Missy, do you want to watch television while your sis helps me clean up? I'll show you the best channels. I have cable, so there are lots of good shows to choose from."

Janice had already rinsed and stacked the dishes when Henrietta returned. After she arranged the utensils in the dishwasher and put the leftovers in the refrigerator, Henrietta motioned to the table.

"Let's sit in here. You said you wanted advice, and I thought you might not want to talk in front of your sister."

"That's true. I don't know where to start."

"I've got all day. Just say what pops in your head."

"I don't remember ever seeing my uncle. I was amazed when he named me in his will. Tell me about him."

"What do you know about the Reids?"

"Not much, but more than I want to know."

"I hope you don't mind some plain speaking about your kin."

"I could probably tell you things you don't even know," Janice said wryly.

"John was the best of the three brothers. Your dad, and the younger brother, Albert, who's still living in this county, received money when their parents died, same as John did. They frittered it away and John was determined they weren't going to get any of his. He intended to give his money to the church until he heard that you and your sister had been taken away from your parents. He did a lot of investigating before he finally decided that you needed and deserved his property, and that you'd take care of it."

"He must have done his investigating secretly. I didn't know anything about it."

"John was a closemouthed man. He didn't tell everything he knew. Now that you've got his property, what are you going to do with it?"

Briefly, Janice explained what she'd been doing since she'd left VOH, stating that she wanted to make a new start in Stanton.

"I didn't have any idea the house was such a mess until I got here. I envisioned the house like it had been in its heyday. Lance Gordon took me to see the house yesterday, and I think it could still be a nice home. But it will take a long time and a lot of money to restore the house to what it used to be. Just to get a few rooms ready so Brooke and I can live there will take weeks. And I can't afford to live in a motel while I renovate the place. Lance suggested an apartment, but usually they have to be leased for a year, and I'd hoped to move into the house before then."

With a wise look, Henrietta said, "Not all apartments are like that."

"I don't intend to use all of Uncle John's money to fix up the house, so I'll have to find a job. If I'm working, it will take that much longer to finish the house."

"I have an idea about where you can live. Anything else bothering you?"

"Yes." Janice explained about the warning note and her tires. "I wonder if it's safe for me to take Brooke to that house. Lance told me yesterday that Uncle John had committed suicide in the house and that a lot of people think the house is haunted. I didn't sleep much last night after I heard that."

An angry look crossed Henrietta's face. "I'd have had to see John pull the trigger to believe he killed himself. I don't know why he even went to Mountjoy that day."

"In his letter to me that I read a few days ago, he mentioned that there was something mysterious going on at Mountjoy, and he intended to investigate."

Surprise flitted across Henrietta's face, and she shook her head. "That's the first I've heard about that. But as I said John was closemouthed. I had gone to the hospital in the county seat to visit my sister, and when I got back John wasn't here. He hadn't driven his old truck for months, but my neighbor saw him drive away in it. When he didn't show up for several hours, I notified the police. They saw his truck parked in front of Mountjoy and they found John inside."

"But what made them think he'd committed suicide?"

"He'd taken his pistol with him, and he was killed with it. Of course his fingerprints were on the gun. I have no doubt that somebody tolled him out there and shot him. And, between us, I lay the deed at the door of his kin, figuring they'd inherit his property. They were always trying to con money out of him. Soon as John was buried, his brother Albert started acting like he owned the county. He went to Santrock and had a fit when he learned that John had left everything to you."

"That note I received probably came from him, too."

"Either him or one of his worthless kids." With a keen glance, she added, "How'd you turn out so well, kid?"

"I'm not quite sure. It certainly wasn't from my parents' examples. My dad was out west somewhere, maybe Colorado, when he met Mom. Her family disowned her when she married my father, so they had no input. But mostly, I owe my character to Miss Caroline at the Valley of Hope. If I hadn't gone to VOH when I did, I can't imagine what my life would be like now. Even as a kid, I vowed if I ever got the chance, I'd make something of my life."

"Well, you have that chance, and I'm going to help you. My health ain't too good, and I'm not able to work anymore. If it hadn't been for your uncle, I'd probably be in a nursing home instead of living in this comfortable house. He also paid me a good salary during the years I worked for him, and I have a little nest egg salted away. I figure I owe him. I'm gonna pay him back by helping you."

Henrietta stood up and motioned to Janice. "Come with me." She stuck her head into the living room. "Brooke, we're going downstairs for a minute. Call if you need us."

Entranced in a Disney program, Brooke only nodded her head.

Henrietta opened a door at one side of the kitchen that led downstairs and into a large, paneled room. Blue carpet covered the floor, light entered through three small windows near the ceiling. A queen-sized bed and a dresser stood at the far end of the room. An upholstered couch and two chairs were grouped around a television. At the foot of the stairs were a set of cabinets and a kitchen unit that contained a sink, stove top and microwave oven.

"There's a bathroom to the left of the bedroom area," Henrietta said. "And that's a sofa bed that Brooke can sleep on. It's yours as long as you want it, free of charge."

Janice turned incredulous eyes toward Henrietta. How could she accept such generosity from a stranger?

Chapter Six

When the first shock of surprise passed, Janice shook her head and opened her mouth to refuse.

Henrietta forestalled her refusal. "This is no time to act on pride. When John decided to move to town, he fixed up this apartment for me, so I'd have some privacy. I haven't had any use for it since he died. I can't handle steps very well, and I'm hardly ever in the apartment. The appliances need to be used, so if you live here, it'll be a help to me."

"I don't know what to say."

"Say nothing—just accept it. It's the perfect setup for you. The school is only three blocks from here. Brooke can walk back and forth to school. I'll be home most every afternoon, and if I'm gone, I'll let you know so you can be here when she comes home. You can spend your time working on Mountjoy without worrying about her."

Tears pricked Janice's eyelids, and she said, "I feel like crying."

Henrietta hugged her shoulders. "Everybody needs to cry once in a while, so go ahead."

Janice swiped at her eyes. "I don't suppose I can ever repay you, but I pray that God will. Let's tell Brooke—she's been worried that we wouldn't have a place to live. I'll move in tomorrow as soon as I take her to school."

"There's an outside entrance to the basement so you can come and go as you want to."

Janice felt like a big burden had rolled off her back. She curled up in a big, comfortable chair in the living room and spent the afternoon listening to Henrietta's memories of John Reid. In Henrietta's comfortable presence, it was easy to push the threat of danger into the background.

But when Henrietta drove them back to the motel, Janice saw two cops in the parking lot, and her fears returned. After thanking Henrietta for her kindness, Janice took Brooke to their room and told her briefly what had happened to her car. She tried to allay her sister's fears by being nonchalant before she went downstairs to meet the cops.

Chief Goodman wandered around the parking area studying the ground intently. He waved to her.

"Howdy, Miss Reid." He nodded toward the other officer. "This is my deputy, Winston Goodman—and he's also my brother."

"Hello, Mr. Goodman," Janice said. The chief of police bestowed a fond glance on his brother. Winston was several years younger than Chief Goodman. His luxuriant dark brown hair spread back from a broad forehead and hung straight to his shoulders. The hair was so evenly colored that Janice suspected Winston touched up his hair to remove signs of aging. She didn't like his bold, appraising glance when they shook hands. Obviously Winston was cut from a different mold than the amiable chief of police.

"Have you any news for me?"

"Not a thing, so far," Chief Goodman said. "We've dusted the car for fingerprints, but since only the tires were touched, I figure we'll find all the prints belonged to you and your sister. We're finished with the car now, so you can have the tires replaced tomorrow."

"We'll find the culprits, Miss Reid," the deputy said. "A lot of people think we're hick policeman, but we always track down our man."

"I'm glad to hear that," Janice said. Winston handed her a card. "Here's the place to get your tires fixed," he said. "They'll either come here and replace the tires or tow the car to the garage."

As she entered the motel, Janice wondered how she would get Brooke to school the next morning. Lance or Henrietta would take her, but she didn't want to bother Lance on the first day of school, and she didn't want to trust Brooke to Henrietta's erratic driving. It was less than a mile from the motel to the school, and she supposed they could walk that distance.

Looking at the card Winston had given her, Janice noted that the tire shop opened at seven o'clock each morning, but there was also an emergency number for weekend problems. Surely her situation could be considered an emergency and Janice dialed the number.

A man answered and Janice explained her problem. "Would it be possible for you to come early in the morning, so I can have the car ready in time to take my sister to school?"

"I'll do better than that," he answered. "I occasionally work on Sunday in an emergency. I'll come by and tow your vehicle into the garage. I'll have it back to you by seven o'clock in the morning."

Janice watched from the window until she saw the wrecker approaching and went downstairs to meet the mechanic. She paid him in advance by check. The next morning, when she looked out the window, her car had been returned.

The driveway and parking lot in front of the school was a frenzy of activity when Janice tried to maneuver her car into a small corner space. Several buses waited in line to unload their passengers as Janice and Brooke left their car and walked into the building.

Janice saw Lance at a distance, shepherding a group of small children down one hall, and he waved to her. Following directions from the guidance counselor, Janice found the sixth grade classroom where Brooke was assigned. Several students were already in the room, and Janice was relieved to see that Taylor Mallory was one of them. Taylor hurried toward the sisters, took Brooke's hand and led her to the teacher.

"Mrs. Hayman, here's the new student, Brooke Reid."

Janice extended a hand to the teacher. "And I'm Janice, Brooke's sister and guardian."

"Welcome to our school, Brooke. We'll do what we can to make you feel at home."

Brooke's teacher, Vivian Hayman, appeared to be in her thirties. As orderly as the students were on the first day of school, Janice decided she was a no-nonsense teacher.

Brooke looked afraid and vulnerable, but knowing she couldn't stay any longer, Janice told Brooke she'd pick her up after school. Remembering the many new schools she'd entered when she was a child, she understood the uncertainty her sister was experiencing.

Since they'd unpacked only two suitcases, Janice soon checked out of the motel and drove to Henrietta's place. She carried the boxes into the apartment then returned the U-Haul trailer to the garage where her tires had been replaced. The next stop was at Mr. Santrock's office. Fortunately she found him at work. He accompanied her to the bank to make arrangements for her to take control of John Reid's finances.

Mr. Santrock protested when she said she wanted to cash one fifteen-thousand-dollar certificate of deposit and put the money in a checking account.

"But I'll need ready cash when I start renovations at Mountjoy," she said. "I looked the property over on Saturday, and I intend to fix up the downstairs so Brooke and I can live there while we work on the rest of the house."

The lawyer shook his head and sighed. "I'd hoped that you'd change your mind about that once you saw how dilapidated the house is. But my conscience is clear now that I've advised you against it," he said with a smile. "So if I can be of any help, be sure to call on me."

Following his advice, she left the remainder of the investments as they were with the interest being paid into a savings account. Janice felt like a millionaire and she wondered aloud if she was capable of handling so much money. The lawyer assured her that she could come to him for advice at any time.

Janice bought a sub sandwich from a deli on Main Street and returned to the apartment. She swept and dusted the rooms before she unpacked her summer clothes, for September was always a warm month. She reserved one side of the closet and some of the dresser drawers for Brooke to put her things.

"Hey, Janice," Henrietta called from her kitchen. "Are you there?"

Janice moved to the stairs and looked up at Henrietta. "Yes. I'm about settled in. I'm ready to go and walk home with Brooke."

"I've fixed supper for the three of us, so don't worry about cooking."

"Now, Henrietta," Janice started to protest.

"It's just for today until you have time to lay in some groceries. Or," Henrietta added, laughter in her voice, "when I take a notion for company. I like to cook."

"You're going to spoil us."

"Best I can tell you're overdue for some spoiling. No girl as young as you oughta be carrying such a load of responsibility."

"I'm used to it. But I am worn out mentally and physically tonight, so it will be nice to eat with you. Cooking isn't one of my talents. What time do you eat?"

"How about half past five?"

Janice nodded her head. "That will give me time to take Brooke with me to the grocery store. I don't know all of the food she likes, so it's better for her to help shop."

It took less than ten minutes to walk from Henrietta's house to the school and she had five minutes to wait. A dozen school buses were lined up ready for the students. Janice sat on a concrete bench until the bell rang. She was thinking about Lance, wondering when she'd see him again, when he walked out of a nearby door.

"Oh, hello," he said, with his usual friendly nature. "I should have called this morning to see if Brooke needed a ride to school. But the first day of school is always hectic, especially with the kindergarten kids who are scared of the big school."

"A mechanic replaced my tires last night, so I drove Brooke to school. And Henrietta Cunningham is letting us stay in her basement apartment until I can get Mountjoy ready to live in."

He nodded approvingly. "I saw Henrietta talking to you yesterday after church. You're in good hands with her."

Lance was pleased about these living arrangements. If Henrietta took Janice under her wing, she'd see to it that Janice didn't make any rash decisions. Lance knew it wasn't wise to set himself up as her advisor.

"And Mr. Santrock took me to the bank this morning and helped me take care of things there, too," Janice continued. "I've never had to deal with any money, except a weekly paycheck before, but he was very patient with me. I moved into the apartment this morning and returned the U-Haul. We're eating supper with Henrietta this evening. She didn't have to twist my arm very hard to get me to agree." Wryly, she admitted, "I guess everyone knows I need a lot of looking after. It's humbling to admit I have to depend on others, but I'm thankful there are people willing to help me."

"Put Linda on the list of those who'll help you settle in Stanton. She told me to invite you to attend our Sunday school class. You'll get a lot of support there."

"Thank you. We'll be there next Sunday."

"I'll probably see you before then." The closing bell rang, and he hurried away. "Take care," he called over his shoulder.

Brooke's backpack was full when she came out of the building. Janice took the heavy pack and slung it over her shoulder as they walked away from the school.

"Lots of homework, huh?"

Brooke rolled her eyes and groaned. "Yeah! Mrs. Hayman is a hard teacher, but I like her."

"How you'd get along?"

"All right, I guess, but some of the kids in my class don't seem to like me."

That news distressed Janice, but she said lightly, "It's probably because you're new. Be nice to everyone, and when they know you better, they'll be friendly."

"I hope so," Brooke said, her eyes uncertain. Then she

brightened. "But Taylor and three of her friends are planning a pajama party in a few weeks and they invited me. Can I go?"

"Probably, but I won't say yes until I learn more about it."

"Oh, look," Brooke said, pointing. "There's my dog!"

Sure enough, the mongrel Brooke had fed a couple of times stood on the sidewalk ahead of them, head on his front feet, tail wagging, watching them. Janice had never seen a more pitiful dog. His ribs showed plainly and his black hair was filthy, probably because he'd been living on refuse from trash cans.

"I had some cookies left from lunch," Brooke said. She rummaged in her backpack and pulled out a package of cookies. The dog's tail waved back and forth when Brooke approached him.

"Careful," Janice cautioned, although she didn't think the dog was dangerous. Brooke took the cookies out of the wrapper and tossed them close to the dog. With two gulps, the cookies disappeared.

"Poor doggie," Brooke said, and her lips trembled.

Poor me, Janice thought, for as they continued toward Henrietta's house the dog followed them. She felt sorry for the animal, but she had too much on her plate right now to adopt a pet.

The dog didn't try to follow them into the house. He sat on the sidewalk and watched as they entered their apartment. But the dog obviously needed some care. Perhaps Henrietta would call animal control or the local animal shelter. But Janice doubted that she would be able to convince Brooke that calling animal control was the thing to do. When they went to the grocery store, Brooke insisted on buying some pet food.

"The dog knows where we live now," she said, "and we can put some food out for him."

"We can't take the dog on Henrietta's property."

"There's an empty lot beside her house. No reason I can't put some dog food on it, is there?"

"We'll see."

"I'll have to think up a name for him. I don't like to keep calling him 'dog.'"

Janice still thought the animal should be taken to a shelter, but Henrietta agreed with Brooke.

"I don't want a dog digging up my flowers," she said, "but an out-of-town man owns that vacant lot next door. He won't mind if you scatter some food there."

While they ate the roast beef, baked potatoes, green beans and slaw that Henrietta had prepared, she asked, "What are your plans for tomorrow?

"I'm going to Mountjoy and figure out what to do next."

Even without knowing the danger that seemed to lurk at Mountjoy, Henrietta immediately advised, "It ain't wise for you to go by yourself, and I can't walk through all that underbrush to go with you."

"I'll admit I don't want to go alone, but I wouldn't be so skittish about it if there wasn't so much undergrowth. The first thing is to have a path cleared from the highway to the house."

"I agree. The local earth-moving company usually has an ad in the Saturday newspaper. There's a stack of papers on that table. Check through them, and you'll find one of his ads. You can telephone in the morning. Or you can stop by his place of business. Once you get a road so you can drive to the house, I can go with you."

Henrietta stood with difficulty and said, "These sore knees are sure a bother to me, but I could be in worse shape."

The next day after she walked to school with Brooke, Janice made arrangements for a bulldozer to come to her property on Wednesday. Encouraged by this quick response, she visited several contractors that Henrietta had mentioned asking them to give an estimate on needed repairs at Mountjoy. She couldn't believe that none of the three contractors would even give her a tentative date when she might expect their help.

Disillusioned, she returned to the apartment, moped for a while, then tapped on Henrietta's door.

"Come in."

Henrietta was knitting an afghan. She smiled cheerily at Janice and put her knitting aside.

"Sit down. I need to rest my eyes. What's troubling you?"

"I've been to three contractors and they're all too busy to work for me."

"Nonsense." Henrietta snorted. "They continually harp about their lack of business. They need the work, but they're afraid to work on your property."

"Afraid! Because they think the house is haunted? Lance mentioned something about that."

"The story spread around after John's death that Mountjoy was haunted and most people won't go near the place. Hard to believe, in this day and age, that sensible people still believe in ghosts."

Henrietta struggled to her feet. "I'll find a contractor for you, but we'll have to go see him, for he doesn't answer his phone regularly. Cecil Smith ain't afraid of anything and he's not superstitious."

Henrietta walked into her bedroom and came back with her purse and car keys. "He's not the best carpenter I know, but he does work hard, and he won't rob you. That's more than I can say for the other contractors."

Janice insisted on driving, but Henrietta shook her head. "I drive better'n I give directions."

With a few jumps and starts, Henrietta soon had the car on the highway east of town. She was a slow driver, but her tendency to roam over the center highway lines kept Janice on the edge of the seat. She was relieved when they turned off the highway onto a narrow road.

Cecil Smith lived five miles from Stanton in the most ramshackle place Janice had ever seen. Even the worst of the places where her parents had lived seemed like a mansion to Mr. Smith's home. His appearance wasn't much better.

He wore a faded red T-shirt tucked into a pair of ragged coveralls that hung loosely on his tall, lanky body. But he seemed clean, and keen blue eyes glowed from under his bristling gray brows. Long, scraggy hair hung over his shoulders and white whiskers covered his face, so it was difficult to tell where his hair stopped and the whiskers began. Smith hoisted himself from a rocking chair on his porch and came to meet them.

"Hiddee-do, Henrietta. What can I do for you?"

"I've brought my young friend, Janice Reid, to see you."

"Reid, huh?" Cecil Smith said, peering at Janice with interest.

"She's John's niece and inherited Mountjoy."

"Mr. Smith," Janice said. "I need a contractor to look over the house and give me an estimate of how much it will cost to put it in living condition."

He squinted at her curiously. "You're aimin' to live there?"

"Yes."

"I've got a little job that'll take me the rest of the day. I could meet you about six o'clock this evening, if that suits you."

"That suits me fine. A bulldozer will clear the road this week, so you could probably start to work in a few days. I want to move in as soon as possible, so I can stop imposing on Henrietta."

"Henrietta thrives on being imposed on, so don't worry about that," the contractor said. "I'll do what I can do to help you, but from I've heard, that house ain't worth fixin' up."

"That may be true," Janice agreed. "That's what I want you to tell me. If it isn't, I'll make other arrangements."

As they drove back to town, Henrietta said, "There used to be some good pieces of furniture in that house."

"They're still there. If I can salvage enough for four rooms, so Brooke and I can move in, I'll store everything else and work on it as I can."

Was it stubbornness to insist on moving to Mountjoy when everyone seemed to think it was a bad idea?

Chapter Seven

Henrietta drove at a snail's pace, pointing out the homes of her friends. Janice answered when necessary, but the clock on the dashboard indicated that school had already been dismissed.

Finally, as discreetly as possible, she said, "Could we go a little faster? School is over for the day, and I'm worried about Brooke. I've told her not to walk home alone, but she might walk with a friend. If she comes home and neither one of us are there, she might be afraid."

"Sorry, honey," Henrietta said. "I start talking and I forget the time." She tromped on the gas pedal and the car shot forward so rapidly that, in spite of the seat belt, Janice thought her head might go through the windshield. "We'll go to the house first."

When Brooke wasn't at the apartment, Janice said, "I'll walk over to school and probably meet her on the way."

But she didn't meet Brooke, and she was uneasy. What if something had happened to her sister? Would whoever wanted Janice out of Stanton stoop to harming Brooke?

When she turned the corner of the school, Lance and

Brooke were sitting on a concrete bench chatting amicably. Brooke jumped up gave Janice a hug. "I thought you'd forgotten me."

Janice leaned over and kissed her sister's forehead. "I'd never do that. Henrietta and I went out in the country and we were late getting back."

"Mr. Gordon waited with me. I could have walked home by myself but he wouldn't let me."

Janice's eyes met Lance's blue ones and she murmured, "Thanks." To Brooke, she said, "You can start walking alone later on, when you know the town and its people a little better." Turning to Lance, she said, "I'm sorry if I delayed you."

"I never leave until all the students are gone, except for the ones involved in sports. It's the coaches' responsibility to see that they're protected."

She took Brooke's hand. "Let's go." To Lance, she said, "I'm meeting Cecil Smith at six o'clock. I couldn't find any other contractor to even give me an estimate on the work at Mountjoy." She rolled her eyes. "For reasons that you might guess."

He nodded understandingly. "If you don't mind, I'll go with you. Smith is reliable enough, but he might be held up and be late in keeping his appointment."

She looked directly at him, pleased, surprised and aggravated at the same time. "I don't need a nursemaid," she said.

"Look at it this way—I wouldn't want Linda to be alone on your property."

"I've imposed on you enough."

"You're not imposing. You haven't asked me to do anything for you. I'll pick you up at Henrietta's around quarter to six."

With a smile, Janice said, "Henrietta will be pleased. She's fusses over Brooke and me like a mother hen with a dozen chicks. She insisted that I must get the driveway cleared and stoned right away so she can drive to the house."

"I'm glad she's looking after you."

"Truth to tell—I rather like it. I've never had any coddling in my life."

In spite of Henrietta's insistence that they eat with her, Janice prepared supper in the apartment. She'd bought a frozen lasagna at the grocery store, and while it baked, she made a salad. Deli cookies and ice cream would have to do for dessert. She wasn't used to cooking for two yet. When she was ready to go to Mountjoy, she opened the door to the upstairs so Henrietta could monitor Brooke's activities.

Cecil Smith was already waiting for them when they arrived. Lance parked behind the contractor's truck, which was as ramshackle as his house. The truck was piled high with lumber, tools, gadgets, buckets, chains, several ladders and a lot of other stuff that Janice couldn't identify.

"Cecil carries his office and workshop with him," Lance said humorously. "Strange to say, he can find what he wants without any trouble."

Lance shook hands with Smith. "Glad to see you, Cecil. It's good you can help Janice."

"I don't know that I *can* help her, but I'll take a look."

"Let's take your ladder," Lance said. "The ceilings are ten feet high, and you may need a long ladder to see everything."

Lance and Cecil carried the ladder and maneuvered their way through the brush and heavy tree foliage along the narrow path that Lance had cut on their previous visit. Janice carried two flashlights and a small case holding a conglomeration of tools.

"Shame this property has gone to rack and ruin," Smith said. "It used to be a showplace."

"I'd like to have it look like that again."

"Big job for a young woman like you."

"Maybe *too* big a job for me. Your assessment of the work that has to be done will determine my decision."

"We crawled in the window when we were here Saturday," Lance said.

"Did you look around for a key?" Cecil said. "It's my experience that everybody leaves a key somewhere handy."

A tall, lanky man, Cecil was able to run his hand across the top of the door frame. With a self-satisfied look, he picked up a key and waved it at them. He pulled open the decrepit screen door and turned the key in the lock. The door was stuck, but when Lance put his shoulder against the door, it squeaked open.

Cecil whistled while he sauntered around the first floor rooms. Janice recognized it as an off-key version of "She'll be Coming Around the Mountain." Lance and Janice followed for the most part in silence, although Lance occasionally asked a question or made a comment.

"Let's take a look at the second floor," Cecil said.

"Wonder if that key will work in the door to the stairway," Lance said. "The door was locked when we were here a few days ago."

Cecil handed the key to Lance, but as they approached the door, they saw that it stood ajar. Lance glanced quickly at Janice. "I know that door was locked. So that means somebody has been here since we were."

Smith cackled with laughter. "What kind of somebody? The kind that walks on two feet or the kind that floats around in the air?"

Janice supposed that was Cecil's idea of a joke, but she didn't find it amusing. Hesitantly Lance pushed open the door and muttered, "What do you make of that?"

Cecil and Janice peered over his shoulder. "There ain't any steps!" Cecil said. "Maybe the second story never was finished."

Lance ran his hands over the walls. "There have been steps here, but they've been sawed away. Strange! Let's bring the ladder so we can see what's upstairs."

They carried the ladder through the hall and propped it against the floor of the upper story.

"Are you going up?" Lance asked Janice.

"I'd like to."

Lance looked at Cecil, who tested the ladder by placing both feet on the bottom rung. "It oughta be safe enough."

"I'll go first, Cecil, and you hold the ladder while Janice climbs. You come up last, if that's all right."

"Right as rain," Cecil said.

The ladder stood at a forty-five-degree angle, so the climb wasn't too difficult, but Janice welcomed Lance's extended hand supporting her last two steps. When Cecil joined them, they started a tour of the four upstairs rooms that were separated by a wide hallway. One room was empty, but the others were fully furnished.

"So there were steps at one time," Janice said and Lance nodded. She wondered at the concerned look on his face. "But what could have happened to the furniture in this room?"

"When Mr. Reid got sick," Lance said, "they probably took the furniture from this room to make a bedroom downstairs. Henrietta can tell you, and she'll probably clear up the mystery of the missing steps."

The other three rooms had furnishings typical of the late nineteenth century. Each bed had a six-foot-high oak headboard with a footboard about two feet in height. Each room had a dresser and a table that matched the beds, and an armless high-backed wooden rocker. Small electric lamps stood on the tables. Soiled, tattered paper covered the walls, and a few ragged rugs lay on the pine floors. Filthy bedspreads and quilts covered the beds. Every window was broken, and flimsy, dirty, torn curtains hung through the openings.

Cecil pointed to the many wasp and yellow jackets' nests near the ceilings. "You'll have to get rid of those pests before you can live here," he said.

While Janice considered the value of the furniture, Cecil and Lance checked out the structure of the house.

"I don't see any sign of leaks except where the rain blew in through broken windows," Cecil said, pointing to brownish spots on the floors. "That's what made the stains. The roof must still be in good shape."

A massive cupboard almost covered the rear wall of the hallway. Lance peered inside. "It's empty. Looks like this piece of furniture was built right here—it couldn't have been brought up the stairs." He pushed on the cupboard and couldn't budge it. "Sure is heavy."

"Let's go downstairs to talk over what you can do," Cecil said.

Lance went down the ladder first, because if Janice slipped, he wanted to be in a position to catch her. He'd learned that Janice resented help, so he couldn't make an issue of assisting her.

Janice and Lance sat side by side on the deacon's bench. Cecil pulled a ladder-back chair with a woven seat from the living room. He sniffed the air like a dog on a scent.

"There's a funny smell in here," he said. "I can't place it."

"I've been noticing it, too," Lance said. "I didn't notice it when we were here before. It smells like turpentine or ether."

Janice had moved into a lot of smelly houses, so she wasn't concerned with the odor. "What do you think of the house?"

Cecil pulled on his whiskers, hummed a little tune and

gazed at the ceiling. "It'll take a lot of work to make this place the way it was a hundred years ago. But as far as I can determine, the structure is good, so termites must not be working on it. It'll take a lot of money."

"Which I don't have," Janice said. "How much will it cost to get the downstairs rooms in good shape so my sister and I can live here? The upstairs renovation will have to wait."

Cecil studied the ceiling again and drummed his fingers on the arm of his chair. Lance winked at Janice, obviously amused by Cecil's idiosyncrasies. Wasps, buzzing around the ceiling, accompanied the contractor's humming.

"Lance," Cecil said, after several minutes had passed, "you've had experience with a lot of construction at the school so speak up if you think I'm wrong. It's my opinion that this house needs a good cleaning more'n anything else." He appraised Janice with a keen glance. "You'll have some expense to make the house fit to live in, but if you just do the downstairs, you can be comfortable without spending a lot of money."

"I agree," Lance said, "but Janice knows I have reservations about her living here. It's too isolated."

Cecil shrugged his skinny shoulders, peering at Lance under his shaggy brows. "That's not for me to decide nor you neither, unless there's something I don't know."

Lance colored slightly, admitting, "It isn't any of my business."

"I'll give you an idea of what you'd have to do before you can move in," Cecil continued. "First off, you've gotta replace all the broken windows to preserve the house. If you put new locks on the doors, that'll give you protection from ordinary circumstances. You'd have to get rid of the curtains and the carpets. Later on, you might want to refinish the floors, but if they're clean, you can manage if you add some rugs, here and there."

"You've encouraged me already, Mr. Smith. What else?"

"Your biggest expense will be getting the plumbin' checked and repaired. After ten years of neglect, you could have damage to the pipes. The gas furnace is old, so you might be better off to replace it. You can get somebody from the county seat if the local guys won't work here. And I'd get all of this brush cleaned off the place, not only so you can see out, but so you can tell if anybody is looking in."

"Can you give a ballpark figure on how much this might cost her?" Lance asked.

Cecil gazed around the ceiling for a while, closed his eyes and whistled a tune. He took a ragged notebook and a pencil out of his shirt pocket. He chewed on the end of the pencil and scribbled down some figures.

"Not countin' the curtains and rugs, and leavin' the upstairs as is except the windows, and not painting the outside, I'd say she could get by with around ten thousand dollars. You got that much?" he asked.

Janice nodded. That sounded like a lot of money to her, but she'd expected it to be more. The certificate of deposit she'd set aside to renovate Mountjoy would be enough, with some left for the driveway. The money in her personal savings would take care of their living expenses until she finished working on the house. She'd papered and painted her apartment once, so she could do a lot of the work herself. But should she spend so much money on an old house that someone was determined she shouldn't occupy? She'd never had to make a decision of such magnitude before, and it wasn't easy.

Lance watched as Janice weighed her options. Her troubled eyes indicated uncertainty. Janice was too young to be thrown suddenly into the guardianship of her sister, owner-ship of this property and a sizable amount of money. Little wonder she seemed bewildered, but he'd leave it to her law-yer and Henrietta to advise her.

"When could you start work?" she asked Cecil in a weary voice.

"Like I said—I've got a couple of jobs to finish, which will take me about a week. There's some other work pending, but nothing I can't postpone." He whistled again and stared at the ceiling. "I could start a week from this coming Tuesday," Cecil decided. "That'll give you time to clear the road, so we can haul in the materials we need."

"What do you think?" Janice asked, looking directly at Lance.

"If you're determined to live here," he said, trying to keep concern out of his voice, "Cecil's suggestions seems reason-able to me."

Janice stood and walked through the four downstairs rooms trying to envision the house with the improvements Cecil had suggested. Lance and Cecil watched her silently. When she returned to the hallway, she sat wearily on the bench beside Lance, and he wished he had the right to put his arm around her slumped shoulders.

"The only other alternative is to sell the property, and I don't want to do that. Besides, I don't think it will seem so scary when we get all of the underbrush cleared away and we can see to the highway. Could I be ready to move within a month?" she asked Cecil.

He whistled a line of "Amazing Grace." "I'm not the fast-est carpenter in the business," he said, "and I'd judge it'll take two months."

"I'll be free while Brooke is in school, so I'll work right along beside you."

"I can help with cleaning the yard," Lance said, and when Janice started to protest, he held up his hand. "We have a men's service club at the church, and we often take on projects like this. We've built a porch for one family this summer, we roofed a house and we mow a few yards every week for elderly people—Henrietta's for example. I'll talk to the men, and if there are enough of them free, we can come Saturday to work on your yard. You'll be surprised at what a change we can make with one day's work."

"But I don't *want* people working for me unless I pay them," Janice protested. "I want to be independent."

"Being independent can be mighty lonely, miss," Cecil said. "There are some things you can't pay people to do. And I doubt you could find anyone around Stanton who'd even take the job of cleaning up this place, no matter what you paid. It's hard to find people who'll take on a grubby, dirty job, and that's what this one will be."

Most of her life Janice had been on the receiving end of charity and she hadn't liked it. In spite of Miss Caroline's kindness, it had been charity. That was why she'd worked so hard to make enough money to be worthy of being Brooke's guardian. She didn't want her sister to grow up with the burden of being a charity kid. But she still had enough humility to take advice.

Turning to Lance, she said, "I'll appreciate having your men's group clean the lawn."

Lance didn't think she really appreciated it and he wondered why Janice found it so difficult to accept help.

As he'd promised, the man came with the bulldozer on Wednesday and when he finished on Thursday evening, Janice couldn't believe the difference his work had made in her property. All of the multiflora rosebushes that had taken over the driveway had been pushed to one corner of the lot. The man and his helper said they'd come back and destroy the brush when conditions were suitable for burning.

The original driveway had been located, subsequently graded, and ditches laid out on each side for proper drainage. A wide parking area was cleared in front of the house. Several loads of coarse limestone had been put on the driveway and covered with a layer of finer stone.

While the men worked, Janice started assessing how much renovation she would have to do in the kitchen. Without water, she couldn't do much, but she did clear the shelves of items that would have to be thrown away and put them in large plastic garbage bags. She put usable dishes and pans on the table. The refrigerator was empty, but had an unpleasant odor, so she propped the door open so it could air.

With an old broom she'd found in the pantry, she scraped everything out of the cabinets and off the pantry shelves. Then she swept up the refuse and dumped it in the garbage bags. The work was strenuous and at the end of two days, she was bushed.

But she was now convinced that Cecil's estimate was correct and that the house needed cleaning more than anything else. The furniture was well built. Although the stove and refrigerator were questionable, they didn't seem to be more than ten years old and she'd certainly used older appliances than that in her childhood. She wouldn't know for sure until she tried them, so she reserved an opinion on whether she'd have to buy appliances. But the red-checked linoleum seemed solid, and she thought restoring the kitchen would take a minimum of money. The kitchen had been her greatest worry.

As the work on the driveway progressed, Janice kept wishing that Lance would stop by so she could ask his opinion if the work was done satisfactorily. He didn't come, and she didn't want to put him on the spot by asking him to approve the work. Although she was convinced that the contractor had earned the money, Janice's hand shook with uneasiness as she wrote his check for three thousand dollars. How long would her money last if she had many more bills like this?

On Thursday evening, after the road was completed, Janice took Henrietta and Brooke to see the house.

"He did a good job on this road," Henrietta said when Janice turned her car into the driveway.

Henrietta walked slowly through the rooms on the first floor, nostalgically remembering the days she'd lived at Mountjoy. "Except for the filth, nothin's changed," she said. "I figured thieves would have hauled everything away by now."

Janice looked around for Brooke before she answered. Her sister still stood in the center hall, as if she were glued to the floor, looking around in dismay.

"Cecil said it was probably because people think the place is haunted," Janice said quietly, "and they're afraid to steal anything."

"So much the better for you," Henrietta answered. "There have been some strange things happening out here, according to rumor."

Joining the others in the living room, Brooke wailed, "I don't want to live here. It looks awful and the place stinks."

"It will look a lot better when it's clean," Janice assured her, wishing she hadn't brought Brooke to see the house until it was in livable condition. The child's attitude depressed her. Did the house remind her of some of the unsavory places they'd lived during her childhood?

"Besides a good cleaning, what else is necessary to make the downstairs livable?" Janice asked.

"The davenport and chairs in the living room will have to go. You could refinish them and have them upholstered, but that would cost a lot of money. Besides, they're uncomfortable, to my notion. They'd bring a good price in an antique store if you want to sell them, and you could use the money to buy a new couch and some chairs."

"Cecil said there was room to store them in the outbuilding back of the house, so I think I'll tear the upholstery off and put them in the building. I can buy secondhand furniture and refinish the antique pieces when I have more time and money."

Following Henrietta's advice, she took inventory of what was usable in a notebook, separating what she could sell and what she'd have to buy. Except for a few tables and two rocking chairs, she'd need to replace the living room furniture. In the hallway, beside the deacon's bench, there was a closed cupboard, constructed of pine and poplar lumber, that would be great for storing their outdoor garments.

"John had the kitchen overhauled and bought new appliances when the county water and sewer system was laid out this way. He got sick right soon after that and the kitchen in the town house was newly fixed when we moved, so he left all of these things here. He never did give up the idea that he might move back to Mountjoy. We took the washer and dryer to town with us so you'll need new ones."

Janice shook her head. "I'll go to the coin laundry in town. I'm used to doing that."

Henrietta peered at the dishes Janice had put on the table. "We took most of the dishes and pans with us so there's not much here but odds and ends."

"I'm used to odds and ends," Janice said.

A pie safe with punched heart tin inserts in the doors stood in one corner of the kitchen. "I used this to store the canned goods and cereal. I kept the onions, potatoes and such like in the pantry."

"I worked in there yesterday. It's a huge room. The floor covering seems all right."

Henrietta nodded agreement. "It's the same vinyl tile that was here when I came, but it still looks good."

The dining room had a cherry corner cupboard that reached the ten-foot ceiling and a walnut extension table with matching chairs. "John's mother bought the table and chairs sixty years ago," Henrietta explained, "but that cupboard is as old as the house. An antique dealer once offered John three thousand dollars for it."

"Really!"

"But John was tenderhearted about the past, and he didn't like to change things. I don't suppose his local kin have any idea how valuable these things are, but if they'd inherited, the furnishings would have been sold right away. They'll do anything for money."

Henrietta pointed to the sideboard made of solid oak, neatly carved, with a good gloss finish. A large German beveled mirror was attached to the solid base. "This is a family piece, too."

"I'll keep the dining room furniture and anything else that belonged to the family."

"This room was the parlor in the old days," Henrietta said, when they came to the room across the hallway from the dining room. It was furnished with a high-backboard poplar bed, a matching chest and table, as well as two trunks.

"When John got so poorly that he couldn't climb the steps, he brought this furniture downstairs. These old houses didn't have any closets—that's why there's so many cupboards and such."

Henrietta flipped back the quilt from the bed and poked around in the mattress. The mattress looked clean, but it smelled of mildew.

"Nothin' wrong with this that a good airin' won't take care of," Henrietta commented. "Guess the mice had enough other things to chew on that they didn't bother the mattress. Well, Janice, it looks to me as if you're in pretty good shape. I don't feel up to climbing the stairs, but I reckon everything is about the same."

"The furniture on the second floor is all right, but what happened to the steps?"

"What do you mean?"

"There aren't any. Come and see."

When Janice opened the door to the stairway, Henrietta stepped into the stairwell. A startled gasp escaped her lips, and she stared, a stunned expression on her face.

When she found her voice, Henrietta said, "What has happened here? Who tore out these steps?"

"Then this happened after you and Uncle John moved?"

"Of course it did," Henrietta snapped. "Who did it? And a more important question—why did they do it? Makes no sense to me."

"Cecil, Lance and I climbed to the second floor by using a ladder, and except for the one room, the furnishings were still there. We couldn't figure out why the steps had been removed."

Shaking her head, Henrietta stepped out into the hall. "Appears like visitors ain't welcome on the second floor." Concern evident in her eyes, Henrietta glanced from Janice to Brooke. "Maybe you'd better not be in any hurry to move."

Hoping to reassure Brooke, whose hand clutched the bottom of her sister's denim shirt, Janice said lightly, "We'll not move for a while. It will take several weeks for the house to be livable."

Henrietta opened her mouth to speak but closed it after she took a look at Brooke's frightened expression.

"What's your next move?" she asked Janice.

"I can't do much until Cecil replaces the windows and puts locks on the doors. After that, I can start cleaning. In the meantime, I'll shop for curtains, and the few household articles I'll need."

Henrietta nodded approvingly. "There are several used furniture stores in the area, so furniture ain't no problem. But curtains will be. These windows are taller and more narrow than modern windows and store-bought draperies won't fit. If you have them custom-made, it'll cost a fortune."

Grimacing, Janice said, "I might find curtains to fit these windows in Goodwill stores."

Henrietta put her arm around Janice and hugged her tightly. "I'm proud of you, girl, and I know John would be, too. Not many women your age would take on a project like this. They'd sell the property and all this old stuff and buy everything new. You're making decisions I wouldn't even want to make at my age."

"I've always felt hard toward my parents for not taking care of us, but I suppose everything works out for good. If they'd been good parents, I'd never have learned to make decisions when I was a child. And if we'd continued to live with them, Uncle John wouldn't have left this house to me."

Henrietta squeezed her shoulders again then released her. "As for curtains—can you sew?"

"I took sewing lessons in vocational classes before I went to VOH. I could probably remember the basics. Why?"

"You can make the curtains out of bed sheets, which wouldn't cost much. King-size sheets would be long enough to cover the windows. If you want to tackle the curtains, you can borrow my machine, which I seldom use. It's a portable, and you could bring it here and cut and measure as you go."

"That sounds like a good plan. I'll do some shopping tomorrow while Brooke is in school. Saturday, the men from the church are coming to clear the property of underbrush."

"We'll need to fix lunch for them, too," Henrietta said, "for it'll be an all-day job."

"What kind of food should I buy?"

"There are sometimes ten of them, so we can figure on that number. Let's think about the food as we go back to town. My old legs have had all the standing they want."

Janice locked the house and held her mentor's arm as they moved to the car. Henrietta had solved several of her problems, but she was disturbed about Brooke's reactions to the house. After her first outburst of dissatisfaction, she hadn't said a word. Now she drooped silently in the back seat. Janice had thought her sister would be excited to have a house of their own. She remembered she'd promised Brooke if she was unhappy she could sell Mountjoy and return to Willow Springs—a promise she might have to keep if Brooke's opinion didn't change soon. But she'd go ahead with her plans, as the house would bring a better price if she made some inexpensive improvements.

"A picnic-type lunch is the kind to have, for it's supposed to be hot the rest of the week," Henrietta said, interrupting her thoughts. "Besides, there's no place fit to eat inside the house."

"So we'll need sandwiches."

Henrietta nodded. "You can get containers of chicken salad and ham salad at the grocery store deli. And don't forget cheese cubes and crackers. Apples and bananas will go well, and I'll make a batch of cookies." She grinned. "I've seen those men eat before, so I know they have big appetites."

Janice was making mental notes as Henrietta talked. "What about beverages?"

"Get canned pop and bottled water, and a big bag of ice. We can put the beverages and ice in my big cooler. They'll probably bring something to drink, but it would be hospitable for you to provide something."

Janice nodded emphatically. "I want to pay my own way."

When Janice went to pick up Brooke on Friday evening, Lance waited for her.

"We'll start working at Mountjoy about eight o'clock tomorrow. Can you come out for a while and tell us what trees and shrubs you want to keep?"

"You guys will have a better idea about that than I will, but I'll be there early. Henrietta and I are preparing lunch for you."

"That isn't necessary."

"I know, but we want to do it."

How had it happened that in a few short weeks, Lance Gordon had become so interested in her welfare?

Chapter Eight

The next evening as Janice stood on the front porch of Mountjoy and looked toward the highway, she couldn't believe the transformation in her property. Several trees had been cut down and the logs sawed into lengths, usable for the fireplaces in the house. Two large oak trees and several spruce trees dotted the landscape. The hedge close to the house had been pruned to a height of two feet.

A lilac tree, several forsythia bushes and a rambler rose had been shaped into attractive shrubbery. After the brambles in the backyard had been cut down, the men piled all of the discarded shrubbery on the stack of brush left by the contractor who'd made her road.

"When the contractor burns this, several of us will come and help keep the fire from spreading," Lance said.

While the men had worked, Janice had swept the front porch. Using a container of hot water she'd brought from Henrietta's, Janice started cleaning the kitchen. She hummed contentedly as she washed the interior of the refrigerator, which seemed in excellent condition.

When she turned to the cabinets above the sink, her contentment disappeared like air from a deflated balloon. She'd cleaned everything out of these cabinets a few days ago, but on the bottom shelf was a plastic cup, with a sketch of a cemetery headstone inscribed with her name. A cry of dismay escaped Janice's lips as she backed away from the cabinet, her hand clutching her throbbing throat. *Another warning—a warning of death!*

She reached for the cup, intending to throw it away, but Henrietta called from the front porch. "Hey, Janice. Where do you want to picnic?"

Janice slammed the cabinet door, leaving the cup where she'd found it. She hurried to meet Henrietta, who stood at the foot of the steps, holding a lawn chair.

"How about the porch?"

"Looks good to me. I've got a folding table in the car and we can put the food on it. I brought a chair for myself. The rest of you are younger than I am, so you won't mind sitting on the ground or the porch floor."

Trying to force the warning of danger from her mind, Janice unfolded the chair for Henrietta. "You sit here while I carry the food from the car. I intended to come back and help load the food. You should have waited for me," she scolded.

"I was curious to see what was going on," Henrietta said. "I left Brooke at the church for the youth meeting, and I'll pick her up about three o'clock."

As she settled into the chair, Henrietta gazed with appreciation over the lawn. "They've sure done a lot of work. Mountjoy is going to live again. I'm grateful to you, Janice, for deciding to make your home here."

Janice didn't answer, because the cup with the gravestone was imprinted in her mind, and she couldn't think of anything else. But she didn't want to worry Henrietta or Lance, so she decided to say nothing about it for the time being. As she carried baskets of food from Henrietta's car, she wondered momentarily if she should report this harassment to the chief of police. She didn't think it would do any good, as he hadn't made a report to her about his investigation of the damage to her tires.

Lance tarried after the others left Mountjoy, and he scanned the contents of the outbuilding.

"I'll help you sort out the good items later on. Looks like there may be several cans of paint and stuff like that. Cecil will no doubt haul the junk away for you."

"I keep getting further into your debt," she said, "but I wouldn't have a clue about what to keep or throw away. If we get rid of some of the junk in this building, I can use the space to store the antiques that I don't want to use in the house."

Lance twisted his shoulders and swung his arms in a circular motion. Janice's pulse quickened as she noted the play of his muscles through the sweat-stained shirt that clung to his back and shoulders. She flushed when he intercepted her glance and she turned away, afraid of what her eyes might reveal to him.

"I'll probably have a lot of stiff joints tomorrow," he said, "but we've accomplished a lot."

"Beyond my greatest imagination," Janice said. "It's beginning to look like a home. With such a large front yard, I'm surprised there isn't more land behind the house."

The boundary fence was only a few yards from the porch. A barbed wire fence separated her property from her neighbor, where a weathered barn stood close to the fence. "Who owns that property?" she asked.

"Probably Loren Santrock. His home is just over the hill, a mile along the highway, and I think his line extends this far."

Hesitating to advise Janice, but feeling that he must, Lance said, "There are advantages and disadvantages to what's been done here this week. You have no trouble driving in here now, or in viewing the land surrounding the house. But on the other hand, anyone else can easily access your property, too."

Janice laughed at the concern on his face. "Don't worry about it. I won't move until I can lock the windows and doors. And I can phone for help if I'm in trouble. We'll be all right," Janice said with more assurance than she felt.

"You might consider putting a lock on the gate, too, so you can secure it when you come home at night. The gate and fence aren't much good, but they'll do for now."

"I'll ask Cecil to take care of it for me."

"Will I see you at church tomorrow?" he asked.

"Yes, Linda invited me to Sunday school, and Brooke wants to come, too."

As she drove down the driveway in front of Lance, Janice kept thinking about the cup she'd found in the cabinet. Someone had been in the house since she was there with Henrietta two days ago. If the person who'd put the cup in the cabinet had intended to scare her, he'd succeeded. But she wasn't yet intimidated to the point where she'd cancel her plans to live at Mountjoy.

The Outreach Class of Bethesda Church met for coffee and rolls before the Bible study started. Leaving Brooke at the door of her classroom in the main building, Janice entered the annex and walked down the hallway looking for the meeting room. Her hands were moist and her heartbeat accelerated. Right now, she was less intimidated by the mystery at Mountjoy than she was of meeting a group of new people. She took a deep breath and paused with her hand on the doorknob.

Rapid steps approached behind her and she turned when Linda Mallory called, "Janice, wait for me."

The words were music to Janice's ears.

Linda hurried down the hallway. "I'd expected to meet you at the front door," she said, "but Taylor and I overslept this morning."

"I'm not at my best meeting new people," Janice admitted, "so I'm glad you made it before I went inside."

"Lance will be along soon, so you'll know two people, at least. He had some things to do in preparation for the worship service."

There were about thirty people in the room and it sounded as if all of them were talking at once. The chattering was interspersed with a lot of laughing. When Linda entered the room with Janice in tow, she shouted over the conversations, "We have a guest this morning. Make Janice Reid welcome."

They welcomed Janice like a long-lost friend rather tha someone related to the infamous Reids. As often occurre when she least expected it, Janice recalled a Scripture she'o learned at VOH. "I was a stranger, and you took me in."

Philip Long, the class teacher, had been one of the men who'd worked at Mountjoy on Saturday, and he personally introduced Janice to his wife and several other people. She h d always feared to make friends because when she was a chi , she'd have a special girlfriend, only to lose her when her p ents made a sudden move. But she was soon seated at a ta beside Linda, being served chocolate milk and a breakfast roll, and her anxiety about meeting new people had disappeared.

When Lance strolled into the room, he made a beeline for her, shook her hand and said, "Sure is nice to see you this morning. This is a loud bunch, but we enjoy one another." He sat beside her, and she felt sheltered between Linda and him.

"Everyone has been friendly to me."

It was no easy task to get the attention of the thirty or so people when Philip called the group to order. "Lance, how about leading us in prayer," he said.

Everyone automatically clasped the hand of their neighbors and Janice's hand trembled slightly when Lance gently squeezed her fingers. His prayer was quiet and personal and Janice had never felt nearer to the presence of God than she did when she heard Lance pray.

"We have to wrap up some business about our fall festival project before we start today's lesson," Philip said. "For the benefit of our visitors, I'll explain that we're spearheading a food and clothing drive for needy families in the county. For the past few years we've sponsored a food booth at the town's fall festival which takes place the first weekend in October. All of us will be needed to work in the booth during the festival. Do we have all of the committees filled?" he asked the secretary.

"No one has volunteered to gather the food that's been promised and bring it to the booth."

"Who hasn't been assigned to a committee?" Philip asked.

The secretary flipped through a notebook she held. With a pointed look in his direction, she said, "Lance hasn't volunteered for anything."

A loud sound of good-natured catcalls echoed around the room.

Lance laughed, throwing up his arms in self-defense. "Hey, I'm a busy man. Remember, I'm the guy who looks after your kids."

"A poor excuse is better than none," Philip said. "Put him

down to head that committee, but we will give him some help. Any volunteers?"

"Most of us are already committed to baking and cooking," the secretary said. "Why don't we ask Janice to help him? She needs a job."

Loud clapping indicated agreement and Janice glanced timidly at Lance. She couldn't tell from his expression what he thought about having her for a helper.

"That's fine with me," Lance said. He looked at her and she nodded agreement.

Janice enjoyed the give-and-take between the teacher and the class as they discussed the Bible lesson, but her mind was busy with thoughts of Lance. Circumstances seemed to throw them together. Although he had been willing to help her at Mountjoy, she didn't want to infringe on his personal life.

Outwardly Lance seemed nonchalant about this new association with Janice, but inwardly, he was excited. He'd told himself over the past few days that he had to back off and stop seeing Janice so often. Now he'd been given a new reason to seek her company. Was it a good idea for him to see so much of Janice?

Chapter Nine

Stanton didn't offer many choices in bargain shopping, so Janice spent Monday in the county seat. She went to a secondhand store and found a couch, a matching chair and twin bedsteads for a reasonable price. She intended to take the antique bedroom furniture upstairs where it had been originally. If they remained at Mountjoy she'd arrange for separate rooms for Brooke and herself, but she had to conserve her money for the time being.

She located a huge furniture warehouse where she could buy a stove, refrigerator and new mattresses for their beds. She made note of the information so she could check with Henrietta. More and more, Henrietta was filling the role of the grandmother she'd never had.

After visiting several stores and looking at curtains, Janice decided she *could* make stylish window coverings out of sheets. She would buy Venetian blinds for the lower sash of the windows to provide privacy and thread long panels through large ornamental loops to fall gracefully to the floor.

Janice met Cecil Smith at the house early on Tuesday

morning. He took measurements of all of the windows and drove to a lumber supply company to place the order. There wasn't much Janice could do about cleaning the floors until Cecil finished his carpenter work. But she had brought water from Henrietta's to continue cleaning the cabinets in the kitchen and the pantry shelves.

Cecil had contacted a plumber, who would arrive the next day to check the water and sewer lines. Cecil advised her to stop by the water office to make an application.

This was the first time Janice had been alone at Mountjoy, and she was overcome with a sense of desperation when she realized how much there was to be done to make this place livable. She was also afraid to go into the kitchen and learn if the cup with the tombstone was where she'd left it.

Again, a Scripture verse she'd learned at VOH popped into her head. *Sufficient unto the day is the evil thereof.* It had taken Janice a long time to make any sense out of that verse until Miss Caroline had explained that worrying about tomorrow wouldn't solve anything. She'd taught her students to trust God for tomorrow and enjoy each day in His presence.

Knowing that fidgeting around waiting for Cecil to return would only give her more concern, she walked into the kitchen intending to continue cleaning the cabinets and pantry. Fearfully, she opened the cabinet where the foam cup had been. It was gone! Had there been a cup in the cabinet Saturday, or had she dreamed it?

Janice cleaned the pie safe which held Lysol, detergents and other cleaning supplies. After ten years, they'd be worthless. She brought a rusty garbage can in from the side porch and dropped the bottles and cans in it. Mice apparently couldn't find a way into the second shelf, which held napkins, towels and other paper products. The items were dusty and had picked up a musty smell, so Janice disposed of them, too.

The drawer below the two shelves was full of towels and dishcloths, many of them no longer usable. Salvaging one cloth that was mostly intact, Janice wiped the dust off the shelves. Her hands halted in midair when she glanced at the refrigerator. Although she'd left the door ajar on Saturday, it was closed now. Almost afraid to open the door, Janice jerked on it quickly and stumbled backward.

The cup that had been on the table on Saturday was now in the refrigerator. Angrily, she grabbed the cup, flattened it with her feet and dropped it in the garbage can. If Cecil saw the warning, he might refuse to work on the house, too.

When her heartbeat slowed, Janice continued to work on the pie safe until she had the shelves cleared of debris and ready for washing. Remembering a small wire brush she'd left on the pantry shelves, Janice decided to use it to clean grime from the metal doors.

She walked to the pantry, and as the door squeaked open, a sound of thunder nearly deafened her. She heard running steps on the second floor, followed by groaning. The house creaked as if it would collapse around her.

Janice had had all she could stand. She bolted out of the house, ran off the porch and into the yard. Gasping for breath, she thought her heart would never stop pounding. She leaned against one of the spruce trees and stared at the house. Obviously, since the cup had been moved, somebody had been in the house and perhaps was still there.

Fifteen minutes later, when she heard Cecil's ancient truck in the driveway, Janice steeled herself to meet him as if nothing had happened in his absence. When Cecil looked at her suspiciously, she doubted that she'd succeeded. To forestall any questions, she said, "How'd you get along with your orders?"

Whistling, he stepped out of the truck. "Not bad. They'll bring some of the windows this afternoon and the others as soon as they come in. There are lots of old houses in this county so these odd-sized windows are still available." He eyed her with concern. "What have you been up to?"

"Cleaning out the kitchen cupboards. Not much else I can do without water."

Cecil took a battered lunch bucket out of his truck. "I'll stay here in the shade and eat my dinner. You wanna share my grub?"

"No, thank you. I'll go to my apartment and have a sandwich. I'll bring food with me tomorrow."

Janice stepped into her car and drove away, wondering if she could find the nerve to return to Mountjoy. She knew she hadn't imagined those noises or the cup. It was a continuance of the campaign to drive her away from her inheritance. What was so important about the house that her relatives were determined to have it? According to Santrock, the house wouldn't bring much on the real estate market, so why was her presence a threat to anyone? The farther she traveled from the house, the more determined she was that she wasn't going to let her harassers obstruct her plans for the future. Her mother had always said that the Reids had a stubborn streak, and at this moment, she was all Reid.

When she parked in front of Henrietta's house, the dog Brooke had befriended, and had named Hungry, sat on his haunches on the sidewalk. Janice stepped inside the apartment and filled a bowl with dog food, drew a pitcher of water and walked to the vacant lot next door. Usually the dog waited until they left before he came to eat, but today he approached

Janice cautiously. She kept her eye on him as she poured the dry food into the metal pan that Henrietta had provided. She sloshed water into the big bowl on the ground.

"Hello," she said softly as the dog inched his way toward the food. "You don't have to be afraid. I'm friendly and although it's against my better judgment, I've allowed Brooke to feed you. I know how it feels to be abandoned, and how scary it is for new people to look after you."

The dog was lapping the water now and as he took a bite of the food, Janice knelt and reached out a hand to touch him. He dodged away, but as she continued to talk softly to him, he returned to the food and allowed her to put a hand on his head. She felt around his neck for a collar, but there wasn't one.

"I don't know how to find your home, but I'll look after you as long as I can."

Janice felt so safe under Henrietta's roof that she knew it would be difficult for her to return to Mountjoy. She placed slices of bologna and cheese between two slices of whole wheat bread, peeled an orange, filled a glass with ice cubes and tea that she'd made earlier in the day. She'd almost finished eating when she heard the upstairs door open.

Henrietta stepped out on the landing. "How'd things go this morning?"

Janice was tempted to tell Henrietta the details of her disturbing morning, but she couldn't worry this woman who'd been so good to her. She'd have to bear the suspense alone. She'd even considered calling Miss Caroline and shifting her problems to her former teacher. But her old mentor had new youths to advise now. Janice took the last bite of her sandwich, picked up the tea glass and walked to the foot of the stairs.

"Cecil ordered the windows and some of them will be delivered this afternoon. I'm going to take down the curtains today."

"I wish I was twenty years younger and I could pitch in and help you."

"You're helping me by giving us a place to live and keeping an eye on Brooke. And you're a great advisor."

Although life hadn't taught her to be demonstrative, Janice climbed the steps, leaned forward and kissed Henrietta's dry, weathered cheek.

"You're like a mother and grandmother all rolled into one. If God hadn't sent you to help me, I'd probably have left Stanton after the first weekend."

"And I'd have missed a great joy in my life. I've never been around young folks much—seems like my ministry was to elderly, sick people. It's like a ray of sunshine to have you and Brooke in the house."

For the rest of the week Janice delayed her arrival at Mountjoy until she knew Cecil would be there, and she always left when he did. He replaced the door from the kitchen to the back porch and put new locks on the massive front door. Over the next five days, he repaired or replaced the downstairs windows, intending to rebuild the stairway so he could put in new windows upstairs.

Excitement about the fall festival took center stage in Stanton during the month of September until an alarming incident rocked the complacency of the little town.

Cecil relayed the news to Janice when she went to Mountjoy on Monday morning. "Did you hear about the big drug bust?" he said.

"A drug bust in Stanton?"

"Yep. Chief Goodman was out patrolling in his personal car about two o'clock this morning. A guy ran a stop sign and the chief pulled him over. Goodman found a lot of illegal drugs in the car. Don't know if the guy was selling drugs, or if he'd picked them up here in Stanton. Talk on the street is that there are some people in the area producing the drugs."

"Oh, I hope not," Janice said. "I thought I was bringing Brooke to a quiet, stable little town. I'd hate to think she'll grow up in an environment where drugs are sold on the street."

"I wouldn't worry. Chief Goodman and his brother are on the job."

Janice conceded that the chief of police was a competent man, but she didn't think much of his brother. She hadn't noticed that he shirked his duties, but she didn't appreciate his come-hither looks when he met her. She ignored him as much as possible, and she'd concluded that he treated all women like that. His flirting wouldn't necessarily keep him from being a good officer.

"Besides, there's a state police detachment in town," Cecil continued. "If there's any drug problem, the state guys will ferret it out."

"I hope so."

"I brought a Dumpster with me this morning. Before I start on the stairs, I can help you carry out a lot of the old stuff that you want to get rid of."

"Cecil, you're a treasure!" Janice said sincerely. "I want to get rid of the trash so I can clean the kitchen and close it off from the rest of the house to keep out the dirt while you work on the upstairs. Then I can bring Henrietta's sewing machine and start making draperies for the windows."

After they carried bags of trash to the Dumpster, Janice went to the front porch to clean the new windows Cecil had installed. She'd already cleaned the oval window in the front door and the leaded-glass panes looked as good as new. As she sprayed the windows with cleaner and wiped off the grime, she admired the sheen and shine of the new glass. A car with two men in it slowly approached the house. She went inside where Cecil was sawing boards to repair the stairway.

"We have company coming," she said. "I don't know who they are."

Groaning a little, Cecil unlimbered his long body and stood. He walked into the living room and peered through a window. Amusement lit his faded eyes when he turned to face Janice. "That's your kin—Albert Reid and his boy, Bob."

Grimacing, Janice said, "My father's brother! Now I wonder what they want."

"No good, I can guarantee that."

"Stay with me, Cecil."

"You'd better believe it." He brushed his hands across his pants legs. "Want me to get rid of them?"

"No. I'll have to meet them sooner or later."

When the older man set his foot on the first step, Janice walked out on the porch. She hoped that the butterflies in her stomach hadn't sent a message to her face.

"What can I do for you?" she asked, noting the physical resemblance between this man and her father.

Her uncle spat a stream of tobacco juice on the grass. "Just thought we'd be neighborly and pay a visit."

"I'm not ready for visitors yet. We're still working to renovate the house."

While they'd talked, the younger man had wandered around sizing up the house. He was near the corner, apparently intending to circle the building when Cecil moved to Janice's side.

"Looking for something, Bob?"

Bob stopped suddenly, surprise on his face. Cecil's truck was parked out of sight behind the house and the Reids must have thought she was alone.

"No, just looking around."

"Janice, this is your kinfolks, Albert Reid, and his son, Bob. They must know who you are."

Janice nodded her head to acknowledge the introduction.

"As long as we're here," Albert said, "we might as well look around the old place. I haven't been here since brother John moved to town."

She wondered if he'd emphasized that point to throw her off the scent that he'd been trespassing in her house. Feeling it wasn't wise to antagonize them, Janice said, "I'd rather you'd made your visit after we had the place looking better, but since you're here, come on in."

Janice didn't trust the two men and when they stepped inside, Albert turned toward the kitchen, while Bob started to the rear of the house. She looked pointedly at Cecil. He caught her meaning and tagged along behind Bob, whistling a dismal tune.

"I see you've put in new windows," Albert said.

"All the windows were broken."

He peered around the kitchen, went to the cellar door, lifted it, sniffing. "Funny smell in here—smells like bleach."

"I've been cleaning with bleach and other cleansers, so there would naturally be several odors. That's better than the musty smell that was here."

"What's Leroy doing these days?"

Janice figured he knew that her father was in prison, but she said evasively, "I don't keep in touch with him." Starting toward the door, she said, "Is there anything else you want to see?"

"Oh, I might take a look upstairs. I used to sleep up there when I was a little shaver."

"That won't be possible—the steps have been dismantled."

"Why'd you do that?"

"*I* didn't do it. It was that way before I came."

With a suspicious glance at Janice, he headed toward the stairwell. When Albert saw the empty space, he looked sharply at Bob, who'd come into the central hall with Cecil tagging at his heels.

"There's some kind of hanky-panky goin' on here, niece. You'd better find another place to live. I wouldn't want anything to happen to you like it did to brother John."

Over Albert's head, Janice exchanged glances with Cecil, and he winked at her.

"That's about all there is to see, Albert, so you'd best be on your way," Cecil said. "Me and Janice have got a lot of work to do today."

Bob slanted an angry look toward Cecil, and he said, "Come on, Dad. I don't want no part of this haunted house anyway."

"What was their *real* reason for coming to Mountjoy?" Janice asked herself as she observed Bob's reckless speed down the driveway.

Chapter Ten

Although school had been in session for several weeks, Janice still wasn't willing to let Brooke walk home alone. It shortened her working time at Mountjoy, but she considered her sister's welfare her first priority. As they walked home from school the day the Reids had visited her, Brooke said, "Let's eat out tonight. Okay?"

"Don't tell me you're getting tired of my cooking already?" Janice said with a grin.

"No. No," Brooke stammered. "Taylor told me that they're having a cheeseburger and French fries special at the diner tonight. I thought it might be fun to go there for our supper."

Since it didn't take much persuasion to avoid cooking, Janice said, "I'll agree we can't turn down a special like that." Thinking that since she'd had a cheese sandwich for her lunch, she'd aim a little higher for her dinner.

Hungry was waiting for them at the corner of the street, and he bounded ahead of them toward the vacant lot. He looked expectantly at Brooke. "You feed your pet and keep him company for a bit," Janice said.

The dog's appearance had improved greatly since he'd been getting proper food, and Janice didn't hesitate to let Brooke play with him. Having the dog for a companion was good therapy for her sister. Janice had often wished for a dog when she was a child, but when there was hardly enough food to feed the family, she hadn't asked for a pet.

"Are you hungry now? Or do you want to wait a while before we go to the restaurant?"

"I was thinking about six o'clock," Brooke said. "There's a television program I want to watch."

"Fine. I'll do some laundry."

"Will that give you time to shower and change into some clean clothes?"

Janice looked down at her jeans and shirt, which were wrinkled but not dirty. "We're only going to the diner—not a Broadway show. I think my clothes are appropriate enough."

"It'll make you feel better to take a shower," Brooke insisted.

Janice wondered at the unusual ideas in Brooke's mind. She frowned a little, realizing how inadequate she was to mother an eleven-year-old child. She made a mental note to buy a book on child psychology so she could brush up on what to expect as her sister matured.

She put the last load of clothes in the dryer at five o'clock. Feeling somewhat disheveled after sorting and folding clothes, Janice decided a shower would be welcome. Brooke was immersed in the television show, but when Janice finished her shower, put a robe on and left the bathroom, Brooke said, "I laid out that new dress you bought last week. Tonight would be a good time to see how you like it."

"Maid service 'n' everything," Janice said. "Brooke, what are you up to?"

Brooke wouldn't meet her gaze. "Nuthin'. I just wanted to help."

"I bought that dress to wear to church. I'll stick out like a sore thumb if I wear it to the diner."

"You should dress up more, Janice. Mrs. Smith always dressed up when we went out to eat."

"Mrs. Smith is forty years older than I am, too," Janice retorted.

But Brooke was insistent, and she handed Janice a bottle of perfume. "Put some of this on. I like to smell it."

Still baffled about Brooke's behavior, Janice took the bottle of spicy Parisian Night perfume that her supervisor at the store had given her for Christmas. She sprayed a soft mist on her wrists and behind her ears, thinking she definitely needed some advice on how to handle her sister. Who could she ask? Being childless, Henrietta wouldn't know any more than she did, so Linda Mallory would probably be her best source of information.

Without any more argument, Janice put on the ivory two-piece dress. With its button-front jacket, princess seams and front slits, double collar and full-length sleeves with gold trim, the polyester poplin dress flattered her brunette features. The knee length elasticized-waist skirt had a kick pleat in the back. Getting into the spirit of the occasion, Janice put on a gold choker necklace and small gold-plated earrings. She slipped her feet into a pair of ivory and brown sandals.

Brooke turned off the television, although the program wasn't finished yet. "Are you ready to go?"

Janice pirouetted before her sister. "I guess so, if you're sure my appearance suits you."

Giggling, Brooke answered, "You look good enough to go on a date."

Picking up her purse, Janice said, "Run upstairs and tell Henrietta we're going out. We might as well walk to the diner—no need to take the car for three blocks."

The cheeseburger special had apparently enticed many people, for the parking lot was crowded and a long queue of people waited to place their orders. Taking Janice's hand, Brooke tugged her past the ordering line toward the far corner of the restaurant.

"Well, look who's here," Taylor Mallory said, and Janice saw Taylor and Lance sitting at a booth. Taylor stood up and waved, "Come and sit with us. You won't mind will you, Uncle Lance."

"Well, no…" he said, and the surprised look on his face mirrored Janice's amazement. He moved over and Taylor motioned Janice to sit down beside him. Her amazement shifted to anger, which increased when Brooke and Taylor starting giggling and made no move to sit down.

With a wave of her hand, Taylor started out of the restaurant, and Brooke said, "Have fun. Don't stay out too late."

Lance was stunned into speechlessness, but he finally muttered, "Do you have the feeling that we've been set up?"

Without meeting his eyes, Janice said angrily, "I assume that you're as surprised as I am about this little escapade."

"Why, of course. Linda had a dinner meeting at the church and Taylor suggested that we could eat out tonight." He laughed. "Their little scheme worked, although I don't care much for their choice of restaurants. What are we going to do about it?"

Scooting out of the booth, Janice said, "I don't know what you're going to do, but I intend to find my sister. If Linda isn't at home, those kids are prowling around alone and I don't like it."

She started toward the door with Lance right behind her. "Let's go in my van," he said. "We can cover more territory that way."

Janice nodded and walked silently to his vehicle.

When he started the engine, Lance asked, "Any ideas where they might have gone?" he asked.

She shrugged her shoulders. "I have no idea what goes through the mind of an eleven-year-old. Let's check our apartment first."

They drove to the apartment, but it was empty. Janice went upstairs and tapped on Henrietta's door. When she received no answer, she remembered that Henrietta had also gone to the meeting at the church. She ran downstairs and back to Lance's car.

"No sign of them here," Janice said, her anger giving way to concern. "With all the trouble I'm having taking possession of the Reid property and trying to protect Brooke from harm, she pulls a stunt like this. What do we do next?"

"Let's drive around a bit. It's been less than fifteen minutes. They couldn't have gone far."

He eased out on Main Street and drove several blocks before they found the two children strolling along window-shopping. Brooke must have known that Janice was angry, because her face turned beet-red when Janice stepped out of Lance's car and confronted her.

"What do you kids think you're doing?" Janice said. "Get in the car."

Wordlessly, Brooke and Taylor crawled into the back seat of the van, and when Janice sat beside him, Lance looked at her and lifted his eyebrows.

"Please take Brooke and me back to our apartment."

The drive was made in silence, and after thanking Lance for his help, Janice herded Brooke into the apartment.

"Are you going to send me away, Janice?" Brooke whispered, tears welling in her eyes.

"Of course I'm not going to send you away. But I do want an explanation of your actions tonight."

Brooke curled up on the couch and clutched a pillow to her stomach. Without meeting Janice's gaze, she said, "I told you before that Taylor wants her mom and dad to get back together again. If you and Mr. Gordon would get married, Taylor thinks her mother would have to move out of his house. That way, Taylor thinks her parents would marry again. And I'd like that, too—I don't want to live in Uncle John's house."

Brooke spoke logically, as if a situation that involved six people could be solved so simply. There was no sign of penitence, but Janice tried to control her anger.

"Marriage is a serious matter and Taylor is selfish to try and manipulate her parents' decisions."

Brooke opened her mouth to speak and Janice silenced her with a brusque wave of her hand.

"Taylor probably has no notion of why her parents separated, and regardless, you had no reason to interfere. Do you realize that you put me in an embarrassing position tonight? If Mr. Gordon wants to get married, he'll choose his own bride—he certainly doesn't need a couple of kids to arrange a blind date for him."

"But…"

Janice shook her head. "I'm not finished yet. Besides, I don't want any arguments. You interfered in a situation that wasn't any of your business, and I don't want it to happen again. Promise me."

"All right, I won't do it anymore. But I still think you and Mr. Gordon ought to get together."

"It is none of your business, Brooke. Can't I get that through your mind?"

"Am I going to be punished?"

"Do you think you should be?"

"Maybe." She peered up at Janice anxiously, "Can I still go to Taylor's slumber party?"

"I don't know. It's possible that Linda will cancel the party after she hears what Taylor has done."

"I'm hungry. Will I have to go to bed without any supper?"

Janice stood and moved to the kitchen area. "What do you want to eat?" Her anger had cooled now, and remembering the times she'd gone to bed hungry as a child, she certainly wouldn't punish Brooke by withholding food from her. She was still so confused and angry that she didn't have an appetite.

"A bowl of tomato soup and a grilled cheese sandwich."

"You prepare the sandwich while I heat the soup."

While Brooke ate, Janice undressed and got into her pajamas. Long after Brooke was in bed asleep, she sat listlessly in the chair—wondering what it would have been like to have shared the evening with Lance.

Although Linda was as angry at her daughter as Janice had been with Brooke, she went ahead with plans for the sleepover because the invitations had already been given. She told Janice that if she canceled the party, she'd have to give a reason, and she wanted as little gossip about the girls' stunt as possible. It bothered Janice that Brooke still didn't feel guilty about trying to bring Lance and her together, but she wouldn't punish her by taking away the opportunity for her sister to be with her friends. She gave permission for Brooke to go to the sleepover.

The day of the party, Janice was making curtains at Mount-joy when her cell phone rang.

"Hello," Lance said. "Are you by yourself?"

"No, Cecil is working on the steps to the second floor." She hadn't told Lance that she was afraid to be alone at Mountjoy.

She sensed his hesitation before he said, "We haven't had a chance to talk about what happened the other night. I realize you were embarrassed by the situation, but it would have been a pleasure to have dinner with you."

"Thanks for letting me know that. I was so angry and afraid that I wasn't very diplomatic. Nothing personal."

"I've been thinking that the kids may have had a good idea. Since you'll be alone for the evening, let's have dinner together."

Her pulse beat rapidly, and Janice disguised her elation by saying teasingly, "Are you sure you aren't using me as an excuse to get out of a house with five girls?"

"I do wonder if the walls are thick enough to muffle their merrymaking, but that isn't the reason I'm asking."

"With Brooke in Linda's care tonight, I'd love to accept your invitation. Are we going to have cheeseburgers at the diner?" she added, mirth in her voice.

He laughed in a mellow tone that always thrilled Janice. "I think we can do better than that. There's a good Italian restaurant a few miles south of town. Would you like that?"

"Very much."

"Then I'll pick you up about six o'clock."

Janice cradled the phone in her hand after Lance hung up, and she stared dreamily out the window without seeing the wooded hills in their autumn beauty beyond the house. With the suspense hanging over her head, was she foolish to become involved romantically with Lance? Janice knew she was lonely. She'd been lonely all her life—even in a crowd of people she'd often felt alone.

She wanted someone to care for her and she'd be vulnerable in a relationship with Lance. He'd asked her once to be his friend, but often she'd wondered how it would be to be more than a friend to Lance. If she dated him and lost her heart to him, and he wanted nothing but friendship, she'd be hurt again. She'd had so little love in her life that it seemed she had a void where her heart was.

Janice had never felt that her parents loved her. Brooke loved her, but it was a childish love—a dependent love. Miss Caroline and Maddie had loved her unselfishly, but she sensed that a special love between a man and woman would be different. After she'd guarded her heart for years, she wanted to be sure that she didn't lose it to Lance if he didn't reciprocate her feelings.

Stirring from her reverie, Janice put her sewing aside and turned off the sewing machine. She wandered down the hall and waited until Cecil finished sawing on a piece of lumber before she said anything.

"If you'll lock up before you leave, I'm going back to the apartment."

"Sure, go ahead. I've got another hour's work before I finish."

"Brooke is going to a slumber party tonight and I'll have to be sure she has all of her things together before Linda Mallory picks her up. See you tomorrow morning."

Her phone rang again as she walked to the car. She answered to Lance's voice. "I forgot to mention this, but I thought you were very attractive in the suit you had on a few nights ago. I'd like for you to wear it again."

Janice's heart skipped a beat, but she said lightly, "Thanks for the suggestion. Now I won't have to decide what to wear."

How could Lance have noticed what she'd worn that night? She been so angry at Brooke that she had no idea whether Lance had been in a suit and tie or in casual dress.

After Brooke left for the night, Janice showered and changed into the ivory and gold suit. She hadn't told Brooke she was going out, but she'd have her phone if her sister called. She did take the precaution of telling Henrietta where she was going.

Her elderly friend was eating peanut butter, cheese and crackers while watching the evening news, when Janice tapped on the door.

"Come in for a snack," Henrietta said. "I should have asked you to have supper with me since Brooke is gone. It slipped my mind about the sleepover until I saw Linda pick her up. I'll share my peanut butter with you."

"Thanks, but I've had a better offer," she said, laughing. "Lance is taking me out to an Italian restaurant for supper."

Henrietta didn't blink an eye, or act as if one invitation was a prerequisite to marriage as some people might have done. "I'll agree it *is* a better offer. That restaurant serves delicious food."

"Since Linda is supervising Brooke tonight, I can go out without being concerned about her."

"I'm here to look out for Brooke whenever you want to go out. It's wonderful that you're so devoted to your sister, but you need a life of your own."

"You have my phone number if you need to reach me."

"Take my advice and leave the phone at home."

"Maybe you're right." Janice heard a knock on the apartment door and said, "That must be Lance."

She hurried down the stairs, laid the phone to one side, picked up her purse and hurried to open the door.

"Ready?"

Lance looked more handsome than usual in an indigo merino V-neck sweater, a small-checked light blue dress shirt with open collar and a pair of black slacks.

"Yes. I've been upstairs telling Henrietta I was going out."

In silence they walked to the car, where he opened the door for her. "How were things at your house when you left?"

"Noisy," he said, with a wide grin. "But I'm used to kids, so it really didn't bother me. However, after I've been around children all day, I prefer quiet evenings. How's the work progressing at Mountjoy?"

"Not bad. For a man who moves as slow as Cecil does, he accomplishes a lot."

"He makes every move count. I'll want a tour of the house in a few days."

"I think you'll be amazed at the changes. Cecil has all the windows replaced and new locks for the doors. I thought that would take care of intruders, but I'm not sure it has. Almost every day something is out of place, and I'm sure Cecil and I haven't moved them."

She told him about the moving cup with the tombstone on it and the sounds she heard when she was there alone. "I assume that's what you heard when you investigated Mountjoy before I came."

He darted a quick glance toward her as he turned into the restaurant's parking lot. When he parked and turned off the engine, he said indignantly, "Why haven't you told me that before now?"

"I haven't told anyone. I knew if I told you or Henrietta, you'd insist that I shouldn't move to the house. Also, I kept hoping it was just my imagination."

"You should report this to the police."

She shook her head. "No! It would terrify Brooke if the police start investigating. Besides, they haven't found the people who slashed my tires, so I don't have much confidence in the local police. Surely when I move in, and my relatives know I'm not going to be intimidated, they'll leave me alone."

He walked around the car and opened the door. "If it is Albert and his kids."

Still seated, she glanced upward in surprise. "Who else could it be?"

"I don't know, but despite the bad reputation the Reids have, I've never known them to be really violent about anything. They're too shiftless to exert that much energy."

"Well, let's forget it tonight. I'd like a few hours away from my troubles, and I'm certainly not going to ruin your evening by complaining."

He took her hand and pulled upward. "Then I won't bother you about my troubles, either," he said with a grin.

As they entered the restaurant and waited to be seated, she said anxiously, "I didn't know you had any trouble."

"What! When I deal with four hundred elementary school kids every day?" In a lower tone, he said, "I had to suspend a fifth grader for bringing a bag of marijuana to school today. That wasn't a pleasant experience."

"Where did he get it?"

"He said he found it, but the chief of police is investigating his family. Goodman is desperate to put a stop to drug trafficking around here but he hasn't had a lead to where that carload of drugs came from. The man driving the car he apprehended a week ago posted bail and promptly disappeared. Frankly, I think it's a bigger problem than we suspect."

"This way," the hostess said, and led them to a secluded table in the rear of the restaurant.

"It's an interesting place."

"This restaurant was established in an old warehouse," Lance explained. He motioned toward the ceiling where the furnace pipes and supporting beams had been incorporated into the décor. "It's a little noisy, because there isn't a ceiling to muffle sounds, but at least our next-door neighbor can't hear what we're saying. This restaurant started last year, and it's a popular place."

The menu had a large variety of Italian entrées, but Janice had made her choice when the waitress came.

"I'd like the vegetable lasagna, please, and the small Caesar salad. Also, hot tea."

Lance ordered spaghetti and meatballs, a Caesar salad and a soda.

As they sipped on their beverages, Lance leaned back in his chair and said quietly, "It's been so long since I've been out on a date, I hardly know how to act."

Her heart quickened from the tender expression on his face. "You're doing fine so far," she said, and ducked her head to hide her warm cheeks.

"I suppose if I wanted to impress you, I'd pretend to be very experienced in the dating game," he countered, a mischievous gleam in his blue eyes.

"That wouldn't impress me," she said, a smile hovering around her lips. "It would probably scare me away. At VOH Miss Caroline discouraged any affection between the boys and girls. I double-dated a few times when I got out on my own, but I was more interested in making money than a social life." She glanced at him shyly. "I can't help wonder why you asked me out."

"Because you're the only woman I've wanted to date for a long time. See, I told you I'm not experienced along this line—I shouldn't have admitted that."

The waitress brought their salads, and after she left, he said, "Why did you agree to come out with me?"

"Maybe because you've been so helpful, and I feel safe with you. More likely because the idea appealed to me."

They didn't talk about anything else personal after the waitress brought their entrées. They ate slowly, speaking of church activities, in particular the class project. When the waitress removed the plates, she brought a dessert tray. Janice chose the carrot cake, while Lance took blackberry cobbler à la mode. While they lingered over their dessert and coffee, a man paused at their booth.

"Hey, Dale," Lance said heartily and pulled out a chair. "Sit down."

"I'm meeting a couple of guys," the man said and his eyes moved around the room. "They aren't here yet, so I'll visit 'til they come if I'm not bothering you."

Lance signaled for the waitress and asked for another cup of coffee.

"Dale, this is my friend, Janice Reid."

"Any relation to Brooke?"

"Her sister," Janice answered. Puzzled, she turned to Lance. Smiling, he explained, "This is Dale Mallory, Taylor's father."

Janice saw little resemblance between Taylor and her deeply-tanned, brown-eyed father. His neat mustache set off a well-shaped chin and generous mouth. He was small-boned and of medium height, but he had wide shoulders and muscular arms.

A smile lit his pleasant eyes when he said, "Taylor talks about Brooke a lot." He reached his hand across the table. "I'm pleased to meet you."

"Taylor's having a sleepover tonight and Brooke was invited," Janice said. "Lance was kind enough to invite me out so I wouldn't get lonesome."

"A poor excuse is better than none," Dale said, humor in his eyes as he clapped Lance on the shoulder. Janice liked him at once and she wondered why Linda had divorced him.

"I see my buddies coming. Thanks for the coffee, Lance. Nice to meet you, Janice."

After he left, Lance asked for the check and paid their bill. When they returned to the car, Janice said, "He seems like such a nice man—no wonder Taylor wants her parents to remarry."

"He is a nice guy, and I've never thought he was guilty of embezzlement. Dale and I have always been friends. Linda has never told me why she divorced him and I haven't asked."

"Do you think they'll get back together?"

"It's hard to tell. Linda is stubborn."

Arriving back at the apartment, Lance turned off the car engine and turned to face Janice in the semidarkness of the street light. "So where do we go from here?" he said.

Janice took a steadying breath. "Where do you want to go?"

Blue eyes, soft and tender, gazed into hers. "I'm not sure. I asked to be your friend, but friendship may not be enough. My interest in you is such a new feeling that I suppose I'm being cautious."

"I understand exactly what you mean. We both need to be cautious. I feel like I'm living under a cloud with all the suspense at Mountjoy, and I have a responsibility to Brooke. I'm living one day at a time—too stressed to deal with anything as important as the future."

"We could see each other occasionally."

She opened the car door. "Which we must do if we fulfill our obligation about the fall festival. That'll give us a lot of time together. It will be wonderful to work with you—I've enjoyed this evening so much. Thanks."

He walked with her to the door. Would he kiss her, she

wondered? Should she let him kiss her on the first date? He towered over her and her heartbeat raced, but he didn't kiss her. Instead, he cupped her face softly with his hand, and ran his fingers over her lips in a caress more intimate than a kiss.

Chapter Eleven

The next two weeks passed quickly as Janice worked long hours at Mountjoy. She was bone tired when she left the house each evening, but rejoiced in the rebirth of her ancestral home. Perhaps her persistence had removed some of the stigma from the house, she thought, because she was able to hire more workmen. The plumber found that most of the water lines were still usable. By the time a heating contractor had installed a new furnace, Cecil had finished his carpenter work. Janice completed and hung the curtains. On hands and knees, she'd scrubbed floors and applied wax to the clean wood. The antique furniture had been cleaned and polished. And she'd paid a paperhanger to replace all of the wallpaper.

After the steps had been replaced, Lance helped Cecil take the antique bed upstairs to make room for the twin beds. She locked the door to the second floor because she didn't want visitors up there until she had time to clean those rooms. She'd emptied the trunk in the downstairs bedroom and had taken the blankets and quilts to the Laundromat.

The day before the fall festival started, all of the furniture

Janice had ordered was delivered. She hung one of the quilts in the hallway and laid another one over the back of the couch. She'd already paid Cecil for his work—a bill she thought was so reasonable that she'd added an extra hundred dollars to it. While she waited for Cecil to load all of his tools and equipment into his truck, Janice walked from room to room, a satisfied feeling warming her heart.

The late afternoon sunlight slanted through the upper window sash of the living room and Janice looked lovingly around the room. When she brought the television and her knick-knacks from the apartment, the house would be complete—by far the nicest place she'd ever lived. A feeling of thanksgiving swelled her heart—gratitude to her uncle for his generosity, but also to God for helping her make the right decisions.

Janice felt a presence in the room behind her, and she stiffened, but immediately she sensed that it was Lance. He placed his hands on her shoulders and she leaned against him.

"Doesn't it look pretty?" she said and Lance answered absentmindedly, "Very pretty." He was looking at her profile in the mirror over the fireplace as it was reflected in a sunbeam. Janice had been too busy to visit a hairdresser and her hair was longer than it had been when he'd first met her. A stray brown curl had escaped the scarf she'd tied around her head. He leaned forward and kissed it.

Janice turned to him in surprise. He grinned sheepishly as he tucked the curl under her scarf. "I was tempted—I couldn't help myself."

"I wanted you to look at my furniture," she scolded gently, but her spine still tingled from the unexpected pleasure his caress had caused. Disturbed at her inner trembling, she moved away.

"I want to look at everything," he said. "Give me the grand tour."

Lance hadn't been to Mountjoy for over a week, and he was amazed at the improvement Janice had effected. "You have a fine home."

"Then you agree that it's all right to live here?"

"I'm not sure it *is* all right. There are undercurrents of unrest in Stanton. Something fishy is going on around here and Chief Goodman doesn't know which way to turn."

Cecil joined them in the kitchen, shook hands with Lance and Janice, thanking her for the opportunity to work at Mountjoy. "It's been a pleasure to work for you, Miss Janice. I hope you're happy here."

"I hope so, too. I'll expect you to paint the outside as soon as spring comes. Stop by and see me anytime."

When Cecil left, Janice sat at the kitchen table and motioned for Lance to sit with her.

"I kept hoping my tormentors would give up, but I received another warning note in the mail yesterday. I can't understand who's trying to scare me. If it is Albert Reid and his family, they have nothing to gain. Uncle John had an addendum to his will that if I didn't inherit, Bethesda Church would get his estate."

"I lie awake at night thinking about you living here alone. You must talk to Chief Goodman. I'll go with you if you don't want to go alone," Lance said.

She shook her head. "He wouldn't believe me. Besides I don't want his brother snooping around Mountjoy."

Annoyance crossed Lance's face. "Why not? Has he given you any trouble?"

"I don't like the way he looks at me."

He relaxed visibly, thankful that the officer hadn't crossed the line of decency. "Winston considers himself a ladies' man, but it won't do any good to complain to the chief of police. He thinks the sun rises and sets in his brother."

"I'd just as soon have a cloudy day as to have Winston nosing around Mountjoy."

"Janice," he said sternly. "You must have some protection."

"Maybe I should bring that puppy Brooke has befriended with us. We've been feeding him for weeks, and he seems like an intelligent dog. I'm not used to having animals in the house, but we could make a home for him on the front porch."

Vastly relieved, Lance said, "You should bring him. He's been hanging around Stanton for a couple of months. If anyone has offered a reward for return of the dog, we would know it by now."

"I don't intend to move until after the fall festival, so I'll be available to do my share of our assignment. Actually, I should do most of the work. With your job, you don't have any free time except at night, and then I need to stay at home with Brooke."

"I have to go now—I have an appointment with a parent at six-thirty. If it's okay, I'll stop by your apartment after that, and we can decide on what needs to be done."

"Yes, that will be fine."

"The class has rented a sales wagon. Refrigeration is limited, but the wagon will be in place on Thursday. So Thursday evening, we can pick up enough supplies to fill the refrigerator. Over the weekend, we'll have to keep in touch with the workers and be sure we get supplies to them as needed. I'd suggest that we collect the food the farthest from the festival site Thursday night. During the rest of the time, we can bring supplies from the nearest homes. We may have to buy items at the grocery store if enough hasn't been donated."

"Sounds like a lot to do."

"It's usually a relaxed, entertaining weekend." He put a brotherly arm around her shoulder and squeezed her gently. "You have a nice home."

Lance arrived at the apartment soon after seven o'clock. Janice hadn't considered how low the ceilings were until Lance stepped aside.

"It's a nice apartment." With a glance at Brooke, who was doing her homework, he said in a low voice, "Sure I can't convince you to stay here?"

With a slight smile, she shook her head.

They sat at the kitchen table and made a list of the food to be contributed. Lance gave her directions to the homes and businesses she'd have to contact, and Janice agreed to take care of all the Friday deliveries, since he would be in school. On Saturday they would go together in Lance's car to pick up food and deliver it to the sales wagon.

"By the way," he said, "Linda said to tell you she'd look after Brooke on Saturday. There'll be a carnival. Linda will stay with Taylor all the time—they'd like for Brooke to go with them."

Brooke was watching television, but she must have also been monitoring their conversation, because she stuck her head around the side of the chair where she was lounging.

"Please, let me go, Janice. I haven't been to a carnival for a long time."

Janice nodded. "I've been wondering what to do with you while we collected food. I'm glad Linda will look after you."

As Lance walked to his car, he considered the sweetness of Janice's smile. He remembered the first day she'd come to Stanton, and how he'd wondered what it would take to get Janice to smile. She smiled often now, and he believed that it was because of the friends she'd made in Stanton. In spite of the disquieting situation at Mountjoy, Janice seemed to be adjusting to the new environment. He hadn't noticed any conceit in Janice, and he knew she wasn't aware of how enchanting she was when she smiled.

A worship service on Sunday night in the elementary school gym, sponsored by Stanton's churches, closed the fall festival. Janice was on the platform with a group from the Outreach Class singing an anthem when Cecil ran into the gymnasium. He made eye contact with Janice and motioned for her to join him. She hurried to Cecil with Lance close behind her.

"There's a fire at Mountjoy. I called the fire department, but you'd better come right away. I think it's that pile of brush the contractor left, but I couldn't be sure."

"Ask Linda if she'll look after Brooke for me," Janice said to Cecil as she ran out of the building.

"Let's go in my van," Lance said.

As he rushed out of the parking lot, she said, "If that house burns after all the work I've put into it, I don't know what I'll do. It just dawned on me that I haven't insured the house."

"Don't borrow trouble," he said, laying a comforting hand on her shoulder. They continued the rest of the way in silence, and when they rounded the curve in the road, they saw the blaze.

"It's the brush pile, not the house," Lance said.

"I'm thankful for that, but as dry as it's been, it could spread. That's the reason the contractor hasn't burned the brush."

"The fire truck is already there," Lance said, as the revolving lights on the truck flashed intermittently with the flames.

The gate was ajar, but Lance parked along the highway. "Let's walk from here, so we won't be in the way of the firemen."

He took Janice's hand and they ran toward the fire. She heard the crackling of the flames, and flying sparks pierced the darkness. Another fire truck approached, sirens blowing. The wind blew smoke in their direction. Almost suffocated, Janice gasped for breath.

"There's a streak of fire heading toward the house," Janice cried, and Lance squeezed her hand.

"It will be all right now, thanks to the quick thinking of Cecil and the response from the fire department. They'd better stop that fire snaking under the fence though. There's a good stand of timber on the hill, and you don't want it destroyed."

Lance's thoughts were busy, thinking of how timely this fire was—when a large number of the residents were in the gymnasium. If Cecil hadn't been coming by, the fire might not have been detected until it was too late.

The heat was intense, and Lance halted when they were several yards from the fire. One of the firemen recognized Lance and walked toward them.

"Quite a blaze," Lance said, "but looks like you'll be able to control it."

"Yes—as long as the wind doesn't pick up."

"This is Janice Reid. She owns the property," Lance said. "Do you know what started the fire?"

"Not yet. But the way it was burning when we got here, I figure a match triggered the blaze." He looked keenly at Janice. "You got any idea who might have set the fire, ma'am?"

Janice steeled herself to avoid Lance's eyes. "Nobody I'd want to accuse," she said.

A police cruiser rushed through the gate and up the driveway, sirens blaring. Janice moved toward the vehicle, but when she saw it was Winston, rather than Chief Goodman, she stopped.

"What's going on here?" he said importantly, striding toward them.

"Pretty obvious, ain't it?" the fireman said. "That pile of brush is burning and we're trying to keep the fire from spreading."

"Arson, eh?" Winston said. "We'll have to check that out. You need any help?" he asked.

"No," the fireman said. "We've got everything under control."

"I'll go down to the road and keep thrill seekers out," he said, and looking at Janice, he added, "but we'll be on this case the first thing tomorrow."

"Thanks," she said.

After Goodman left, the fireman said, "There's no need for you to stay any longer, Miss Reid. We won't leave until the fire is controlled."

"I should go," Janice said to Lance, "and find where Brooke is."

"I'll get in touch with Linda and find out," he said. He took his phone from his pocket and soon had Linda on the line. After a few minutes, he hung up. "She's at your apartment, waiting until she heard from us. I told her to go on home— that'd we be there soon."

Driving into Stanton, they met a steady stream of traffic driving past Mountjoy to see what havoc the fire had caused.

"Is this another attempt to drive me away?" Janice asked wearily.

"I'm afraid so," he answered, hardly knowing what to say. What if the next attempts would be personal attacks on Brooke or Janice?

Janice must have been thinking along the same line, and said, "I'll talk to Chief Goodman tomorrow morning and tell him what's been going on at Mountjoy. He already knows about the mutilation of my tires."

Smothering a sigh of relief, Lance said, "I'll go with you."

She desperately felt the need for his help, but she said, "Oh, don't bother—it's a school day."

"If you'll wait until midmorning, I'll take my lunch break and go with you. What will you tell him?"

"Just the basics—nothing about what we suspect."

Since Janice and Brooke had gone with Henrietta to the worship service, Lance drove directly to their apartment. Janice checked to be sure that Brooke was all right, then she closed the door.

"I'll wait for you to go with me," she said, feeling the crushing weight of despair. "I hesitate to bring my troubles out in the open, but I don't know what else to do."

Lance's strong arm went around her and she leaned her head on his shoulder, marveling that she could feel his heartbeat in steady rhythm with hers. His fingers touched her chin and lifted until their eyes met. He kissed the end of her nose and unwillingly let her slip from his arms.

"I've enjoyed your company so much this weekend that I'm sorry it ended this way," Lance said in a tender voice. "I don't know how or when, but I have faith that you'll be able to make your home at Mountjoy. Good night, my dear."

The chief of police had mixed reactions when Janice apprised him of the sounds at the house, the warning letters and the cup with the tombstone on it. At first, his face registered disbelief, then he became angry.

"If people would stop keeping things from the police, we might not have so much crime in this county. Why didn't you tell me about these crazy stunts?"

His attitude annoyed Janice. "You knew that my tires had been mutilated. Have you found who did that?"

He looked at her angrily. "No, but I've tried."

"And what can you do about these other incidents?"

"I don't know. Forbid you to move out there, maybe."

"Something you don't have the authority to do," Lance interjected.

"Do you think she should move into that house?" Goodman demanded of Lance.

"No. I've been against it from the first, but it isn't my decision."

"Let me ask you both a question," Janice said. "If you didn't have a home and you inherited some property that had been in your family for over a hundred years, what would you have done?"

Goodman grinned sheepishly. "Probably the same thing you're doing. I shouldn't have lost my temper, but I'm having a rough time. Drugs popping up here and there and freakish things happening to you. If I don't solve at least one of these crimes in the next few weeks, I figure the town council will appoint a new chief of police. And I wouldn't blame them if they did," he added grimly.

"Oh, it's not as bad as that," Lance assured him. "Stanton has had crime sprees before."

"But nothin' like what's going on now."

Janice stood and the chief said, "When you figuring on moving?"

"This week. I can move all my things in two carloads, so it won't take long."

"Be careful, and let me know if anything else suspicious happens. Don't take any chances."

The next day, not meaning to eavesdrop, Lance overheard Brooke and Taylor talking in the hallway where they waited for Lance to finish his work and take them home.

"Things aren't going as I'd hoped they would," Taylor said. "My mother won't even talk to Dad. My grandmother comes and picks me up when I spend nights with them. And Uncle Lance doesn't act around your sister the way he ought to if he was gonna fall in love with her."

Lance started to join them, but stayed in his office. If the two girls planned some outlandish scheme like they'd done before, he'd better learn about it.

"I know," Brooke said mournfully. "He spent two evenings in our apartment while they planned for the festival. And he never touched her. Not as much as a peck on her cheek as he was leaving."

"But I haven't given up yet. Dad admitted to me that he still loves Mama, but I know he's been out on dates. Why are parents so stubborn?"

"I haven't seen my parents for a long time—so I don't know much about how they should act."

"I've thought about it a lot, and the best I can come up with is to see if I can't trick my mother into having a housewarming for you and Janice after you move. That'll give a reason for them to be together, now that they won't be working on the fall festival any longer."

"What do you do at a housewarming?"

"I'm not sure, but I've heard about them."

Lance shuffled his feet, closed the office window loudly and moved into the hall. He ignored the guilty expressions on the girls' faces, because he approved of Taylor's plan and he intended to help it along. Once she had the idea, he knew Taylor wouldn't waste any time putting her plans in motion. He figured she would broach the subject to her mother that evening.

Chapter Twelve

Although he left his sister and niece to their privacy most of the time, Lance did share dinner with them. He prepared his own breakfast, and ate lunch at school, but he reserved the dinner hour for his family.

"Brooke and Janice are moving this week," Taylor said as soon as Lance had said grace and the serving dishes were being passed. "They intend to stay at Mountjoy this weekend."

"Does Brooke like their home any better now?" Lance asked.

"Oh, yes. She thinks it's cool."

"I'll have to stop by and visit," Linda said.

"That would be really nice, Mom. Why can't we have a housewarming for them?" Taylor said, her eyes sparkling as if she'd suddenly had the inspiration.

"Well, I don't know…" Linda hesitated. "I suppose it would be a nice gesture. What do you think, Lance?"

"I think my niece has come up with a super idea. If they're going to move in this weekend, why don't we have it on Saturday night?"

"But who would we ask?" Linda asked.

"Why not the members of our Sunday school class?" Lance said, for he'd been planning in advance, too. "Taylor can invite a few of Brooke's friends from school."

"That could number up to fifty people," Linda said, a frown on her face.

"If it's an open house, everyone wouldn't be there at once," Lance said. "But even if they were, there's a lot of space at Mountjoy. It's unbelievable the changes Janice has made in that house."

"I didn't know you'd been keeping up with the renovations," Linda said, casting an oblique glance at her brother.

Lance felt his face coloring. Linda was apparently unaware of how much time he *had* spent at Mountjoy. "Yes, I've helped Janice and Cecil with some decisions. The four downstairs rooms and the wide hallway look lovely and will accommodate a lot of people. She hasn't done anything to the upstairs except sweep the floors and dust the furniture."

"Is this going to be a secret?" Taylor asked, squirming restlessly in her chair.

"I think not," Linda said. "Surprises often backfire. Isn't it better to tell them, Lance?"

"Yes. Why not call a few people and ask them to pass the word."

"Presents?"

"Janice won't want them," Lance said, and Linda stared at her brother, a speculative gleam in her eyes. "Just ask everyone to bring something to eat."

Lance was proud of his manipulation, for he'd dreaded what might happen on Janice's first night in the house. It did disturb him when Brooke invited Taylor to spend the night with her, and Linda agreed. But perhaps the presence of another person, even a child, would intimidate any would-be harassers.

When Linda first mentioned the party to Janice, she hesitated. "It's nice of you, but I don't want anyone to go to so much trouble for me," she said.

"But your friends want to see what you've done with the house," Linda insisted. "We'll have a good time visiting and eating."

"Then Brooke and I will be happy to have you."

"We'll bring refreshments with us, so don't worry about it."

Janice was relieved that they wouldn't be alone in the house the first night. She wondered how much Lance had to do with the party. It didn't enter her mind that Brooke and Taylor were still scheming to bring them together.

Thirty or more guests filtered in and out of the house during a three-hour period, and Janice's plan to renovate the house was vindicated by the many compliments she received from guests who came to the housewarming.

By ten o'clock, everyone was gone except Lance, who stayed for an extra cup of coffee. He could hardly bear to leave Janice and the two girls. While Janice helped Brooke and Taylor settle in for the night, he tried to think of some way to watch over them. He finally realized that his prayers were all the protection he could furnish.

Reluctantly, he left at midnight, cautioning, "Please don't take any risks. Keep your phone close beside you, and if anything happens, call me immediately."

"I'll be alert," Janice promised. "I doubt if Brooke and Taylor will sleep at all tonight, so I'll probably be awake, too. Thanks for helping with such a nice party. I've never been the guest of honor before, and I liked it."

The first night, and the next week, passed peacefully. Now that she was in her own house, Janice started working four days a week at SuperMart. Because of her experience, she was put to work on the register, and she worked enough hours to continue her health insurance, to which she added Brooke. She earned enough for their weekly expenses and was relieved that she could save her inheritance. She'd made many friends through the church, and Brooke was happy at school. If it wasn't for the mysterious cloud hanging over Mountjoy, Janice would have been happy.

Hungry adapted to his new home quite well. At night, or when Janice was gone, she kept him in the doghouse on the front porch on a long leash, so he wasn't too confined. The rest of the time she let him roam at will.

A week after she started working, a state trooper approached Janice as she left the store.

"Are you Janice Reid?" he asked.

She gave him a brief nod.

"I'm Sergeant Baxter, WV state police. Do you mind if I do some checking around your property? We're not satisfied that the fire a few weeks ago was accidental, but the sheriff isn't eager to share any of his findings with us. I'd like to look over the site."

"Certainly," Janice said, and when he followed her home, she wondered if he wanted to see the site of the fire or if he was looking for something else at Mountjoy. Since she didn't know how long the cop would stay, Janice called Lance and asked him if he would bring Brooke home.

She watched Sgt. Baxter as he walked slowly around the property for almost an hour. She figured that Baxter was in his early forties. He was a tall, rawboned, clean shaven man. A handsome square face surrounded his intelligent hazel eyes. Janice had immediately sensed the strength and determination of the man, and it pleased her that he was taking an interest in Mountjoy's mystery.

When Lance brought Brooke home, she invited him in for a cup of coffee. While Janice prepared the coffee, Lance watched the policeman from the window. Brooke took a glass of milk and some cookies and went across the hall to watch television.

"I'm glad the state police are taking an interest in what's going on at Mountjoy," Lance said quietly. "Did you tell Baxter about the harassment you've had?"

"No, but I'm tempted to."

"Good idea. Goodman hasn't done anything to help you."

When Baxter came to the door to thank her, Janice asked him to come in. She introduced him to Lance, who shook hands, saying, "You must be the new man who joined the local detachment a few weeks ago."

"Sit down and have some coffee with us," Janice invited. Baxter accepted, walked to the sink and washed his hands.

Janice stuck some donuts in the microwave to heat while she poured his coffee. When the three of them were seated at the table, she asked, "Have you heard about the strange things that have been happening here?"

"What kind of things?" he asked, and she couldn't tell from his expression how much he knew.

Janice explained about the threatening notes, the mutilation of her tires, the strange sounds and the items that had been shifted in her home.

He frowned. "Why hasn't this been reported to us?"

"I didn't say anything at first because I didn't want my sister to be scared to live in the house. After the fire, I did report the harassment to the chief of police."

Sergeant Baxter grinned slightly. "The chief resents us, I think, and he's tight-lipped about what goes on in Stanton. If you have any more problems, feel free to telephone us. We're doing a lot of investigating in and around Stanton right now."

"Sheriff Goodman says that Mountjoy is within the city limits and this is his jurisdiction," she said. "That's one reason I didn't consider contacting you."

"The parameter of the town isn't too well-defined," Baxter said with a smile. "If you have anymore trouble, call me."

He accepted a warm roll, but before he ate it, he took a large swallow of coffee. "Just the way I like it," he said. He scanned Janice with piercing hazel eyes that seemed to search her thoughts.

"Do you have any idea who or why anyone would want to drive you away from Stanton?"

"Away from Stanton or only Mountjoy?" Lance asked.

The sergeant threw him a startled glance. "You think if she left here, the harassment would stop?"

"I don't know, but it's my opinion that Mountjoy is very valuable to someone."

"You haven't answered my question, miss."

"You asked more than one question."

"Then answer *all* of them."

"I suspect who might be trying to drive me away, but I have absolutely no proof and I won't name them. No, I don't know why my presence here is a threat to anyone."

"Well, be careful, Miss Reid and please contact us if you need us."

The townspeople lost interest in Janice's affairs when they started gearing up for Christmas. City workers had decorated the town in October. Bethesda Church was planning elaborate Christmas activities, including a cantata. The choir director insisted that Janice should participate in the cantata, but she refused because she couldn't leave Brooke for evening rehearsals. However, Henrietta, who constantly fretted because

Janice didn't have any life of her own, insisted that Brooke could stay with her during cantata practice. Janice was hesitant to leave Mountjoy and return after dark, but she knew she couldn't live in fear all of her life, so she agreed to sing in the musical.

Her life was busier than it had ever been, and Janice realized that she was happier than she'd ever been also. How much Lance had to do with that she wasn't sure. They saw each other often, but he still seemed to be playing the role of a big brother, rather than showing any romantic tendencies toward her. Of course, they seldom saw each other alone.

Her emotions about Lance were so confused that Janice wished she had a confidant in Stanton. During her years at VOH, she'd had Maddie, and she could confide anything to her. But because Maddie's college schedule and Janice's working hours often conflicted, she'd only talked by phone to Maddie a few times since the move to Stanton. And most of those conversations were made with Brooke in the room. She could talk to Henrietta about most things, but not her feelings for Lance.

Linda was the nearest friend she'd made, but lately she'd sensed that Linda wasn't as friendly as she had been at first. Besides, she couldn't talk about Lance to his sister. So when Janice answered her phone two days before Thanksgiving and she heard her Maddie's voice, she said, "Oh, I'm so glad to hear from you. I'd love to see you."

"Then you won't mind having me visit you on Thanksgiving Day?" Maddie said in her quiet, lilting voice.

"Mind!" Janice shouted. "That's the best news I've heard for weeks. What time will you get here?"

"A college friend is driving to Virginia to spend Thanksgiving with her grandmother. Her route takes her near Stan-

ton, and she's offered to leave me at your house about noon
on Thursday and pick me up the next day. She has to be back
in Morgantown to work on Saturday, and so do I."

"Oh, yes, yes," Janice said, and gave Maddie directions to
Mountjoy. "Don't expect to get any sleep Thursday night. I
have so many things to tell you that we'll talk all night."

"I have some news, too," Maddie said mysteriously. "I
can't wait to see you and your home."

Henrietta had already invited Janice and Brooke for
Thanksgiving dinner, so Janice called immediately to see if
they could bring another guest.

"Of course, your friend is welcome. And I'll hold dinner
off until one o'clock, so she'll have time to get here."

Looking forward to Maddie's visit lifted Janice's spirits,
and she hummed as she went about her work. As she dusted
the furniture in her bedroom, she picked up the picture of
Maddie that had been taken when she graduated from high
school at VOH. Thick, curling black lashes framed light blue
eyes with an iris of a darker blue. Dark blond, wavy hair
swung around her graceful shoulders. Her lips were full and
rounded over even white teeth. A dainty, exquisite nose was
the focal point of a delicate face with a complexion blend of
gold and ivory.

Maddie had a petite, slender, perfectly proportioned body.
Because she looked fragile and appealing, many people mis-
took the tenderness and peace in her eyes to be innocence, so
that Maddie was often thought to be much younger than she
was. In spite of the death of her parents, Maddie had blossomed
into a young woman who looked upon the world with optimism.

When Lance heard that Maddie was coming, he said, "Will
I get to meet her?"

"I *want* you to meet her. We're going to Henrietta's for the noon meal, but maybe you can come to my house for a snack about six o'clock. I warn you though that you can't stay long. Maddie and I have a lot to talk about."

Maddie and her friend arrived in Stanton by eleven o'clock, and Maddie had time to look over Mountjoy before they went to Henrietta's.

"I can't believe you really own this place," Maddie said, as they walked through the comfortably equipped downstairs rooms. Tears formed in Maddie's eyes. "I'm so happy for you," she said and hugged Janice again. "You look happier than I've ever seen you."

They were overjoyed to be together again and the hours flew by fast—too fast, Janice thought as they sat at Henrietta's table enjoying the bountiful meal that could have fed twenty people instead of four. When they started home, Henrietta insisted that they take some leftovers, which included a pumpkin pie. Janice didn't argue because she knew the pie would be better than anything she could provide for their evening snack.

In the company of Brooke and Henrietta, Janice and Maddie didn't have an opportunity for confidences, although Maddie's questioning eyes caused Janice to blush when she mentioned that a friend was coming to meet her. She was a little fearful, too, that when Lance saw how unbelievably lovely Maddie was, he might not have eyes for Janice Reid any longer.

She needn't have worried. Lance conceded that Madison Horton was a beautiful young woman, but he noticed that Janice was more lovely than ever as she glowed in the presence of her dearest friend.

Soon after they'd eaten a light meal of sandwiches, fruit and pumpkin pie, Lance said his goodbyes. Brooke had agreed to sleep in the living room and leave the twin beds to

Maddie and Janice. As she unfolded Brooke's bed, Janice said, "Even if you don't have school tomorrow, don't stay up later than eleven o'clock."

Brooke cuddled down in the blankets. "I'm sleepy *now,* but I have another show to watch. 'Night."

As soon as they changed into their pajamas and got into their beds, Janice said, "You, first. What's your big news?"

Maddie's blue eyes sparkled with excitement. "I'm going to Hawaii for Christmas."

"That's wonderful. On a guided tour?"

Maddie shook her head. "You remember Linc Carey, don't you?"

"How could I forget Linc Carey?" Janice asked in a teasing tone. "Morning, noon and night, I had to look at his photograph stuck up on the mirror of our dorm dresser. Now I remember—he lives in Hawaii."

Maddie's face flushed. "Because he was my father's friend, and several years older than I am, I suppose I was a silly teenager to idolize him so much. But after he accompanied Daddy's body home from Hawaii, he kept in touch with Mother and me, and he became my hero."

"And wrote to you, didn't he?"

"Mostly he just sent cards to Mother for Christmas and Easter. After Mother died, I had a few notes from him. Anyway, I've always been interested in Hawaii since Daddy was killed there. I'm doing a history paper on Hawaii's role in World War Two. I hadn't heard from Linc for over a year, but I wrote to him asking if he could send me some research material. I explained why I wanted it. He sent me an invitation to spend Christmas in Hawaii at his expense and do my research on site."

"How long will you be gone?"

"About six weeks. I'll be back for the second semester. He has a live-in housekeeper, so we'll be properly chaperoned. If he's anything like he used to be, I'll have a joyous Christmas."

The rest of the night, Janice talked about the three months she'd spent at Stanton, and after assuring herself that Brooke was sleeping, she told Maddie about the efforts to scare her away from Mountjoy. Her friend couldn't enlighten her about the mystery, but it helped Janice to talk to her about it.

And just before they settled for the night, Maddie teased, "And what about Lance? Am I right in assuming that Miss Independent has finally given her heart away?"

"Not yet, but I like him more than anyone else I've ever known. What's it like to be in love, girlfriend?"

"I've been more or less in love with Linc Carey since I was a kid. I only saw him that one time, when he stayed with us for a week. I suppose I'm in love with a memory. But I know that isn't what *real* love is like. So you tell me—how do you feel about Lance? Is he in love with you?"

"I think so, but before I came, he'd decided that he was a confirmed bachelor, so he's a little afraid of what he feels for me. Afraid of giving up his freedom, I think. I felt that way at first, but I've learned that being Miss Independent is a lonely way to live. Lance has been so helpful and understanding of the things that have been happening to me. I appreciate that, but that doesn't have anything to do with my deep feelings for him. I want to be with him all the time. I feel as if part of me is missing when we're away from each other, but I feel complete when we're together." Janice blushed and lifted timid eyes to her friend. "Does that make any sense?"

"I don't know whether it makes any sense, but it's beautiful. Let's pray now, and ask God to show you without any doubt that you and Lance share a love that will last a lifetime."

As they joined hands, Janice said, "Let's pray, too, that this vacation will give you the chance to see if you really love Linc, or if your feelings for him are only a crush."

Chapter Thirteen

The short interlude with Maddie provided the impetus Janice needed to face a busy holiday season. She worked five days a week at SuperMart, practiced three evenings each week on the cantata and made plans for Christmas. After thinking about it for several days, Janice called Henrietta.

"I want to have Christmas dinner at Mountjoy," she said, "and invite the ones who've been so helpful to me this fall— you, Lance, his family and Cecil."

"I'll help with the cooking."

"I want to do it all myself."

"You'd better check the Mallorys' plans before you go further. Lance and Linda's parents live in Florida, and sometimes they go there to visit their folks for Christmas."

The next day when Janice telephoned Linda about her plans, she said, "We'll be home on Christmas day, but Taylor and I leave the next morning to visit my parents. I'm annoyed at Lance because he won't go with us, and have half a notion to go as soon as school is out and leave him home alone on Christmas."

"If you decide to leave early, Lance can spend Christmas with us, so he wouldn't be alone."

"That wouldn't be the same as being with family," Linda said tersely, and Janice felt like cold water had been thrown in her face.

"Does that mean you'll be available to eat with us at Mountjoy?"

"I'll talk to Lance about it and let you know."

Janice knew it wouldn't be much of a celebration if Lance didn't come, but she'd already committed herself to Henrietta. And she definitely wanted to invite Cecil, because he was a childless widower, and she intended to look after him because he'd been such a help to her.

Besides, she wanted to have a memorable Christmas to make up for the many times they didn't have anything when they were younger. By Christmas morning, her parents were usually in a drunken stupor and then slept all day. Many a Christmas, she and Brooke had nothing to eat except crackers and peanut butter.

Depressed by Linda's attitude, Janice was encouraged when Lance phoned the same evening she'd talked to Linda.

"Set a plate for me on Christmas. Thanks for the invitation," he said.

"Great. Since it's the first real home I've ever had, I wanted to try a celebration at Mountjoy this year. I may be a flop as a hostess, but I'll never know until I try. I suppose Linda will let me know about Taylor and her."

"Oh, she's coming," Lance said. With a good-natured laugh, he said, "She's been trying for weeks to get me to go to Florida. I told her from the outset that I wasn't leaving Stanton this Christmas and insisted that she go on without bothering about me. For some reason, she thinks she has to mother me."

"Won't you miss being with your parents?"

"Mom and Dad live at their farm in this area from April through August, so it isn't as if I don't see them a lot. I've gone to Florida a couple of times for Christmas since they've been there, but I still prefer snowy weather on Christmas rather than lounging on the beach."

Janice consulted with Henrietta about the menu for Christmas dinner, and she heeded the older woman's advice to "keep it simple."

When Henrietta shared her recipes with Janice, she insisted that she'd bring the hot rolls, which Janice accepted, because she didn't think she could make bread. They agreed on ham, candied sweet potatoes, green beans, buttered baby carrots and cranberry salad.

"That probably doesn't sound like much of a feast to most people," Janice said, "but I don't think I can handle anything else. What should I make for dessert?"

"Bake a cake."

"What's a simple recipe for a woman who's never before baked a cake?"

Henrietta handed her a recipe for a pineapple cake, which did look easy. "You don't even need icing for this cake—just put on a dollop of whipped cream. It's delicious."

"We're going to eat at noon since Linda and Taylor are driving to Morgantown to catch a plane for Florida the next morning."

Although she saw Lance often when she picked up Brooke at school, and at cantata rehearsal, days passed and she didn't have a private word with him. One night after choir practice, Lance asked her to stay behind for a few minutes.

"We haven't been alone for weeks. Can you find time for dinner and maybe a movie?"

"Brooke has been invited to another overnight party next week, but I think there's cantata practice that night."

"Practice is over by seven o'clock. Let's have dinner and catch a late movie. What do you say?"

"I'll look forward to it."

"There's a good steak house at the county seat. Will that be all right?"

"I love steak, and I'd even settle for hot dogs, as long as I don't have to cook the food. I'll eventually get the hang of cooking if Henrietta doesn't lose patience with me."

Janice dressed in white slacks and a red sweater with green holly on it for their date. She enjoyed Lance's compliments on her appearance. He always looked good to Janice, as he did tonight in a blue turtleneck sweater and brown trousers. The restaurant was busy and they had to wait several minutes to be seated.

While they waited for their order, Janice said, "This may be a strange thing to ask, so don't answer if you'd rather not. Is Linda jealous of you?"

Astonishment lit his blue eyes. "Jealous of me! Why should she be?"

"I'm serious. She's obviously unhappy because you won't go to Florida with her. Do you have any other reason for not going besides what you've already told me?"

He colored a little. "I'd be miserable in Florida wondering if you're having more trouble."

She reached her hand across the table and laid it on his. He gathered her fingers into his warm grasp. "Does Linda suspect that?"

"Maybe. It's obvious that I'm interested in you." He was thoughtfully silent during most of their meal, and while they waited for dessert, he said, "I've been thinking—you may be right. Although I dated only a few girls when I was in high school, Linda found fault with all of them."

"When was she divorced?"

"The year I built my house."

"Whose idea was it for her and Taylor to move in with you?"

"I really don't know. Frankly, I moved away from home to give my folks some time for themselves. And I also wanted some privacy. I hesitated about taking Linda and Taylor into the house, but I didn't want them neglected."

"It seems as if Linda has gotten cooler toward me. She wasn't very gracious when I asked the three of you over for Christmas. I wouldn't have mentioned it, but I don't want to be the cause of family trouble."

An unaccustomed look of anger lit his eyes. "Let's get this straight. As long as you and I enjoy seeing each other, nobody can stop me from being with you. My sister doesn't control my life, and I may have to tell her that. In fact, I've been a little disturbed lately about her tendency to control Taylor's visits with Dale's family. She suggests other things to interest Taylor on days she's supposed to see her father."

"Maybe Taylor wasn't too far off-base when she took it into her head that if you married, her mother would have to move."

His smile was unpleasant. "I'm beginning to understand a lot of things. As I told you, I've never known what caused Linda and Dale to divorce, but I'm going to talk with Dale. Linda was probably trying to control his life, and he got tired of it."

"I wouldn't have brought this up, but I've noticed that Brooke isn't invited to do things with Taylor the way she was when we moved here. Brooke hasn't said anything about it, but if dating you is going to break up a friendship that Brooke enjoys so much, then I won't go out with you anymore. I suppose that indicates that I'm letting Brooke control *my* life, but I want her to be happy."

Lance lifted her hand and kissed her fingers individually. "Linda is five years older than I am, and even as children, she 'mothered' me. She can't keep me from dating you. I like your company and Linda isn't going to interfere with us. I'll take care of the situation between Brooke and Taylor, too."

It was so late by the time they finished dinner that there wasn't time to go a movie, so they drove slowly back to Stanton. When they entered Mountjoy's driveway Lance said, "I guess I'm as controlling as my sister, but I'm afraid for you to stay alone tonight. You should have spent the night with Henrietta."

Laughing lightly to disguise the fact that this was also a personal concern, Janice said, "How much help do you think Brooke would be if I did have trouble?"

"Not much. Perhaps I shouldn't be concerned since nothing's happened since you moved in."

"Now that my relatives couldn't stop me from moving, maybe they'll leave me alone."

Lance still believed that there was more to the threats than Albert Reid's jealousy over her inheritance. He feared that Mountjoy was connected to a larger problem—something that involved drugs.

He didn't want to frighten Janice unduly, but when he got to the house, he went inside and checked all the doors and windows to be sure they were locked. He even unlocked the door to the upstairs and looked through the empty rooms, opening the wardrobe doors. He didn't know what else he could do to assure her safety.

Standing by the door, he felt as bashful as a teenager. Why

didn't he kiss her as he wanted to? He didn't think Janice would mind, but he didn't want to rush things. "Be sure you have your cell phone with you and call me if you have the least bit of trouble."

Knowing he couldn't stay any longer, he hugged her and murmured, "Goodbye." He waited until she'd locked the door behind him, glad that the dog was on the porch. While Hungry was on guard, no one was likely to break into the house.

The house seemed strangely quiet and Janice quickly got ready for bed. She was ashamed of her fear, but she pushed the trunk in front of the bedroom door. If anyone tried to break in, there would be a noisy barrier that would wake her up.

Thinking about the evening with Lance, she wondered if he was falling for her. His interest in her was obviously more than mere friendship, but why wouldn't he tell her?

Smiling to herself as she contemplated a future with Lance, she snuggled down in bed. Enjoying the warmth of the room, she soon went to sleep.

Something woke her, and she sat up in bed, her heart pumping. She sniffed trying to identify the strange odor. Her head ached and she thought she was going to be sick. Discomfort overriding her fear of the empty house, she hurried to the bathroom.

The nausea passed and she decided that nothing she'd eaten could have made her sick, Janice went back to the bedroom. She blockaded the door again, but she opened the window for fresh air.

She had just gotten settled in bed again, but sat upright quickly when she heard stealthy footsteps overhead. How could anyone have gotten in? She'd followed Lance as he'd searched every possible hiding place on the second floor.

Knowing she hadn't imagined the footsteps, Janice hoped it was an animal walking on the roof, but she knew it wasn't.

After about fifteen minutes the noise ceased. Wrapped in a blanket, she leaned against the headboard and stayed awake the rest of the night. At daylight her head ached, her eyes stung from lack of sleep and she was exhausted.

By the time the phone rang at seven o'clock, she had gotten enough energy to go to the kitchen where she was drinking coffee and munching on toast.

"Hi," Lance said. "Everything okay?"

"I don't know, Lance," she said, weariness evident in her voice as she related the events of the night.

"I checked the upstairs before I left," he said. "No one could have been walking there unless they came in from the ground floor."

Grumpily, she said, "Then you think it's my imagination."

"No, I don't. I keep thinking about the sounds both of us have heard. There could be a hidden mike that's controlled by a remote several miles away. Who could have known you'd be alone last night? Do you suppose the house is bugged and someone is listening to your conversations?"

"Could be. How can I find out?"

"I don't know. Wasn't the dog any help?"

"Didn't hear a sound out of him. He probably wouldn't have heard the noise inside the house. I'm tempted to keep him in the house at night."

"I'm all for that. So you didn't get any sleep?"

"Not much. So I've got a headache and not one bit of energy."

"Why don't you sleep in this morning?"

"I'm already up and dressed. I'm picking Brooke up at nine. She'll probably be sleepy, too, so we can both take a nap. We can't sleep too late though—I've promised to take her up on the hillside today to look for a Christmas tree. We thought it would be fun to cut one on our own property. There should be some evergreens on the hill behind the house."

"What time do you want to start?"

"Now, Lance, I wasn't hinting."

"I know. Let's say about two o'clock, and I'll bring Taylor along. Linda prefers a commercial tree, but Taylor would like the fun of cutting a tree. I'm meeting Dale for breakfast this morning."

"I hope that turns out well for you."

"For *us*," he added significantly.

As they waited for their meal, Lance said, "Dale, I didn't invite you out to be sociable. I want to ask you some questions. You know, I didn't ask what went wrong between you and Linda, but I'm beginning to believe I should have. What caused the divorce?"

Without hesitation, Dale said, "She didn't want me to have a life of my own and I got tired of it. You remember I'd done a lot of bowling before we were married. She kept at me until I quit that. She wanted me under her thumb all the time. When she started doing the same thing to Taylor, we quarreled and she walked out on me. Your parents took my side and she wouldn't go back home. She moved in with you instead. But maybe it's a good thing we separated before I went to prison," he said bitterly.

"Dale, wasn't there any way for you to prove your innocence?"

"I was set up. Loren Santrock was my lawyer, and since he was also a member of the bank's board of directors, he checked everything. But all the evidence pointed to me as the embezzler, and he couldn't prove otherwise. Somebody got twenty thousand dollars of the bank's money, and it wasn't me."

"Linda won't talk about you at all, but I've let Taylor know that I believe you're innocent."

In a meditative mood, Dale said, "The funny thing is that as the bank's auditor, I was the one who found and reported the shortage to the board. Then the books were altered to implicate me. I spent months in prison trying to figure out what happened."

"I suppose you know that Taylor is plotting to get me married, so Linda will have to go back to you."

"Yes, she told me, but I think I've convinced her that it doesn't work that way. She'll soon be old enough to choose where she wants to live. I haven't pressured her, but I won't be surprised if she chooses me, and I'll take her if Linda doesn't stop trying to keep us apart. I love Linda and I'd go back to her in a minute so Taylor can be raised in the family atmosphere she wants. But Linda will have to agree to some changes before I'll do that."

Lance sat at the table after Dale left for work. How could he have been so blind all of these years not to recognize that Linda was a manipulator? He had never doubted Dale's honesty and truthfulness, and he believed that the majority of their family problems had been Linda's fault—perhaps that was the reason she was so bitter about Dale. Her controlling attitude had ruined her own marriage, but Lance was determined that she wouldn't destroy his chances with Janice.

When he returned home, Linda and Taylor were just returning from the sleepover. Taylor wearily struggled out of the car, yawning as she pulled her backpack out of the back seat.

Lance ruffled her already disheveled hair. "Take a quick

nap," he said. "I'm going with Janice and Brooke to cut a Christmas tree this afternoon. I want you to go with us."

"Yeah! I'd like that," Taylor said, stifling another yawn.

"Taylor, I expected you to help trim our tree this afternoon," Linda said sternly.

"Had you mentioned it to her before this?" Lance asked his sister.

"Well, no," Linda said with a quick look toward her brother.

"Then she can come with us, since I asked first."

Taylor moped up the steps. "I'll call you at noon," Lance called after her, "so you can be ready to go with us."

"Don't bring home a live tree and expect to use it here," Linda warned her daughter.

Lance followed Linda into the kitchen.

"You were out late last night," Linda said.

"Yes."

She looked at him expectantly, and when he didn't answer, she said, "And early this morning, too. Anything wrong at the school?"

"No." He straddled a kitchen chair. "Janice and I went out for dinner last night after cantata practice." Watching her closely, Lance saw her hands clench at this news.

"I haven't said anything before, but I don't think you should get interested in Janice. Their family background isn't the best. In fact, I'm sorry that Taylor has become so close to Brooke."

"Did you come to this conclusion because I'm seeing a lot of Janice?"

She looked at him strangely but didn't answer.

"Linda, I don't mean to be unkind, but I'm thirty years old. I have one mother, and I don't need another one. I like Janice—I don't know how much yet—but enough that I don't

want you interfering in our relationship or trying to come between Brooke and Taylor. For my sake, I expect you to continue being friendly to Janice. If I have to choose between you
and Janice, you might not like my decision."

Linda stared at him with cold, proud eyes, and her annoyance was evident.

"Do I make myself clear?" he asked. When she nodded,
he turned and left the kitchen, praying that Linda *had* gotten
the message. He didn't want to hurt his sister, but he wouldn't
allow her to mess up his chances with Janice. Janice was sensitive about her past, and if she ever had an inkling that Linda
disapproved of her because of her family, she might stop seeing him.

A brisk breeze wafted wispy snowflakes around them as,
wrapped in heavy coats and hoods, the four of them started
up the hillside. Lance carried a chainsaw. They were breathless before they reached the top of the hill, which leveled off
into sparse forestland of tall, deciduous trees, with a few evergreens among them.

"With Mountjoy's high ceilings, we can get a large tree,"
Janice said, "but these are *way* too big."

"Let's keep going," Lance said. "We may find a clearing
where the evergreens will be smaller."

Soon they reached a section of land where a wide strip of
forest had been cleared for a power line. Various sizes of pine
trees grew beneath the electric wires. "This is more like it,"
Janice said excitedly. "We should find a great one here."

As they searched for the perfect tree, they came suddenly
upon a cultivated area surrounded by a thicket of evergreens.

"Oh, look Uncle Lance—here's a cornfield," Taylor called.

Lance looked quickly at Janice, and she was surprised at

his expression. Taking a second look, Janice knew they hadn't discovered a cornfield. Several rows of plants had already been harvested, leaving behind stalks where the plants had been cut two inches or so from the ground. The field was enclosed by a close-woven fence about five feet high.

"Stay away from the field, girls," Lance called sharply. "Come back. We'll look someplace else for a tree."

"How come?" Taylor turned around and asked, but she and Brooke obeyed him.

"For one thing, there aren't any trees in that field. It's also muddy, so please do as I say and walk around that area."

"What is it?" Janice said quietly.

"I have a feeling someone has been growing marijuana on your property."

Janice looked again at the field. "So there *is* a connection between Mountjoy and the local drug trade!"

"Looks like. Sometimes people lay booby traps in these patches to catch intruders before they get to the field—that's why I didn't want Brooke and Taylor walking in there. We may even be too close already. Let's get away from here and cut our trees farther down this power line."

"Shouldn't we notify the police?"

"Yes, as soon as we return to the house. It's too late to find the growers, but no doubt this is one of the reasons you've been warned away. You got to Stanton about the time marijuana is harvested, and they didn't want you to find this place."

"Why would I be a threat to them?"

"If you'd have walked up here and notified the police, they would have destroyed the plants. That would cost the growers a lot of money. I can't even estimate the street value of a field of pot this size."

"Is that the reason I haven't had much trouble lately?" she asked.

"Could be. Now that they've harvested the crop, they'll likely move their operations next year."

Janice let Brooke talk her into cutting a pine tree that was two feet taller than Lance. The tree *would* look nice in their living room, but she doubted if she could afford to buy enough ornaments to trim it.

"Which tree do you want, Taylor?"

"But Mama said—"

"She said to not get anything for *your* part of the house. Let's choose a small tree for my office, and you can help decorate it."

They agreed on a three-foot-tall cedar.

"How are we going to get the trees back to the house?" Janice asked. "I didn't realize how big our tree would be."

"I'll take the big tree. You carry my chainsaw, and Brooke and Taylor can take turns packing the cedar. We'll make it."

Lance called Sergeant Baxter as soon as they returned to the house. He and another cop came immediately, climbed the hill to see the field and returned soon, affirming Lance's belief that it was a marijuana patch.

"We try to find all of these fields and destroy them before they can harvest the stuff, but we can't find all of them," Baxter said. "We'll get some reinforcements and come back tomorrow to check through all of your woods to see if there are other plantings."

After Lance helped Janice put the tree in a holder, he knew he had to take Taylor home. His worries about Janice had surfaced again, but he tried to conceal his concern from her. But as he put on his coat to leave, she whispered, "Does this mean my troubles *aren't* over?"

Chapter Fourteen

Janice had taken Brooke to children's play practice, and Linda had volunteered to pick her up after practice and bring her home. Even without knowing about Lance's ultimatum to his sister, Janice realized that Linda was friendly again. She welcomed a few hours alone because she needed some privacy to wrap Brooke's gifts and to arrange the decorations she'd bought at bargain prices.

Knowing that Janice would be alone, Lance called and asked if he could stop by.

"As if you have to ask," she said. "You're always welcome. I don't know what I'd have done without you the past four months."

Her statement bothered Lance. Did Janice love him at all, or was she just grateful because he'd been so helpful to her?

"I'll be out soon."

When he arrived, he carried a large box. He set the box on the hall tree while he removed his coat. "This is your Christmas gift," he said, "but it's something you can put to use now, so I brought it early."

"You shouldn't have" trembled on Janice's lips, but she didn't say the words.

"It's a nativity scene I bought in the Holy Land three years ago. I haven't used it, and I've decided this will be perfect for the sideboard in your dining room. Unless you'd rather put the set in another place."

"That's a good place, because I don't have many decorations for the dining room. But this set must be special to you—I don't think I should take it," she protested as he headed toward the dining room.

"I bought the pieces at a gift shop on Shepherd's Field near Bethlehem. They're hand carved of olive wood. I want you to have them."

Janice removed the knickknacks she had on the sideboard, and spread a long white, linen runner across the wide surface. They unpacked the figures of Mary, Joseph and the Christ Child and placed them under the frame of a stable. One by one they arranged the other fifteen carvings around the Holy Family, their hands often touching as they worked.

"I really don't know how to thank you," she said when they stood back to look at the nativity scene. "I value this more than any gift I've ever received, and I'm going to ask you the same question I asked you several months ago. Why are you doing this for me?"

"I didn't know the answer then," Lance said, "but I do now." She read the answer in his blue eyes before he drew her close and lowered his head to hers. She made no effort to avoid his lips, but raised her face eagerly. Her eyes closed as his lips touched hers. She had never dreamed that a kiss could be so tender, yet so magnetic. He kissed her again and again until Janice pulled away breathless.

"I love you," Lance murmured, "that's the reason I gave

you this gift. I was interested in you the first day we met, but my love has grown until it's all-consuming. I'm miserable when I'm not with you. My heart is so closely joined to yours that I want to spend the rest of my life with you. Do you love me enough to marry me?"

Janice's eyes lighted with love and tenderness when she lifted her face. "I love you very much and want to become your wife, but not right away. Everything seems to be going along all right now, but I'm edgy, as if waiting for a storm to break. I'm still not confident that I've seen the last of the trouble at Mountjoy, and until I'm sure, I won't marry you. There are still too many things that are unexplained, and I don't want you harmed because of my troubles."

"Your problems are mine whether or not we're married, but I'll be patient." When he kissed her again, thrilling to her warm response, Lance wondered just how patient he could be.

When Janice received a check from the Christmas club account she'd saved at SuperMart, she gave Brooke some money to buy gifts and used the rest for her own purchases. Henrietta volunteered to help Brooke buy her gifts.

Janice spent sparingly, but she did order a poinsettia from the Willow Creek florist to be delivered to Miss Caroline at VOH. In addition to her presents for Brooke, she bought small gifts for Henrietta, Cecil, Linda, Lance and Taylor to give them on Christmas day.

After receiving Henrietta's instructions, Janice had few qualms about preparing the food for Christmas, but she was fretting about how to arrange the dining room table. She'd found a few usable linen tablecloths with matching napkins in the sideboard. She'd bleached them until they were gleaming white. She spread one of them on the long table. There were only six matching chairs, but since there would be seven of them for Christmas dinner, she brought a straight chair from one of the upstairs bedrooms and washed and waxed it.

Janice had been using mismatched dishes and crystal, but she wanted something special for the Christmas table. She'd looked often at SuperMart's dinnerware display, adoring the holiday-patterned china, although she knew it wasn't practical. If she bought anything, it should be dishes she could use throughout the year.

Henrietta solved that problem when she asked Janice to come to her house two weeks before Christmas. She had a set of bone china packed and ready for her.

"This dinnerware belonged to your grandmother," Henrietta explained. "John brought it with him when he moved to town, but it belongs at Mountjoy. And there's a set of silverware in the box, too."

Despite Janice's protests, Henrietta insisted. "I've got two other sets of dishes that belonged to the Reids, and they'll be yours when I die. They're not as valuable as these, but they're good china, too."

Janice set the table on Christmas Eve morning, handling the pieces of milky-white china with care. She added the Christmas glasses she'd bought at SuperMart and arranged small metallic ornaments around a large candle for a centerpiece. Before she turned off the gleaming chandelier, she looked with pride at the table and at the nativity scene on the sideboard. Her uncle would have been pleased with what she'd done at Mountjoy.

Because it was snowing and the roads were slick, Lance came to Mountjoy to take Janice and Brooke to the cantata. Janice had never participated in such an impressive presentation and her heart was blessed as she sang praises to God for sending Jesus into the world. When Lance took them home, he lingered at the door long enough to kiss her and wish her a Merry Christmas.

By the time Janice checked all the doors and windows to be sure they were locked, Brooke had already undressed and was in bed, anticipating getting up early to open gifts. Janice went to the kitchen to prepare a plate of veggies for the next day's dinner, because she wanted to have the meal ready when her guests arrived. Before she went to bed, she hung a large red stocking for Brooke on the mantel and filled it with candies and fruit.

It seemed as if she'd hardly closed her eyes when Brooke tapped her on the shoulder.

"Time to get up! It's Christmas morning," she shouted and ran toward the tree in the living room.

Yawning widely, Janice slipped into a robe and joined her sister. Happily watching Brooke on her knees pulling packages from under the tree, at first Janice didn't notice that *two* stockings hung on the mantel instead of the *one* she'd placed there the night before.

Pleased that Brooke had prepared a stocking for her out of her meager allowance, while Brooke tried on a pair of fleece-lined boots from her first box Janice squeezed the stocking with her name scratched on it. She couldn't imagine what was in it, but she peered inside and gingerly lifted out a hunting knife, the blade of which was drizzled with red paint.

Feeling faint, Janice smothered a shriek and quickly pushed the knife back in the stocking and stuffed it between some newspapers in the magazine rack. She couldn't let Brooke see the knife. Trembling, she sank down on the couch and feigned an interest in the gifts Brooke was opening.

"Oh, cool," Brooke shouted, as she opened Taylor's gift—a charm bracelet. "I wanted one of these."

Brooke lifted a box from under the tree. "Here's a box for you from Henrietta. Open it—you didn't get anything except her present and what I bought you, which isn't much."

Thinking of the nativity set that Lance had given her and the promise of his kiss and subsequent proposal, she said, "I have all the gifts I want." And one she definitely didn't want, she thought as her trembling fingers struggled to untie the ribbons from the box. What was the meaning of the knife? Was this a new threat to her life? Why did this have to happen today when she wanted to observe the birth of Jesus with her friends? And how did the person get in? The house had been locked up tight when she went to bed.

She'd hoped the threat of living at Mountjoy was over, and after Lance's kiss a few days ago, she'd dared to dream of a pleasant future. How could she entertain her guests with this new danger hanging over her head?

"Hurry up and open your gift," Brooke said impatiently.

She opened Brooke's box first and exclaimed over the white blouse. Henrietta's package contained a pair of tan slacks and a brown turtleneck sweater. "Henrietta has good taste," Janice said through stiff lips. "I would have chosen these clothes myself. What did she get for you?"

"Hey, neat!" Brooke said, as she unwrapped a red-plaid jacket.

Although Janice had been tempted to go overboard in her gifts for Brooke, she'd used restraint. In addition to the boots, she'd purchased a sweater and skirt outfit, two movies for the VCR and a necklace.

When Brooke opened her last gift, they stowed the wrapping in a garbage bag and placed the gifts under the tree so Brooke could show them to Taylor.

"While I put the ham in the oven and start dinner preparations, will you make our beds?" Janice asked. "Then when you finish, we can have a sweet roll and glass of milk for our breakfast."

Hearing Brooke's steps moving toward the bedroom, Janice quickly picked up the stocking holding the knife and went into the kitchen. She pulled a chair close to the cabinets over the sink, stepped up on it and pushed the stocking far back on the top shelf of the cabinet over the sink. She'd decide what to do with it later, but today she'd have to act as if she didn't have another threat hanging over her.

After she put the ham in the oven following Henrietta's written instructions, Janice went into the dining room for a last-minute check. She flipped on the spotlight Lance had brought for the nativity scene. She turned on the chandelier and the table looked elegant with the antique china, the new glasses she'd bought at SuperMart and the gleaming family silverware.

A lump rose in Janice's throat and tears filled her eyes. She leaned her head against the wall.

Oh, God, she thought. *I have You to thank for all of this. When I think of where I came from, I can't believe that this home actually belongs to me. In spite of the trouble I've had here, You've sustained me through it all. And whatever danger the future holds, I believe You will care for Brooke and me. Forgive me, God, for my bitterness, my lack of faithfulness to what I know You want in my life.*

Hearing Brooke coming down the hall, Janice swiped at her eyes and went into the kitchen. She poured a glass of chocolate milk for Brooke and placed a package of sweet rolls on the table.

"I'm going to eat and work at the same time," she said. "I'm afraid I won't have everything ready by one o'clock."

"Anything I can do?"

"You can take Hungry's breakfast to him and wish him a Merry Christmas."

Janice ate a roll and sipped on the milk while she peeled sweet potatoes. A Scripture verse she'd heard at VOH kept whirling in her mind—a verse that seemed applicable to her situation. It was maddening to try to remember what the exact words were. When she put the potatoes on to boil, she said to Brooke, "I'll shower now and get dressed for the day, then you can have the bathroom to yourself."

"After I do that, will it be okay for me to watch one of the new videos?"

"Yes. I'll let you know if there's anything else you can do."

Before she showered, Janice searched for the Bible Miss Caroline had given her when she left VOH. It was in the bottom of a box she hadn't unpacked. She turned to the concordance and looked up the words "beginnings" and "humble," the only two words she could remember from the verse. She soon turned to the eighth chapter of Job.

"'Your beginnings will seem humble, so prosperous will your future be,'" she read aloud.

Janice felt as if *God* had given her a Christmas gift. This had to be God's promise that her future was secure in Him. Her beginnings had certainly been humble and God had already brought her a long way. The verse kept revolving over and over in her head as she dressed for the day and prepared the meal. In spite of the newest threat, she felt secure.

Henrietta and Cecil arrived at the same time. Brooke took their coats and Janice placed Henrietta's pan of tempting rolls on the kitchen table.

Cecil whistled "Silent Night" as he and Henrietta took a tour of the downstairs. Henrietta hadn't been at Mountjoy for a few weeks and Cecil hadn't visited since he'd finished the repair work.

"I can't believe how much you've done to this house in four months," Henrietta said. She fished a handkerchief out of her pocket and wiped her eyes. "John would be proud of you, Janice."

"I'm anxious to get the upstairs rooms looking this way," Janice said, "but my next project is to have the outside painted. I intend to work extra hours at the store all winter to save enough money to pay for it when you start in the spring, Cecil."

"Where'd your pretty poinsettia come from?" Henrietta asked, peering at the large floral arrangement on the library table in the living room.

"From Mr. Santrock and his secretary. He brought it yesterday and asked for a tour of the house. He seemed amazed at the change in Mountjoy. He admitted that I'd made the right decision to renovate the house."

In the dining room, she pointed out the nativity scene. "Lance gave this to me. He'd bought it when he went to Israel. He decided this sideboard was the place for it."

"I agree," Henrietta said, with a sidelong glance at Janice, who sensed that her color had risen.

The minute he spoke to Janice, Lance realized that something was wrong. She wasn't the same as she'd been when he'd said good-night to her last night after the Christmas Eve service. It amazed him that he was so attuned to her thoughts and expressions that he knew instinctively when she was distressed. But she must have hidden her feelings from everyone else, because there was a lot of happy chatter as Janice served the meal. Her preparations had gone well, except the cranberry salad hadn't jelled, but the guests joked about Janice's embarrassment and ate their salad with spoons.

After dessert, Brooke and Taylor went to the living room to watch a video, and the adults sat around the table, relaxing and enjoying a cup of coffee or tea, according to their preference.

"So now you've added entertaining to your other accomplishments," Henrietta said, glancing at Janice, approval in her eyes.

"Other accomplishments!" Janice commented. "They're few and far between."

"After seeing how you've transformed this place, I'd say you have more than your share of talents," Lance said.

Although Linda had been unusually quiet, she said, "That's true. And the meal was delicious."

"I'd never have made it without Henrietta's coaching. But I thank all of you for coming and making this first Christmas in our house so special." She took four desk calendars from a drawer of the sideboard. "I bought calendars for each of you. I hope you'll remember our special dinner throughout the year when you look at the calendar. Each month there's a picture and quotation about friendship. As you turn the pages I want you to remember how much your friendship has meant to me this year."

They seemed sincerely pleased with their gifts and Janice knew she'd made the perfect choice.

They lingered at the table until Lance said, "I'm appointing myself dishwasher." Although they protested, he insisted they leave the work to him.

"At least let us carry the dishes to the kitchen," Linda said, and they all cleared the dining room table before moving into the living room.

"How much longer will the movie last?" Janice asked Brooke.

"Not very long."

"Then please turn down the volume, so we can visit."

Cecil patted his stomach. "I don't know when I've had such a good dinner. I feel a nap comin' on, so the television won't bother me," he said.

"We'll watch the movie as far as I'm concerned," Linda said. "I've watched kids' movies until I'm addicted to them," she added with a smile.

"Then make yourselves at home," Janice said, "while I supervise the dishwashing."

Lance had already rolled his sleeves above his elbows when she entered the kitchen. He was wiping the dishes with a paper towel before washing them.

"I do wish you'd leave the dishes," she said. "It will give me something to do after all of you leave."

Busy at the sink, drawing water and stacking the glasses on the sink ledge, he shook his head. "It's my pleasure, after that wonderful meal."

"This is one time a dishwasher would come in handy, but that's one expense I don't need at this point," Janice said. "Brooke and I don't have a lot of dishes to wash. Maybe after today, I'll do more entertaining—now that I've found out it isn't too difficult."

As Lance washed the dishes, in spite of his protest, Janice started rinsing them and placing them on the drying rack. "I have to keep busy," she said.

"What's wrong?" he said quietly, and she slanted a surprised glance toward him, her face showing the tension that he knew she'd tried to conceal. "And don't say 'nothing.'"

She shook her head and answered quietly, "Let's not spoil the day." They finished washing the dishes talking about the previous night's program, but his concern comforted Janice.

By five o'clock, Linda said, "It's been a lovely day, but I

must go. Taylor and I have an early morning flight out of Morgantown. We need to go to bed soon."

"It's time for me to leave, too," Cecil said. "I've got livestock to feed."

"You stay and have an evening snack with us, Henrietta," Janice said. "We have plenty of ham and rolls left."

When Henrietta agreed, Lance said, "I'll take Linda and Taylor home, but I'd come back for a snack, if I had an invitation. I don't have to get up early tomorrow."

"You're invited," Janice said and surreptitiously pinched him gently on the arm.

When Janice opened the hall cupboard so the guests could get their coats, she heard Taylor whisper to Janice, "I wanted to go to see my dad, but Mom says I have to go to bed early. I'll have to make do with a phone call, I guess. He bought me the prettiest outfit, and I wanted to wear it today, but Mom told me to put on what she'd bought for me."

Not for the first time, Janice wondered what had caused the Mallorys' divorce.

When Janice and Brooke returned to the living room, Henrietta was leaning back in her chair, a faint snore escaping her lips. Janice put her finger to her lips. Brooke grinned and nodded. She spread out on the couch, and Janice, also feeling the need to rest, went to the bedroom and lay on the bed.

After Henrietta finished her nap, Brooke asked her to play checkers with her. "I used to play checkers with Mr. Smith," Brooke said, "so I'm glad Mr. Gordon gave me a set of my own."

"It's an old-fashioned game I used to play as a kid," Henrietta said. "I'm surprised it's still popular."

"Oh, most kids would rather have video games, and I like them, but a game of checkers is fun, too. You want the red or black?"

"I'm partial to red," Henrietta said, and Janice left them to their playing, while she went to the kitchen and put the china into the cupboard. She'd bought disposable Christmas plates and cups for supper, so there wouldn't be any more dish-washing for the day.

When Lance came back, he challenged Henrietta to a game of checkers, which she won.

"I see I'm a little rusty on my checker skills," he said. "Brooke, you play with me." When she also won the game, Lance said, "Well, Janice, you're the only one left. Maybe I can beat you."

"I don't doubt that, but let's eat now."

Henrietta left soon after they'd eaten and Brooke asked permission to watch the second movie she'd received.

"Let's sit at the kitchen table," Janice said to Lance.

Knowing that he'd returned to Mountjoy because he'd seen she was troubled, Janice climbed on the chair, retrieved the stocking and knife and laid them on the table. She sat facing the door, so she could be sure that Brooke didn't walk in on them unannounced. Janice indicated that Lance should sit beside her. She pushed the stocking toward him.

"This was hanging on the fireplace when I got up this morning. I hid it before Brooke saw it."

Concerned over the misery in Janice's eyes, Lance said angrily, "We're going to get to the bottom of this. If the police can't find out what's going on, I'll hire a private investigator. Someone must have a key to your door."

She motioned to the kitchen door. "I had Cecil put a sliding bolt on this door in addition to the lock, so it would have to be the front door. I've moved Hungry's box to the front porch, and I think he would have barked if a stranger had come to the door."

"So maybe it isn't a stranger. We don't know who else be-friended Hungry. Chief Goodman told me he's had an officer tail-ing Bob and Albert Reid, but they haven't been near Mountjoy."

"Nobody can get inside the house, but they do. Maybe they're coming in the upstairs window—you remember I heard footsteps the night I was here alone."

"I so hoped that the trouble had stopped."

"I know. Maybe they're mad we found that patch of mar-ijuana."

"Probably so, but *how* are they getting inside?"

"I don't know, but I have come to terms with my fear." She explained about the verse in Job. "I'm convinced that God controls my future and that He revealed that verse especially for me. I'm determined to get to the bottom of this harassment once and for all. I fear for Brooke more than myself, but I'll try to protect her as much as possible."

"Don't be reckless about it, Janice. You worry about Brooke, but I worry about *you*." His eyes conveyed a message that warmed her heart.

"And I appreciate it."

"But I don't want you to like me out of gratitude—I'm looking for more than that from you."

Her eyes sparkled at him. "I appreciate Henrietta and Cecil, too, but there's a difference in the way I feel about them and the way I feel about you. Or are you hinting for a compli-ment?" she asked mischievously.

In spite of their light words, their eyes spoke volumes about the love they shared.

Lance pulled her to him, but before he kissed her, he said, "In spite of all your troubles, are you happy you moved to Stanton?"

Her kiss as soft and tender as a summer breeze was his answer.

Chapter Fifteen

A train's whistle woke Janice and she sat up in bed.

Immediately she realized that no trains ran through Stanton. The clock showed two-thirty. Again she heard the loud whistle of a train, then the rackety sound of cars on a track. The acoustic phenomenon echoed back and forth in the house, to be replaced with the sound of a jet airplane leaving the runway.

Brooke started screaming and Janice forgot her own fright in trying to calm her sister. When the sounds ceased as quickly as they started, Brooke finally went back to sleep, but she soon woke complaining of a headache and stomach cramps. Since her head hurt also, Janice thought they might be coming down with the flu, but even if they were sick that didn't explain the sounds in the house.

The next morning she took Brooke to the medical clinic, but the doctor couldn't find anything wrong with either of them. Before they returned to Mountjoy, Janice stopped by the library, accessed the Internet and found two records that played the exact sounds she'd heard in the house the previous night and the noises she'd heard when she'd first come to Stanton. At Lance's insistence, she called Sergeant Baxter, and he promised to check the house for hidden microphones as soon as he could.

Perhaps because Janice started keeping Hungry in the house night and day, a week went by without any harassment. When a blizzard hit the region and the schools closed because of icy roads, Janice felt relatively safe because so few people were on the highways. The heavy snow also kept shoppers at home, so Janice wasn't needed at SuperMart.

She didn't want to deprive Brooke of the pleasure of watching television, because there was little else the girl could do while they were snowbound. But after one day of being stranded in the house listening to the Disney Channel, Janice had to find something to do.

Hoping that Brooke would sleep in, Janice got up at six o'clock the next morning, raised the thermostat and opened the stairway door. She went upstairs and lifted the floor register in the room over the kitchen. Brooke had been hinting to host a sleepover and Janice wanted to prepare a temporary room for herself, so Brooke and her friends could sleep downstairs.

After breakfast, when Brooke headed for the television in the living room, Janice said, "I'm going upstairs to do some cleaning this morning."

"Do you want me to help?"

"I'll let you know if I need you."

Janice tied a scarf around her head and put on old jeans and a sweatshirt. She had swept the rooms a few months earlier, but a lot of dust had accumulated since then. She was still sweeping when Hungry wandered in, tail wagging.

"You won't like this dust," Janice said to the dog. "You'd better go back downstairs."

The animal had developed a greater attachment for Janice

than he had for Brooke, but Janice did enjoy his company. Hungry was in a playful mood, and as she swept, he darted around her, barking, trying to grab the broom, succeeding in scattering the dirt that accumulated before her broom.

"Enough is enough!" Janice said. She lightly swatted the dog's thigh with her broom and pointed toward the door. "Get out!"

With tail between his hind legs, belly dragging the floor, Hungry crept into the hall. Without the dog's interference, she soon had the floor swept and the dirt in a dustpan. On hands and knees she crawled around the floor scrubbing the imbedded grime. She enjoyed the emerging beauty of the oak floor, still beautiful even though it showed the scuffs and marks of time.

She'd forgotten about Hungry until he started barking. She was scrubbing near the door and she peered into the hall. The dog was pawing the wall beside the large wardrobe at the end of the hall.

Janice stood, stretched her back and called to the dog. No doubt he had heard a mouse behind the wall, but he paid no attention to Janice's low whistle. Suddenly Janice sensed there was more to the dog's excitement than a mouse, and her blood chilled.

She'd laid her phone on the dresser in the bedroom and slowly she went back to the room, wondering if she was making a mountain out of a molehill. She shut the door of the room and dialed Lance's number. He answered immediately.

"Busy?" she asked.

"Busy looking out the window watching the birds fighting over the food I put in their feeder this morning. What are you doing?"

"I started cleaning one of the upstairs bedrooms this morning, and something unusual happened. Hungry followed me up here, and now he's barking and digging at the wall at the end of the hallway. I can't get him to stop, and it's making me uneasy. Are the roads safe for you can come to help me?"

"I'll walk if I have to, but I think I can find another way. Dale has a four-wheel-drive vehicle. He'll bring me if he's home."

"It might be a good idea for him to come along anyway."

"If I don't call back in ten or fifteen minutes, you'll know I'm on my way."

When Dale and Lance arrived, they had Taylor with them. Janice met them at the door. While the men shrugged out of their heavy clothes and stamped the snow off their boots, Taylor and Brooke gripped hands and whirled around and around.

Dale laughed as he watched the girls. "Looks like everybody has cabin fever. I was just ready to strike out on my own when Lance called me."

Hungry's barks sounded in the distance and Janice motioned the men to follow her. "He may be barking at a mouse, but I don't think so."

"I filled Dale in on a few of the things that have been happening here at Mountjoy," Lance explained as they rushed upstairs.

The men stood for a few minutes and watched Hungry's actions. Lance sized up the large wardrobe.

"Dale, you think you can help me move this piece of furniture?"

"I'll help," Janice said.

"Okay, but be careful. We'll only need to move it a foot or so to see what's behind it."

"The wardrobe is made out of walnut, so it's going to be heavy," Dale said. He opened the door and peered into the dark interior. "Smells like tobacco in here."

"It might scratch the floor, but maybe we should push the wardrobe, instead of lifting it," Lance said.

"Don't worry about the floor," Janice said. "I haven't done anything to this hallway."

The wardrobe slid smoothly away from the wall, and when they peered behind it, Lance whistled. There was a door behind the wardrobe.

"And look here," Janice said, pointing to the back of the wardrobe, where a door had been cut. The door was secured with a small sliding bolt. Dale looked again into the interior of the wardrobe.

"As dark as it is in here, it's impossible to tell that there's a door. There isn't a latch or hinges on this side."

Dale opened the door in the wall and looked upward along a narrow stairway. "This must lead to the attic," he said.

"Cecil wondered why there wasn't an entrance to the attic from the second floor," Janice said.

"So that's how people have been coming into the house," Lance commented. "There's another entrance to the attic somewhere, and the intruders came down these steps, entering the hall through the cupboard. Ingenious plan!" Lance held Hungry's collar to keep him from running up the stairs.

"This looks like a one-passenger stairway," Lance said, "so I'll go up and take a look. Do you have a flashlight, Janice?"

"Yes. I'll bring it."

"Why don't you take the dog and put him outside? He's a problem right now."

Hungry balked and pulled back when Janice tried to get him downstairs. She eventually persuaded him to the front door and out on the porch with some food, where she fastened a chain to his collar. She got a flashlight from the kitchen and peered into the living room. Taylor and Brooke were engrossed in a game of checkers.

Lance stood at the top of the narrow stairs when she returned with the flashlight. Dale was looking over Lance's shoulder. The light revealed a heavy metal door imbedded in the attic wall—a wall reinforced with steel rods.

"Looks like visitors aren't welcome," Dale said.

"What does it mean?" Janice asked Lance.

"I'd say this is where all the noises have originated, and why someone knew exactly when you were alone and what you were doing. They've come into the house through the door in that cabinet."

Janice shuddered to think of this invasion of her privacy and how vulnerable she'd been at Mountjoy.

"Shall we break in?" Dale said.

Lance shook his head. "We shouldn't touch a thing. Maybe you'd better notify the police, Janice, and I mean the state police, not the local chief. Try to get hold of Sergeant Baxter and tell him what we've found."

"What if Chief Goodman intercepts the call and gets here first?"

"He probably doesn't have access to private calls to the state police."

Her face must have reflected the stress Janice experienced because Lance took her hand.

"I'm scared, Lance."

"I know, but perhaps what we find behind that door will solve all of your problems. The sooner we find out the better."

She nodded, dialed the number and asked for Sergeant Baxter. It seemed a long time before he answered.

"This is Janice Reid. My dog has led us to a steel door that goes into the attic here at Mountjoy. I think you'd better come and investigate."

"Right away. Be careful."

"I'll go downstairs and tell Brooke and Taylor that the police are coming," Janice said when she put her phone away.

"I'll come along," Dale said, "and ask Taylor not to call her mother. Linda would demand that I bring Taylor home and I need to stay here. We don't know what we'll find behind that door."

"I don't have a house phone anyway," Janice said. "The cell phone is in my pocket, so she can't call out."

As they'd worked together, Janice had noted that Lance and Dale seemed as close as brothers. Although she'd always felt sorry for Linda about the divorce, she wondered if Dale might be the innocent party.

The police arrived in an unmarked car. The county sheriff accompanied Sergeant Baxter, who said, "We wanted to investigate what you've found as quietly as possible."

"Miss Reid," the sheriff said, "please stay downstairs with the children until we find out what's behind this door."

Frustrated at this restriction, yet knowing the wisdom of it, Janice prepared sandwiches and colas for Taylor and Brooke and encouraged them to watch a movie on television. She made brownies from a mix and put on a pot of coffee.

Dale came downstairs and paused in the kitchen door. "I'm going home for some equipment to disable the lock on that door. Lance is calling Linda to tell her that we're going to stay here for lunch."

"Which is the truth," she said with a wan smile. "The girls are eating sandwiches right now."

"And I smell brownies," he said, a smile touching his brown eyes. "I'll be back soon."

Upon his return, Dale worked more than an hour before he cut through the lock on the steel door. Not a sound had been heard behind the door, but the policemen held their pistols in hand as he worked.

Regardless of what the police had said, Janice thought she had the right to know what was going on, and when she knew that Dale had broken the lock, she ran upstairs.

"All of you out of the stairway," Sergeant Baxter said. "We may stir up all kinds of trouble when we open this door."

Janice stood close to Lance, and he put his arm around her. She didn't realize she was holding her breath until she heard the officer laugh.

"Come on up, folks. We've struck a bonanza."

"Ladies first," the sheriff said.

Janice ran up the stairs with Lance right behind her. They stepped out into a low-ceilinged attic. A safe stood in one corner of the room. Several shelves held a variety of items that Janice didn't recognize.

"What is all of this?"

Picking up a small plastic bag that had a dried green substance in it, Baxter said, "Marijuana. No doubt grown on your farm, miss." Lifting other packets containing pills, capsules and chunks of a pinkish substance, he said, "This is methamphetamine, commonly known as meth. There's probably a meth lab close by."

"Could someone be making meth in the attic?"

"I hope not!" Lance said. "It's extremely dangerous."

"There have been bad odors in the house since I've moved here. I thought it was cleaning supplies I used."

"There's no meth lab in the attic," Baxter said. "Sheriff, we need to call in some reinforcements before anyone knows we've found this cache. I'll stay here and guard our discovery, if you'll go back to the county seat and bring some more officers with you. Try to get an armored car to haul this stuff away. If the drug dealers learn what we're doing, we may have to fight our way out of here. I figure the safe is full of cash, and the street value of this pot and meth is thousands of dollars. The people who own this won't give it up without a fight."

"Shouldn't I call for help on the car radio and stay with you?"

"That call could be intercepted. Since you're driving your personal car, hopefully no one will know we're here. Try to hurry, though. I'm uneasy."

Dale had been looking around the rest of the attic, and after the sheriff left, he called, "Here's the way they've been going in and out." He pointed to an extension ladder leaning against the wall. "If they brought another ladder with them, they could crawl in through the window."

"They didn't bring the safe in that way," Lance said.

"They've probably started using the ladder after Janice came," Dale said. "Up until then, they came in and out of the house when they wanted to."

"But they couldn't have used the driveway," Baxter said, "so they've entered from the vacant land behind the property."

"Sergeant, I'm worried about my daughter," Dale said. "I'd like to take her home."

Baxter shook his head. "If she goes home, she's bound to say something and the news would be all over town at once. I particularly don't want the city police meddling in this. Chief Goodman doesn't have the training to deal with drug trafficking."

"Janice," Lance suggested, "maybe you should take the children into the bedroom and stay with them." When she nodded assent, he said to Baxter, "Can she tell them what we've found?"

"Yes. That probably won't scare them any more than if they keep wondering what's going on."

Lance walked downstairs with Janice.

"Be careful," she said, and her voice trembled.

He drew her close and whispered into her hair. "This may be the end of your troubles, honey. Hang in there a little longer."

Brooke and Taylor sat at the kitchen table, their eyes wide with fright.

"What's wrong, Janice?" Brooke said. She was visibly shaking. Taylor's lips trembled and tears glinted in her eyes. "Why are the police here?"

"The police have found a large amount of drugs in our attic. Actually, Hungry found them. They're going to remove it from the house, and they're afraid the people who own the drugs might try to stop them. They want us to stay out of the way until everything is safe. Bring some snacks and games. We'll wait in the bedroom."

Dale entered the kitchen and put his arms around Taylor. "Be a brave girl, honey. I can't take you home because the police need our help, but I won't let anyone hurt you."

Taylor hugged his neck. "I won't be afraid if you're with me. I love you, Daddy."

A helpless look in his eyes, Dale exchanged glances with Lance and Janice.

During the remainder of the morning, Janice exercised all of her will power to remain serene and pretend that she wasn't worried so the children wouldn't be alarmed. She took a book into the bedroom and kept her eyes on the pages that she turned occasionally, although she didn't read a word. She encouraged Brooke and Taylor to play several board games, which kept them occupied.

An hour passed before she heard heavy treads in the hallway. Someone had arrived, and she prayed it was the police, rather than the drug dealers.

Another hour passed. All she could do was sit, wait and pray that trouble would be averted. She was proud of Brooke and Taylor, who were calmer than she was. After they tired of the games, they propped themselves up on the beds with pillows, put on their headphones and listened to some music.

Janice figured Linda was probably beside herself, wondering why Taylor hadn't come home. But surely knowing Lance was with Dale, she wouldn't worry about Taylor's welfare. When she could no longer sit still, she paced the floor until Brooke said, "Janice, you're making me nervous."

She took a deep breath and tried to relax as she sat down again, but there was a heavy feeling in her stomach. Would her misery never end? When she thought she'd scream if she had to stay cooped up in the room another minute, a soft knock sounded at the door and Janice jumped as if she'd been shot.

"It's Lance," he said, opening the door. "Everything is over now."

Janice hurried toward him. "No problems?"

"No. The money and drugs are in an armored car on the way to the county seat. They didn't count the money, but clearly there were thousands of dollars in that safe, mostly in twenty- and fifty-dollar bills." He ran his hand over her hair. "You've been living in Fort Knox and didn't know it."

"Any clues to who's responsible?"

"Not a thing, but Baxter is going to post two guards upstairs for a few days until they can check out the whole attic."

"That sounds good to me. I've been wondering if I could ever spend another night in this house." She started trembling and, oblivious to the startled children, Lance drew her to him in a close hug.

"I wouldn't have let you stay here by yourself tonight," he

said. "But it might still be a good idea for you to go to Henrietta's for a few nights."

"Are you going to marry Janice, Uncle Lance?" Taylor said hopefully.

Dale, coming down the stairs, heard her remark.

"Mind your own business, girl," he said. "Whether Lance is married or not won't make one bit of difference in bringing your mother and me back together."

She started crying. "But I want to be a family again."

"Well, I'd like that, too," Dale said, with pain marking his eyes, "but your mother and I will have to make that decision. Get your things. It's time for us to leave."

Baxter came downstairs, and Janice moved out of Lance's arms.

"Miss Reid, I'm sorry to impose on you, but I must keep some of my men here for a few days to be sure we haven't overlooked any evidence."

She nodded assent. "What can I do to make them comfortable?"

"Not a thing. They can bring sleeping bags, and we'll provide food for them. One of the troopers will stay in the room, and another will guard the stairway. We'll change men every day."

Dale was helping Taylor into her coat and boots, and Lance and Janice walked to the porch with Sergeant Baxter. A car sped up the driveway scattering snow behind it.

"We made it in the nick of time," Baxter muttered as Chief Goodman and his brother jumped out of the car.

"What's going on here?" the chief of police said.

"What makes you think anything's going on?" Baxter asked.

"Winston saw a whole squad of police cruisers and an armored vehicle in the driveway."

"We uncovered some illegal drugs in the attic. We've taken possession of them," Baxter said.

"Why wasn't I notified?"

"It's a state and county matter."

The chief turned to Janice. "Why'd you call them instead of me?" he said. "I thought you and me were friends."

"I hope we still are," Janice said. "But I thought the situation warranted more help than you could give."

"I told Janice to call the state police," Lance said. "We didn't know what we'd find in that room until they broke down the door."

"I want to see what you found," Goodman said belligerently, attempting to push his way into the house.

"I guess you have the right to know what's happened," the sergeant said. "Come with me."

Dale and Taylor stepped aside to let the three cops into the hallway.

"The chief's car is blocking your vehicle," Lance said to Dale.

"If Janice doesn't mind, we'll turn around in the yard. With the heavy snow, it won't make any ruts. I'll be in the doghouse for exposing Taylor to this danger, so I need to get her home to her mother."

"I'll go with them and get my car," Lance said. "With all the traffic in here this afternoon, the road is clear enough for me to drive my car up the driveway."

Janice waved goodbye to them and turned into the hallway. Her phone was ringing and she took it out of her pocket.

"Miss Reid, this is Loren Santrock. Are you all right? I've just heard that there are a lot of police cruisers at your home. I'm snowbound like everyone else, but if you're in trouble, I'll find some way to come help you."

Janice was warmed by his concern. "Oh, thank you for calling, but everything is all right now. It's been a terrible day. We discovered that people have been using Mountjoy as a headquarters for drug trafficking." She went on to explain how the cache of drugs and money had been discovered. "But the money and drugs are in police custody now, and there will be a constant guard in the house for a few days, while they check for clues in the attic and the grounds. I suppose this is the reason people have been scared away from Mountjoy."

Santrock had always seemed a mild-mannered man, and the venom in his voice surprised her. "This is an outrage!"

"It's good of you to be concerned, but it's all over now."

"You took a chance notifying the state troopers instead of the local police force, who could have gotten there much sooner, but I guess it turned out well for you."

"Yes. This should clear up the cloud that's been hanging over Mountjoy for years," Janice said, and Santrock agreed.

After the trauma of the past few months, Janice found it difficult to be optimistic. But was her trouble over at last?

Chapter Sixteen

The next week was the most peaceful time Janice had experienced since she'd come to Stanton. The temperature warmed, the snow melted quickly, and feeling secure because of the police guard in her home, she went to sleep easily and slept through the night. Detectives spent two days checking the attic, and they found a CD player with the discs that had caused people to think Mountjoy was haunted. Hidden miniature speakers were discovered in the kitchen, the downstairs hallway and on the front porch. After the snow melted, they checked the grounds of Mountjoy and canvassed the rest of her woodland property. She didn't know what evidence they'd found.

The day the police guard was removed, schools reopened, and Janice went back to work. She was the center of attention at work as co-workers and customers quizzed her about what had happened at Mountjoy. Acting on instructions from Sergeant Baxter she said, "It's police business and confidential. I can't tell you anything."

Since the drug dealers hadn't been apprehended, Sergeant

Baxter warned Janice to be alert for anything unusual. She and Brooke had just finished supper a few evenings later when there was a knock at the front door. She wasn't expecting anyone, and Janice hesitated before she went to the door and turned on the porch light. When she saw her visitors, she gasped and looked down quickly to be sure that the storm door was still latched.

Two women and a man stood on the porch, two suitcases on the floor beside them. One woman was a stranger. Janice recognized the other two people and realized her troubles hadn't ended. She remained silent and the stranger stepped forward.

"May we come in?"

"No," Janice answered, her anger rising, a bitter taste in her mouth.

"But these are your parents," the woman persisted.

"I know who they are."

"But I don't understand," the woman faltered.

"And I don't understand who you are and why you're here."

"It would be warmer if we talked inside."

Janice shook her head. "Answer my question."

"Your parents have been released from prison on the condition that they would live with you. I'm their parole officer."

"Whose condition? I didn't agree to be responsible for them."

"Well, after all, you're a daughter—"

"A daughter they haven't contacted for eight years."

Janice slanted a glance at her parents, who had their heads down. She sensed that Brooke was standing beside her.

"Who is it?" Brooke asked.

Her parents looked up when Brooke spoke, and Brooke leaned against Janice.

"Don't you remember me, Brooke?" Florence Reid asked in a querulous voice.

"Janice, is it Mom and Dad?"

"Yes."

"Why are they here?"

"Miss Reid," the parole officer said, "this is ridiculous. Open the door and let us in—it's freezing out here. What kind of a daughter are you?"

"The kind of daughter who's had to fend for herself as long as she can remember. The kind of daughter who had to beg and steal to keep herself and her little sister alive while her parents spent all of their money on drugs and booze. The kind of daughter who was separated from her sister, who was put in a foster home. The kind of daughter who spent four years at an institution for at-risk children. The kind of daughter who's finally gotten to the place where she has a home of her own, and who is *not* going to let her parents spoil her life. Does that answer your question?"

Leroy Reid spoke for the first time. "Let's go, Mrs. Anderson." He turned aside and Janice noticed the hopelessness in his stooped shoulders, but she hardened her heart.

"Oh, let them come in, Janice," Brooke wailed. "It's so cold outdoors."

Brooke's plea softened her attitude. Janice unlocked the door and stood aside to let the three people in. Still seething with anger and resentment, she motioned them into the living room.

"Sit down and speak your piece."

Her father looked around the room. "The old place looks just like it did when I was a boy."

Knowing her father had avoided Mountjoy for years, he must have been desperate to have come here. Unless the lure of John Reid's money had overcome his fear, Janice thought ironically.

"Miss Reid, I'm Annabelle Anderson, your parents' parole officer. They'll report to me regularly, but they need a place to stay, as well as someone to be responsible for them. You're their closest relative."

"I can't deny that," Janice said, "but let me make my position clear. I don't owe my parents anything. The only thing they've ever done for me was to bring me into the world. I don't remember how I managed until I was old enough to fend for myself. But I've been taking care of Brooke since she was born."

Turning to her father, she said, "How did you know where to find me?"

He pulled at his collar. "Albert wrote me a letter and told me John had left everything to you."

"And he wanted you to join him in trying to break the will, is that it?"

Shamefaced, Leroy dropped his eyes and wouldn't look at her.

"Janice," her mother scolded, "you ought to be ashamed talking to your father like that."

"Your parents have both been model prisoners," Mrs. Anderson said. "They're rehabilitated, ready to live productive lives."

"I'm glad to hear it." Janice's head was aching, and the emotional pain in her heart was excruciating. She found no pleasure in tongue-lashing her parents, but the sight of them had unleashed all of the pent-up emotions and horrors of her childhood.

"What is your decision?" Mrs. Anderson persisted.

Janice felt her face warming. "I've told you my decision. They *cannot* live here! Why did you dump this on me without warning?"

The woman shrugged her shoulders and got up. "There was a lack of communication between the prison and the parole

board. Their papers got mislaid and your parents arrived today
unexpectedly."

Brooke had been sitting quietly on the couch, and she
begged, "Don't put them out in the cold, Janice."

Brooke's agony reached Janice's heart and she said, "Very
well. They can spend the night here, but Mrs. Anderson, you
must come back in the morning to make other arrangements."

When she opened the door for Mrs. Anderson to leave, Janice brought in the two small suitcases—the only belongings
these two people had to show for forty years of living. She
set the cases down in the hallway and leaned her head against
the door.

God, forgive me, she prayed silently. *I have neither love
nor respect for these two people. I'm afraid to trust them.
What can I do?*

It took all of the willpower she possessed to go back to the
living room. Silence filled the house, broken only by Brooke's
sobbing.

"We didn't intend to barge in on you like this," Leroy explained, "but we had to tell them who our next of kin was. We
didn't know they'd bring us here."

"Well, you're here for the night, so I'll have to deal with
it. Have you had any supper?"

"No," Florence said.

"Brooke and I had just finished eating, but I'll fix something for you. Come into the kitchen. You can stay here if you
want to, Brooke."

They sat silently at the table as Janice opened a can of vegetable soup. While the soup heated, she prepared two chicken
salad sandwiches, got two apples from the pantry and put the
food on the table. While they ate she washed the dishes she
and Brooke had used for supper.

"I didn't tell Albert I'd help cheat you out of John's money. I didn't answer his letter," her father said.

"Uncle John's estate has already been transferred to me, so I'm not worried about that. This house was in shambles when I came here, and I've spent a lot of money renovating it. I intend to have this house looking like it used to, but I've got a long way to go. I'm working part time to make expenses, and I can't afford to support two more people."

"We'll get out tomorrow morning."

"It's not as easy as that. The parole officer won't allow it. If you did get off of drugs while you were in prison, you'll go back to your old ways if somebody doesn't hold you accountable."

"Do you hate us, Janice?" her mother asked in a quiet voice.

Janice pondered the question for several minutes, and the tension in the room was maddening. "I used to hate you, but at VOH I learned a way to live without hate. But I've never forgiven you for the way we had to live as children. The thing I hate most is that Brooke and I are making a new life, and now you've spoiled that."

"We didn't aim to," her father said.

Wearily, Janice said, "No, I don't suppose you did, but it's too late now. I imagine you're tired. You can sleep in the living room. The couch folds out to a full-sized bed."

"We can sleep upstairs," Leroy said.

"Those rooms aren't ready for sleeping yet. You'll have to sleep in the living room. The bathroom is at the end of the hall."

While her parents ate, she'd noticed Brooke moping toward their bedroom, still crying.

"As you've done it unto the least of these, you've done it unto Me," filtered through Janice's mind while she took cushions and the quilt off the back of the couch. She'd heard Miss Caroline quote that Scripture countless times, and it seemed as if her former teacher was telling her now that she had to look after her parents. She took clean sheets, quilts, pillows and pillowcases from a trunk in the hallway and made the bed as comfortable as she could. There was no door between the living room and the hallway, so she couldn't give them any privacy.

After her parents were settled in bed, Janice went into the bedroom and closed the door behind her. Brooke was huddled in bed, her eyes swollen from crying, her body trembling. Janice sat on the bed and pulled Brooke tightly into her arms.

"Why did they have to come back?" Brooke whispered. "We're getting along by ourselves. I can't even have a sleepover, because my friends might not want anything to do with me now."

How could she comfort her sister when she had so many reservations of her own?

"It they're true friends they won't desert you," Janice said, sounding more certain than what she was. The children's opinions would be tempered by what the adults did. "I won't let them disrupt your life. They can't live here."

"But if they don't, where will they live? What if they're homeless and have to look for food in garbage cans like Hungry did? We took care of him."

The implication being, Janice assumed, that if she'd given Hungry a home, she should do the same for her parents.

"So you want them to live with us?"

"No," Brooke said hesitantly, "but I feel sorry for them."

Brooke had been too young to remember how they'd been neglected as children and Janice hadn't told her.

"Well, I don't feel sorry for them," Janice said bitterly, "but I do feel responsible for them. I'll help them—I only hope I can do it without ruining our lives." She helped Brooke back down and tucked the covers around her. "You go to sleep and don't worry about it. I'll try to work out something."

She closed the bedroom door behind her, took her fleece-lined coat from the hall cabinet and put on her heavy boots. She opened the front door and went out on the porch. Hungry stuck his head out of his house, his tail thumping on the floor.

Shivering from the cold, Janice tied the hood of the coat around her face, stuck her hands deep into her pockets and walked back and forth across the porch. Her parents were only in their mid-forties, but their hair was streaked with gray and their faces were prematurely wrinkled. She'd remembered her parents as being excessively thin, but both Leroy and Florence had gained weight while they were in prison. They looked better than they had the last time she'd seen them. Sorrowfully, she wished that she had one pleasant memory of her parents.

Her fingers wrapped around the phone in her pocket. Janice longed to call Lance and tell him what had happened. It was only ten o'clock, and if she called him, she knew he'd come to her immediately. She also considered calling Miss Caroline. But when it was all said and done, the decision was hers and no one else could help her.

"God," she whispered, "I don't know what to do. I know the Bible says to 'honor your father and mother,' but how can I? They're not honorable people. You know what they've done. I have a responsibility to Brooke, as well as to them. Shouldn't she be my first priority?"

Her parents had destroyed her childhood. Was it right that they ruin the rest of her life? John Reid had given her a chance to better herself, but now the bottom had dropped out of her plans for the future.

She didn't know how long she paced, but when her legs

got so tired she couldn't stand any longer, she sank down on the floor, leaned against the wall of the house and rested her arms and head on bended knees. She was no closer to a solution to the dilemma than she'd been an hour ago. She knew she'd have to go in the house soon, because her feet and hands were getting numb.

Overwhelmed with the enormity of the burden that had been placed on her, Janice muttered, "God, what can I do?" Hungry heard and came to nuzzle against her.

Although she thought she hadn't learned much spiritual knowledge at VOH, as had often happened in the past, a Bible verse slipped into her mind.

"And when you stand praying, if you hold anything against anyone, forgive him, so that your Father in heaven may forgive you your sins."

All of the children who came to VOH had some forgiving to do, and many chapel messages had dealt with forgiveness. Was God telling her through Scripture what she had to do? Janice yearned for God's full forgiveness for her actions and thoughts in the past. Would she ever have the peace of heart and mind she longed for until she forgave her parents?

The sobs that wracked her body were so unusual and so overwhelming that she felt weak. Janice had learned long ago that crying didn't solve problems and she hadn't cried for years. But once the floodgates opened, she couldn't stop crying. Hungry nudged her again, whining softly, licking away the rivulets of tears that coursed down her face. She put her arm around the dog.

Her tears washed away the bitterness she'd held in her heart as long as she could remember. She felt cleansed, a new person inside. She softly hummed a tune she'd sung with Maddie at VOH. One phrase kept rolling through her mind—

"Nothing between my soul and the Savior." She was free at last of the debilitating, unforgiving spirit that had dominated her heart for years.

Stiff from the cold and her hour of sitting on the porch, physically spent, Janice went into the house, taking Hungry to his bed in the pantry. She was at peace with God, but she still didn't know what to do about her parents. The soft warmth within did nothing to soothe the coldness of her body. Undressing, she put on pajamas, wrapped in a terry-cloth robe and laid an extra blanket on her bed. Brooke seemed to be sleeping peacefully and Janice crawled under the covers, but she couldn't sleep. She knew she would have to make a decision in the morning and she spent the night considering her options.

Her parents were still sleeping when Janice left the house to take Brooke to school.

"Should I tell Taylor what happened?" Brooke asked.

"If you want to. You can't keep a secret in a town this size."

Her parents had gotten up when she returned to Mountjoy. They'd folded up the bed and were sitting side by side on the couch.

Janice said, "I've taken Brooke to school. I'll fix your breakfast before Mrs. Anderson comes."

They followed her into the kitchen and sat at the table.

"How long have you been living here?" Florence asked.

"We came to Stanton in August and moved to Mountjoy the last week in October. We had an apartment before then. Nothing had been done to the house for years—it took a lot of work to make it livable."

She sat at the table and drank a cup of tea while they ate their breakfast of eggs and sausage.

"Before Mrs. Anderson comes, I want you to know that I've forgiven you for the way you treated us when we were children. I can't forget it, but Lord willing, I hope to eventually have the grace to put it behind. However, I won't let you move in with us."

"I'm not keen on livin' here anyway," her father said, with a trace of humor. "I've always been afraid of Mountjoy."

She thought wryly that if he'd experienced the things that had happened at his ancestral home the past few months, he would be even more afraid.

"I will help you get a new start in life, but I cannot support you, too. There's still a lot of work to be done on the house, but I'm planning on paying for it out of my salary. I'm keeping the money I still have from my inheritance for Brooke's college expenses."

Hungry started barking and Janice guessed that Mrs. Anderson had returned. But when she went to the door, Lance stood there. He opened the storm door, entered, and took her in his arms. She put her arms around his waist and clung to him as if he was the only anchor in the stormy sea of her life.

"Brooke told me what had happened," he said softly. "Why didn't you call me?"

She motioned him back out on the porch and closed the door. When she shivered at the cold wind blowing across the front of the house, he pulled her close and wrapped his coat around her.

"You don't know how much I wanted to call you, but what could you have done?"

"What I'm doing now," he said, planting a kiss on her soft curls.

Briefly she told him about the mercy God had granted to help her forgive her parents. "So I'm in a better mood to cope with the situation now than I thought I would be. You might as well come in and meet them."

"Just for a minute."

Knowing how much she resented her parents, Lance was relieved to see that her eyes were peaceful and her attitude positive. He greeted the Reids graciously, turned down Janice's offer of breakfast and explained that he had to return to school. Her parents eyed Lance speculatively, but they didn't ask any questions after he left.

Lance hadn't been gone more than ten minutes when Mrs. Anderson came. Janice invited her to join them at the kitchen table and poured a cup of coffee for her.

"What have you decided?" Mrs. Anderson asked directly.

"My parents cannot move in with me, but I do feel a responsibility to help them until they get on their feet. With your help, we can find jobs for them and arrange for housing in the low-income apartments in Stanton. I'll buy furniture for them and some clothes now, but I expect them to pay me back. When I left VOH, I had nothing, so I know how difficult it is to start from scratch, but I did, so I know it's possible. I'll supervise their income and expenses until they prove to me that they're capable of handling their own finances."

Mrs. Anderson turned to Leroy and Florence. "That seems fair enough to me, what do you say?"

"It's morn'n we deserve," Leroy said, "but it's gonna be hard."

"I know it will because you've never been able to handle money," Janice said. "When you get paid, you must put some money in a savings account and keep out some money to pay your loan to me, before you use anything for yourself. If you overspend before the next paycheck you'll do without."

"Janice, you've become hard," Florence said.

"I'm not being any harder on you than I've been on myself. Once you prove to me and to your parole officer that you can take care of yourself, I'll gladly give up my guardianship rights."

"I'll also be checking regularly on your welfare and behavior," Mrs. Anderson said, a note of warning in her voice.

"And I encourage you to go to church," Janice continued. "You can go where Brooke and I go or choose a church of your own. I'll admit I want you to straighten up so Brooke and I won't be ashamed of our parents, but for your own sake, you need to live worthwhile lives. I won't keep you from coming here, as long as you realize that you're visitors. And Brooke can decide if she wants to spend time with you."

Within a week, Janice arranged for an apartment for her parents, and Mrs. Anderson found jobs for them. Since she'd bought used furniture for herself, Janice didn't have any compunction about furnishing her parents' home with secondhand furniture. Florence had taken a secretarial course while she was in prison, and she was hired to work in the office at the apartment complex. Leroy had learned the carpentry trade. He found a job with a local contractor, whose place of business was only a few blocks from the apartment, so Leroy could walk to work.

By the end of the first month, Janice began to breathe easier. She had twice invited her parents to eat dinner at Mountjoy. They seemed to be making friends, and they occasionally attended Bethesda Church. Brooke had come home from school a few times in tears because of comments her peers had made about Leroy and Florence, but her close friends had not turned against Brooke.

Although she was subtle about it, Janice knew that Henrietta created situations to keep Brooke busy, so she could have more time with Lance. One Saturday afternoon, Henrietta asked Brooke to go shopping with her in the county seat because she needed someone to carry her packages. "We'll take in a movie while we're there and maybe eat out, so don't expect her back until evening."

When Lance heard about it, he invited himself to Mountjoy for pizza, which he brought himself. Janice tried her culinary skills at making a chocolate pie—Lance's favorite dessert—and it tasted as good as one Henrietta could have made.

After they'd washed and put away the dinner dishes, they moved to the living room couch. Lance put his right arm around Janice and pulled her close.

"Linda and Dale are finally talking, and Taylor is over the moon."

"I know—Brooke told me."

"I'm not too optimistic yet," he said, "because Linda is proud and stubborn. She'll hesitate to admit that she made a mistake. Dale is determined that she'll agree to some changes before he takes her back. I can't say that I blame him, but Linda won't be coerced."

"Does Linda still love him?"

"Probably—as far as I know she's never considered dating anyone else. But she won't talk to me about it." Linda had been cool toward him since he'd told her to stop manipulating his life and Taylor's.

"So that brings me to us. Everything has settled down for you—the entrance used by intruders into your home has been found and the drugs confiscated, your parents are reasonably settled, and you're living comfortably at Mountjoy. I love you, Janice, and want to marry you. What is there to stop us?"

She could see a look of yearning on his face, and Janice lowered her eyes. Had happiness come to her at last? Would she be the owner of Mountjoy that disproved the old legends that it was an unlucky house? She loved Mountjoy, and all she needed was Lance beside her to make her happiness complete. But if she married Lance, would he expect her to live in his house? And would he want Brooke to move in with her parents? His next words settled that question.

"I'm willing to move to Mountjoy and help you renovate the place. Whether or not Dale and Linda go back together, Linda and Taylor can continue to live in my house. We can remodel two second-floor rooms with a bathroom between them. I can have one room for an office, the other would be our bedroom. Brooke can continue to have the downstairs bedroom."

"I do love you and will marry you," she said. Her words were smothered as he gathered her close in both arms. She lifted her face eagerly, and he kissed her again and again. Breathless, she pulled away and rested her head on his shoulder.

In a quiet voice, she said, "You didn't let me finish. I *will* marry you, but I don't know when. I'm still uneasy because no one has been arrested for the drug activities here at Mountjoy. There are too many unanswered questions. Sergeant Baxter has warned me to be alert for more trouble."

"All the more reason that I should be living here with you. The sooner we get married, the happier I'll be—for many reasons," he added with a mischievous smile. "Do you want a big church wedding?"

"No, I think not—probably just our families. Give me a few days to think about it."

The condition of the envelope should have warned Janice when she picked up her mail at the post office. She was on her way to get Brooke from school, so she tossed the mail in the back seat, picked up Brooke and stopped at the grocery store before she went home. She'd worked eight hours today, and Lance was coming for supper, so she said, "Brooke, bring the mail, and I'll carry in the groceries."

The March day had been warm and balmy, giving a hint of spring weather, and Janice felt that all was right with her world. She and Lance hadn't announced their engagement yet, waiting until they could pick out a ring, but they had agreed on a summer wedding.

She put away the perishable items in the refrigerator, except the pork chops. The last time they'd eaten with Henrietta, she had served a pork chop and rice casserole that Janice thought Lance would like. Now that they were planning to get married, she was constantly pestering Henrietta to teach her how to cook. If Henrietta wondered why, she wisely asked no questions.

Janice browned the pork chops. She put rice, celery and onion in a casserole dish, laid the chops on top of the vegetables and put the casserole in the oven. She was preparing a garden salad and humming a favorite hymn when Brooke wandered into the kitchen, carrying a crumpled, dirty piece of paper.

"Look at this, Janice. What does it mean?"

A cry escaped Janice's lips. She staggered backward against the kitchen cabinet when she read the message.

Tell your big sister that you're next.

The message was unsigned.

"Is it some kind of joke?"

Struggling for normalcy, Janice took the envelope from Brooke's hand and scrutinized it. It was similar to the one she'd received in Willow Creek months ago.

For a moment, she wondered if she should gloss over the situation and pretend there wasn't any problem, but Brooke had to be warned.

"I doubt it's a joke," she said. "The drug dealers probably blame me because their money and drugs were confiscated by the police. That may have been why they sent this. They probably think they can hurt me through you, and that's true. You must be extra careful, Brooke."

"It might be just to scare us," Brooke said.

"It might be," Janice agreed, "but in case it isn't, don't let any strangers in the house and be sure and stay at school until I come for you."

Janice telephoned Sergeant Baxter immediately, and he told her he'd come by in a few hours to get the letter. In an attempt to keep Brooke from suspecting how unnerved she was, Janice watched television with her sister until bedtime. But her mind wasn't on the programs—her mind was burdened with a new threat. How could she keep Brooke safe?

Chapter Seventeen

Janice opened her eyes, wondering why the room seemed so bright. A sudden boom jarred the house and she jumped out of bed. Through the window she saw that the outbuilding was on fire.

"Brooke," she shouted. "Get up!"

With shaky hands, she managed to dial 9-1-1. "This is Janice Reid. There's a fire at Mountjoy." She hurriedly rattled off her address.

She severed the connection, noticing that Brooke was still in bed. She ran to the bed and shook her sister vigorously. "Brooke, get up. The outbuilding is on fire, and this house may burn next. Wrap a blanket around yourself. We have to get out of here. I've got to unlock the gate so the fire truck can get in."

She slipped her feet into her shoes, grabbed a coat from the closet and hustled Brooke outside, put her in the car, started the engine and sped down the driveway. She had just unlocked the gate when she heard the siren. She left the car at the foot of the hill to make way for the firemen. The fire truck and a police cruiser rushed by as she and Brooke walked back to the house. As yet the main house hadn't caught on fire, but as she neared the building, another blast sounded and sparks flew up and settled on Mountjoy's roof.

Even she could tell that there was no way they could save the outbuilding because it was completely engulfed in flames. But within a few minutes, the firefighters were spraying water on the roof and side of the house. A second tanker truck arrived and turned a water hose on the burning building just as the roof collapsed. The heavy onslaught of water kept the fire from spreading to the house or up the hill to the barn on the neighboring property.

By that time a large crowd of spectators had gathered, and Winston Goodman was ordering them to stay away from the fire. Janice, holding tightly to Brooke's hand, stood behind the area the firefighters had cordoned off, her mind too numb to contemplate the meaning of this fire. Chief Goodman scuttled from one place to another, obviously pleased that he was in charge rather than the state troopers.

"Looks like the house is going to be saved, ma'am," he said to Janice, "although the weatherboarding is scorched. You were lucky. Do you know how it started?"

She shook her head. "I have no idea. Brooke and I were asleep. Something woke me, maybe an explosion, because when I opened my eyes, our bedroom was bright like it was in the middle of the day. When another explosion sounded, I called 9-1-1 and got Brooke out of the house as fast as I could."

"What was in there that would have exploded?"

"I don't really know what was in the building. It looked like an accumulation of junk to me, and I decided to let it alone until spring. When Cecil and I put a few pieces of antique furniture in there, I saw a lawn mower. There may have been some gasoline in it—I suppose that could have caused the explosions."

Janice felt someone move in behind her and knew it was Lance before he spoke. She turned quickly, and put her hand in his. His hair was disheveled, and she thought inanely that he shouldn't be out on such a cold night without a hat. He had run up the hill and he breathed deeply.

His eyes were filled with fear, and he gasped, "Are you and Brooke all right?"

"Yes, and the house isn't going to burn."

"Thank God for that. You can't imagine how scared I've been. Dale is a volunteer firefighter, and he called to tell me that Mountjoy was burning. How did the fire start?"

"I don't know. The building was engulfed in flames when I woke up."

A firefighter came toward them, and not until he spoke did Janice realize it was Dale.

"The fire chief is leaving one of the tanks here the rest of the night, and I'm staying with it. I think the fire is out now, but we'll soak this side of the house and roof occasionally just to be sure. It's safe enough for you to go back inside now, Janice. And don't worry about your safety. I'll be outside."

Janice realized she was shivering, because the coat she'd pulled on in a hurry only came to her knees and covered her short nightgown. Her bare feet and legs felt like icicles.

As Lance took her arm and helped her into the house, she said, "I can't understand why Hungry didn't bark, or where he disappeared to. After I thought our trouble was over, I've been putting him in his box at night. He wanders around too much if he's inside, but I haven't heard anything out of him."

"He might have broken loose when the fire started," Chief

Goodman suggested. "He'll probably come back as soon as Winston chases this crowd away."

The house smelled of smoke, but at least it was warm when Janice and Brooke went inside.

Lance followed them and Janice said, "You don't have to stay. The firefighters will be here all night—we'll be fine. Brooke, why don't you go back to bed and get warm?"

"I don't think I can sleep."

"Let's have a cup of hot chocolate then," Janice said. "I have some decaf chocolate mix. Do you want a cup, too, Lance?"

"Might as well," he said, listening as the hall clock chimed three o'clock.

When Brooke went to the bathroom, Lance said quietly, "Was this an accident?"

"How could it be?" Janice said, pouring milk into a pan. "Someone set that fire. Is there never going to be an end to this harassment?"

"There's still something going on that we don't know about. I just can't figure it out."

Janice hadn't locked the door, and as she was stirring the chocolate mix into milk, she heard the door open. "Janice, can you come here a minute," Chief Goodman called. His expression was grave.

"What now?" she said.

"We found your dog—looks like he's been poisoned."

She was speechless. Standing behind her, Lance said, "Is he dead?"

"Not yet, but he's in bad shape. Do you want us to take him to the vet?"

"I'll do it," Lance said. "Keep Brooke in here so she won't see the dog. I'll take care of it."

Chief Goodman seemed bewildered, as if all of these incidents were too much for him. By that time, Sergeant Baxter and another officer had arrived at Mountjoy, and Janice went to bed, although she slept fitfully. The next morning, Baxter knocked on the side door soon after Janice went into the kitchen. She unbolted the door.

"I'd like you to come outside for a minute and look at something," he said.

She followed him to where a stack of charred brush was piled against the house. A fire had been started there, but apparently the brush had been too damp for the fire to spread.

"Janice," Baxter said, "this was an attempt to destroy your home. The dog was poisoned to keep him from barking and waking you."

Janice shuddered. "So someone did try to kill us," she said as she headed back to the warm kitchen.

Baxter followed her in and she poured a cup of coffee for him. "I'm afraid so. If you hadn't woken up, the house might have caught fire, and you'd have perished. I don't mean to pry into your business, but who'd get your property if you died?"

"Brooke. Three years ago when I learned that my uncle had left his estate to me, I made a will making Brooke my sole heir. If I died before she became of age, the money was to be put in trust for her with Miss Caroline, director of the Valley of Hope, as the trustee."

"But if you and Brooke both died, where would the money go?"

Janice felt as if she was drowning. "My parents, I suppose. I didn't make any provision beyond Brooke. But nobody knows this except Miss Caroline."

"There's some clue we're missing in this mystery. I can't sleep nights trying to figure it out."

After Baxter left, without telling Brooke about Hungry, Janice encouraged her to stay in bed. She went into the kitchen to wait for Lance's call after he'd seen the vet. She leaned her head on the table. Was her uncle trying to kill her? Or was it her parents? They would gain a lot if she and Brooke died.

But she couldn't believe that they would try to kill their daughters. They'd been doing so well, seemed to enjoy their work, and were proud of themselves for saving some of their weekly salary. Since they were ex-cons, her parents would be the first suspects.

It was past five o'clock before Lance called, and by that time Janice was pacing the floor with the phone in her hand. If Hungry died, how would Brooke take it? Janice had also grown fond of the dog. After her traumatic childhood, she'd come to believe that she could stand anything, but there had to be a breaking point and she'd about reached it.

Lance wasted no words. "He isn't going to die, but it was close. Another hour and the vet probably couldn't have saved him. She wants to keep him under observation for two or three days."

"That's good. It isn't safe to bring him home. Lance, they've found where a fire was set at the foundation of the house, but it fizzled out."

"Janice, you'll have to leave. If someone wants Mountjoy that bad, let them have it. It isn't worth your life."

"Chief Goodman says he's going to keep round-the-clock police guard around the house until the fire marshal's investigation is complete, so we'll be all right for a few nights. When I tell Brooke about the dog, she'll probably be too upset to come to school. Taylor can get her assignments and we'll work on them at home."

The next call came from her mother, who'd heard about the

fire. Janice believed her concern was genuine, and that her parents hadn't started the fire. She prayed that the police wouldn't investigate them, because it wouldn't take much to destroy their newfound confidence in themselves. When Brooke woke up, Janice told her that the dog was sick and Lance had taken him to the vet. She didn't mention that the dog had been poisoned.

With representatives from the fire marshal's office and policemen in and out of the house all day, Janice had no chance to rest. Her eyes grew heavy early in the evening. She talked with Lance on the phone and told him that she intended to go to bed before long, but that she'd bring Brooke to school the next morning.

"Brooke's already in bed, and I'm headed that way soon. Sergeant Baxter did ease my mind on one count. His detectives quietly checked out my parents. Dad had worked an extra shift at the company, and Mom sat up most of the night with a sick neighbor. I didn't believe they'd fired the building, but it's a relief to know for sure."

"Do you feel safe enough?"

"Yes. Winston Goodman is on guard tonight, and he has his police cruiser parked beside the front porch. I don't have anything to worry about, so I'm sure I'll sleep."

Yawning, Janice started down the hall, and she stopped quickly as a knock sounded on the door. In spite of her confident words to Lance, she was still apprehensive, so before she opened the door, she said, "Who is it?"

"Officer Goodman" was the reply, and recognizing Winston's voice, she opened the door and turned on the porch light. He put his fingers to his lips in a bid for caution.

"Something's come up," he said in a hoarse whisper and motioned for her to join him.

Her concern for Brooke overrode her innate caution, and she stepped outside and followed him down the steps. Feeling a presence behind her, Janice opened her mouth, but her cry was stifled when Winston Goodman jumped forward and put his hand over her mouth. She bit him, and he swore. Grabbed from behind, Janice felt a sharp blow to her head and then darkness.

Chapter Eighteen

Lance didn't know that Brooke wasn't in school until mid-morning when the day's absence list was placed on his desk. Even then, he wasn't too distressed, thinking that Janice had let her sleep in again. But uneasiness kept niggling at his mind, and he telephoned Janice. His anxiety increased when she didn't answer. Except when it was charging at night, Janice kept her phone in her pocket. For months, his emotions had been so attuned to Janice's that he could sense immediately when something was wrong. He was expecting a conference call from the State Board of Education, and he couldn't leave. But after fidgeting in his office for ten minutes without receiving the call, Lance couldn't stand it any longer.

He telephoned the police station, and when Chief Goodman answered, he identified himself and asked, "Who was on duty at Mountjoy last night?"

"My brother."

"Has he reported in this morning?"

"No, but we're shorthanded, and he said he'd do an extra shift. I hadn't expected him to call."

Lance told him why he was uneasy, and the chief said, "Hold on a minute, I'll contact Winston."

After a few minutes, Goodman came back to the line and said, "That's strange. Winston doesn't answer, either. I'll run out there and see what's going on."

"Stop by for me, will you?" Lance said. State board or not, he had a horrendous feeling that something was wrong at Mountjoy.

Everything looked normal when the chief's cruiser turned into Mountjoy's driveway ten minutes later. Janice's car was parked in its usual place. The deputy's car was in front of the porch, but no one was inside. Before Goodman stopped, Lance jumped out of the car and ran to the house.

"Hey," Goodman called. "Lookee here." He'd opened the rear door of the squad car and Lance hurried to his side.

Winston Goodman was lying on the back seat of the cruiser. His arms were tied behind him, his feet shackled, and he was gagged. Leaving the chief to release his brother, Lance rushed to the house. The door stood ajar. He raced through every room. There was no sign of Janice or Brooke.

By the time he got back outside, Winston was leaning against the cruiser, while the chief rubbed his arms to restore circulation.

"I walked around the house about midnight, like I did every hour," Winston said with an effort. "Somebody jumped out of the shadows, grabbed me and knocked me out. The next thing I knew I was trussed up like a turkey in the back seat of my car."

"Did you recognize who attacked you?" the chief said.

"Didn't see nobody," Winston said. "It happened too fast."

"Did you hear anything out of Janice or Brooke?" Lance said.

"Not a thing," Winston said. "After I come to, I thought I

heard a vehicle going down the driveway." Apologetically, he looked at his brother, "Sorry I let you down."

"My fault," Chief Goodman said. "I should have had two men on duty. The state troopers offered to help, but I told them we had enough officers. I'll have to call on them now."

Winston started to protest, but Lance said, "And the sooner the better. If you don't call them, I will."

He had never felt so confused and lost. What could he do? He walked through the house that was as empty as his heart. His mind refused to contemplate what had happened to Janice.

The covers on Brooke's bed were rumpled, but it was obvious Janice hadn't gone to bed at all. He couldn't see any indication of a struggle in the house. Lance went outside, looked around and wondered if Winston had told the truth. For one thing, he doubted if the bruise on the officer's forehead was severe enough to have knocked him out. And in the muddy ground, Lance couldn't see any evidence that there had been another car in and out of the driveway after Winston had arrived.

Chief Goodman notified the state police, then sent Winston back to town for some rest. Lance knew he couldn't return to work, so he called the school, thankful to learn that the call from the state office had been postponed until the next day. He told his secretary he was taking a day of personal leave.

Lance drove to Henrietta's house and told her about the disappearance. He also drove by the housing complex to tell Leroy and Florence what had happened.

"I hate to think this about my own kin," Leroy said, "but Albert might have done it, for he sure wanted our brother's estate. He came to see me after we moved to Stanton asking me to help him get the money. I turned him down cold. I figured John had the right to do what he wanted to with his money."

"I'll suggest to the police that they should investigate your brother and his family."

When he returned to Mountjoy, Sergeant Baxter and two deputy sheriffs had arrived, and they'd persuaded Chief Goodman to leave the investigation to them. Lance told Baxter why he suspected Winston's story.

"By the time we got here," the trooper said, "the two Goodmans had turned their cars in the driveway, and there was nothing for us to see. If no car went out, then the Reids were either carried away or they're still here someplace."

Lance wondered at the officer's words. Could Brooke and Janice have been killed and buried on the grounds?

"As for Winston, we've been watching him for months. There's a police leak somewhere, and we believe it's coming from the city officers instead of the state or county guys. It could be Chief Goodman, but I suspect Winston, and we only have *his* word for what happened here last night. Maybe he was attacked, but I doubt it."

"It will be hard to prove," Lance said.

Baxter nodded in agreement. "We've also been tailing Albert Reid and his boy, who do have an alibi for last night. They were in the local bar drinking and carousing all night, so they didn't take them."

"If they didn't kidnap Brooke and Janice, who did?"

"Probably the people who stored drugs and money in the attic and were raising marijuana on the hill."

"It's worried me that the drug dealers haven't been caught," Lance said.

"The fire marshal has verified that the fire was caused by exploding elements like paint thinner, ammonia, or turpentine," Baxter said. "All of these things are used in making meth, so there's probably a meth lab somewhere on this property. It must be underground because we've combed the rest of this property without any success. Could there be a basement area that we don't know about?"

"Leroy Reid might be able to tell us," Lance said. "Or Henrietta—she lived here for several years."

"We're also working on another angle." Baxter took a bracelet from his pocket. "Do you recognize this?"

Recognition of the item startled Lance. "Yes, it's Brooke's charm bracelet. My niece gave it to her for Christmas."

Motioning to the barn on the adjoining Janice's property, he said, "We found it near the barn, which belongs to Mr. Santrock. We'll get his permission to go on his property. Janice and Brooke may be inside the barn. By the way, when's the dog coming home?"

"The vet said I could pick him up today."

"I want him before we go into that barn. I think the animal was trained for a police dog, because he sure knew what he was after when he led us to the attic."

"I'll go get him after I talk to Leroy about a basement under Mountjoy. Since Janice moved in the house, there's been an offensive odor off and on, sometimes bad enough to cause headaches." He paled when he considered the situation. "But if there's a meth lab under this house, it could have exploded and killed both of them, especially during the fire."

"I know," Baxter said grimly.

Sick at heart, Lance drove to the building site where Janice's father worked to ask if there was a basement under the main part of the house.

"The only basement we've found under Mountjoy is the one that leads from the back porch," Lance told him, "and I think it was dug in the last fifty years to accommodate the furnace and water system."

"I kinda think there was a basement under the house," Leroy said, "but I'll admit to you, Mr. Gordon, all the years of drugs and alcohol have ruined my memory. Albert might know."

"But we don't want Albert to know what we suspect. If he *is* involved in the gang that's trying to destroy Janice, they can't be warned. You try to remember and let me know if you think of anything." Lance gave Leroy his cell phone number before he went to see Henrietta, who also had no knowledge of a basement.

Before he returned to Mountjoy, Lance called the pastor of Bethesda Church and asked him to activate the prayer chain on behalf of Janice and Brooke. He tried to pray for their safety, although he felt so lost and hopeless he couldn't pray. A verse from the book of Romans came to mind. "'We do not know what we ought to pray, but the Spirit Himself intercedes for us with groans that words cannot express.'" When he couldn't come up with a definite petition, he prayed, "God, help us," over and over.

The police couldn't locate Santrock to get permission to search the building, and Miss Banner was worried about him. He hadn't come to the office or called to say he would be late, and the police started to suspect that Santrock had also been kidnapped. Securing a warrant without his permission, they searched the barn, disappointed when they found nothing but farm machinery and several bales of hay.

When Lance arrived with Hungry, the dog was still weak, and he sniffed around the outside of the barn without much interest. When Lance took him inside, Sergeant Baxter held Brooke's bracelet to the dog's nose. Hungry put back his head and brayed like a hunting dog and raced around the barn floor. He started growling and dug frantically beside the bales of hay. The police motioned for Lance to restrain Hungry. They hurriedly pushed the large bales of hay aside and uncovered a trapdoor in the floor. Motioning for silence, Baxter looked significantly at Lance.

"We may have all kinds of trouble when we open this door, so you stand aside, Mr. Gordon."

Baxter reached for the handle, but he pulled back when Leroy Reid stumbled into the barn, puffing like a steam engine.

"Let me get my breath," he panted. "I ran up the hill."

One of the officers uncapped a bottle of water and handed it to Leroy. He took a big swallow.

"Mr. Gordon," he said, "I just remembered. There *is* a basement under the house, and the door goes down from the pantry floor. There was an old house on this spot before my granddaddy bought it. The house belonged to an abolitionist. He had a cellar under his house that led through a tunnel with the opening a mile away. He'd hide runaways in his cellar and then take them out through the tunnel and into Pennsylvania when it was safe for them to leave."

"That's your answer, Sergeant," Lance said. "Janice didn't get to replace the tile covering on the pantry, so we didn't see the door. Will you give me time to find out if the door is still there before you enter the tunnel? It's just possible that the people who've been using Mountjoy don't know about the tunnel. Nobody will be expecting us to come from the house. I'm afraid for them if you attack from this point."

"I'll go with you," Baxter said. "The rest of you stay in this barn and see that no one goes out and pay particular attention to anyone who wants to go in."

Working as quietly as possible, Lance knelt on the pantry floor and, using a knife from the kitchen, he cut a large square in the tile and pushed the pieces to one side. He grinned up at Baxter when a trapdoor similar to the one in the barn was uncovered. He cringed when the hinges on the door squeaked as he lifted it. Baxter handed Lance a flashlight and he sent the beams around the opening.

"The steps look safe enough," he whispered. "I'm going down."

Baxter nodded. "Be careful," he said, drawing his gun. "I'll be right behind you. If there is a meth lab down here, we should have on Tyvek suits before we go in, but it might be dangerous for the girls if we wait. We need to rescue them before the place explodes."

"Yes, we can't wait."

The ten steps led to a cellar under the two rear rooms of the house. He soon found a door that entered a tunnel. Walking rapidly and quietly, Lance hadn't gone far until the tunnel was blocked by a cave-in. So frustrated that he could hardly stand it, Lance started to return to Baxter, but he halted when he heard voices. Apparently the wall of dirt wasn't too thick, because he heard Janice's voice, and he praised God that she was still alive. Then there was a man's voice and, listening intently, he was sure it was Loren Santrock's. So he *had* been kidnapped!

Breathless, Lance motioned for Baxter to follow him to the foot of the steps. "The tunnel is blocked by a cave-in," he whispered, "but I heard Janice's voice. I also think I heard Santrock talking. Is he involved in this or has he been kidnapped?"

"Everybody is a suspect at this point," Baxter said.

"That dirt isn't very thick, and I figure I can tunnel through it. There's a shovel on the back porch. If you can create a diversion of some kind, I might be able to dig a hole big enough to bring Janice and Brooke out this way."

"I'll get the shovel for you," Baxter said. "But don't start digging until you hear something from our end of the tunnel. They might kill the sisters if they know they're trapped."

* * *

Janice felt as if she were walking through a thick fog, and she wasn't making any progress. Her head ached and when she tried to lift her hand, her arm wouldn't move. With an effort she forced her eyes open and looked around. She was in a cave or cellar. Her hands and feet were bound, she was gagged and lying on the damp ground. A dim florescent bulb cast shadows around the room.

The place looked like a laboratory, containing a collection of jugs with tubes running into the jugs from pots on gas burners. The burners weren't lit, but the smell in the room reminded her of the odor that had often infiltrated her house. She'd seen enough pictures of illegal meth labs to recognize the equipment. She had a sinking feeling that this cave was under Mountjoy.

How had she gotten here? The last thing she remembered was when Winston had called her out on the porch. She'd heard someone behind her, and when she started to turn, he'd hit her on the head. No wonder she'd never trusted the guy.

A shiver of panic swept through Janice. What had they done with Brooke? She began to shake as fearful images built in her mind, but her fears were premature. She squirmed on the cold floor until she turned on her side and saw Brooke lying a few feet away, also bound and gagged. Had they killed her? Probably not, or she wouldn't be tied. But as she struggled to scoot across the floor, Brooke opened her eyes. It was maddening not to be able to reach her sister or even communicate with her, but she didn't seem to have any bruises. At least Brooke was alive, but for how long?

Janice kept twisting and pushing until she achieved a more upright position against the earthen wall. The small room opened into a tunnel to the right. Fortunately, none of the burners were active now, but a meth lab was a dangerous place to be. How could they escape?

Alert to a scuffling sound in the tunnel, she batted her eyes at Brooke, hoping she would get the message. Janice closed her eyes and pretended to be unconscious. She sensed that someone was standing over her. Her foot was nudged roughly but she didn't move.

More than one person was in the room now, and she slitted her eyes slightly, seeing four feet and legs. Only two people so far, but there might as well have been a hundred for all she could do about it.

"Can't I ever depend on you to do anything right? If you've killed her or knocked her into a coma, my patience is at an end with you," a voice said. The shock of discovery hit Janice like a jolt of electricity, and her eyes popped open. Astonished, she stared upward into the face of Loren Santrock. Winston Goodman stood beside him.

"Oh, so you're awake after all," Santrock said with a sneer. All vestige of the suave, fatherly attorney had disappeared. How could this man have duped her and everyone else in Stanton? But she'd always known that somebody with brains had to be behind the drug ring.

Her opinion of him must have shown in her eyes, because he gave a bitter laugh. "Surprised you, didn't I, as well as all the other good people in this area? Take that gag off, Winston. I want some information."

The gag had been drawn so tight that Janice's mouth was numb. She licked her lips trying to restore some feeling. Alarm and anger swept through her body when she realized how she'd trusted this man.

She was so furious she could hardly speak, but when the

numbness left her lips, she demanded harshly, "Is this cellar on my property?"

"Yes, right below your bedroom, in fact."

"So that's the reason every now and then I smelled something in my house that made me sick. If this place had exploded, Brooke and I could have been killed."

"The ones who operate this lab are cautious—their lives depend on it. If they're careless, they can be killed. And if the explosion didn't kill them, they know I would."

He wouldn't be telling her this if he didn't expect to kill her, too, so Janice thought she might as well learn what she could. "Like you killed Uncle John."

"Ah, you're wrong there, Missy. I never killed anyone…yet."

"And why did you try to burn down the house to kill me?"

"Do you think I'm crazy? The last thing I wanted was for Mountjoy to burn. I lay those arson attempts at your uncle's door. He'd naturally bungle any job he tried."

"What would he gain by killing Brooke and me?" Janice said. "You're just blaming him to hide your own crimes."

"Believe what you will, but your father wouldn't have been any match for Albert—who would have all of John's money before you were cold in the grave."

He pulled a rickety chair closer to her and sat facing Janice. "Okay, missy, I'm out of patience with you. You've been a thorn in my flesh since the first day you showed up in Stanton, when I had to avoid you because we hadn't hidden everything here at Mountjoy. I've tried everything peaceable to get you to give up this property, and by delaying, you've cost me over a million dollars. But I'm going to get part of that back. You're going to turn all of your money over to me. Thanks to you, our activities are finished at Stanton, but I'm taking your money with me when I leave."

With a harsh laugh, Janice said, "The state police will get you sooner or later. You don't have a chance to get away with this."

"I've been getting away with it for ten years—ever since John Reid moved to town." He shook his head. "I don't know how John got wise to me, but he made a few remarks that made me realize he suspected something. When he came to investigate, one of my men killed him, but I made it look like suicide."

Was there no end to this man's wickedness?

"Where are those CDs your uncle gave you?"

"In the safety box at the bank where you told me to put them when you were giving me 'fatherly' advice."

Laughing, he said, "Well, since I'm well known at the bank, I won't have too much trouble getting them. Where's your key to the box?"

"I won't tell you."

With a significant glance toward Brooke, Santrock said, "Oh, yes, you will. You've got a stubborn streak, so I know you wouldn't bend to my wishes no matter what I do to *you*. But when we start breaking Brooke's fingers one by one, I figure you'll tell me where the key is."

At these words, Brooke's eyes opened, and she whimpered. Janice knew she'd heard everything, but she still played for time. "I'll sign the CDs over to you, but not until I know Brooke is safe. You bring me a note from Lance that Brooke is with him and you can have the money."

"You accused me of being stupid, Miss Reid, but you misjudge me. You think I'd turn her loose when she's heard everything I said to you? I've stashed a lot of money in the Caribbean banks, and I'm leaving the country to live in peace and quiet the rest of my life. You're going to stay tied up here until I'm safely away. After that, you can talk all you want to."

Sensing a slight ray of hope, Janice said, "The key is in the black purse I carry most of the time. It's on the dresser in my bedroom."

Another man had entered the room, someone Janice didn't know, and Santrock said, "I'll wait until dark and sneak into the house by our old route and get the key. I'm trusting you to guard the prisoners. Give them something to eat and drink, and let them walk around for a bit. Then tie them up again."

Santrock left the cellar, and without meeting her eyes, Winston removed Janice's restraints, then set Brooke free. He pointed to a door. "A restroom—only one at a time."

Janice's hands itched to attack Winston, but she'd get along better if she didn't give the men any trouble. She was disturbed to think that Chief Goodman might also be involved in this plot. She'd always liked him.

Janice and Brooke sat side by side after they went to the restroom and Winston retied their legs. The other man handed each of them a sack from a local fast-food restaurant.

"Do you think he'll do any of those mean things he threatened to do?" Brooke whispered so fearfully that Janice was tempted to throw her food at Winston, but she couldn't antagonize him.

Janice squeezed Brooke's fingers. "Don't worry about it. We've been in worse scrapes than this. I'll think of some way to outsmart them."

While they ate the cheeseburgers and fries and sipped on their large colas, Janice looked around the room for a possible escape. There were two entrances to the cellar, and as she eyed the one where her captors hadn't entered, the man who hadn't spoken until now said in a gutteral voice, "Don't get any bright ideas. That entrance from the house has been blocked off for years. You'd get about three or four yards before you'd be stopped by a cave-in."

After they'd eaten, Winston tied their hands again, and Janice closed her eyes with little hope left. She thought of Lance. If he knew she was gone, he must be very worried and without a clue to where she was.

But refusing to believe that God had abandoned them, Janice started to pray. She recalled the time when Paul and Silas were prisoners in Philippi. When they prayed and sang, God had delivered them to safety. Janice started singing, "God Will Take Care of You," praying the words would comfort Brooke. She expected her captors to silence her, but they had huddled in the entrance to the cellar eating their own lunch.

Lance stood beside the wall of dirt, his hands itching to start digging. He thought he heard someone singing. He turned quickly when he heard someone behind him. Two deputy sheriffs, one of them carrying a shovel, motioned him toward them.

When Lance ran to meet them, one of the deputies whispered, "Baxter said to tell you that they had captured Loren Santrock and another man when they climbed out of the tunnel and into the barn. It's hard to believe that Santrock is the one behind this drug trafficking."

The other officer whispered, "One of our men snuck into the tunnel and learned that there are only two guards, but the sisters are tied. I'm going back to the barn, but my buddy will stay here with you. As soon as Baxter knows you have this message, we'll move into the tunnel and start shooting. Hopefully the two guards will race that way to see what's going on. Start shoveling as soon as you hear our fire and get the women out as soon as possible."

It seemed like hours before the gunfire sounded, but Lance and the deputy were poised to start digging. At the first gunshot, they dug frantically, throwing the dirt over their shoulders and soon broke through the thin layer of soil.

Lance quickly crawled into the cellar. "Thank God," he said when he saw that Janice and Brooke were alone in the room and still alive. He picked Brooke up, still bound, and passed her through the hole to the deputy sheriff. He cut Janice's bonds and helped her through the opening.

"Take them to safety," the deputy said. "I'll stay here to stop Goodman and that other guy if they try to come this way."

Urging Janice ahead of him, Lance picked up Brooke and they ran into the safety of the house. He freed Brooke's hands and feet. Oblivious to the shooting and the commotion going on around them, Lance held Janice's trembling body tightly in his arms, as if he never intended to let her go, which he didn't.

"It's all over now, sweetheart," he whispered. "Peace has finally come to Mountjoy. I intend to spend the rest of my life making you happy."

Janice lifted her face and smiled as Lance sealed his promise with a lingering kiss.

Epilogue

Janice lay with her eyes closed for several minutes after she awakened to the roar of Niagara Falls—a sound that had greeted her ears for the past five days. Today was the last day of their honeymoon. She wished they could stay longer, but Lance needed to be home to start preparations for the opening of school.

Listening to Lance's even breathing, she knew he was still asleep, so she slipped quietly out of bed, wrapped a robe around her and sat in a chair by the window. They had been married a week ago in a simple ceremony at Bethesda Church with only their family members and Henrietta present. Lance had encouraged her to have a more elaborate wedding, but after the trauma of her first year at Stanton, Janice didn't want any more public exposure.

For most of the time during the past week, they'd forgotten Stanton and the events that had almost taken her life. Her narrow escape from death had enhanced their love and increased their gratefulness to be together. They'd be leaving for home in a few hours and Janice's thoughts drifted to the past three months.

The discovery of the meth lab at Mountjoy and the treachery of one of the town's most respected citizens had shocked the residents of Stanton. Four men had been arrested in the drug bust, but Loren Santrock escaped imprisonment when he committed suicide by taking poison. No evidence was found to implicate Albert and Bob Reid in the attempted arson at Mountjoy, so Janice was spared the embarrassment of having her family's name besmirched any more than it already was. The authorities had finally conceded that Santrock had lied to Janice and that the Reids weren't responsible for any of the vandalism at Mountjoy.

A Bio-Hazard unit had cleaned out the meth lab in the basement. Janice and Brooke had spent a day in the hospital undergoing tests to see if their exposure to the meth lab had damaged their health. Fortunately, they had suffered no ill effects.

Sheriff Goodman, disillusioned about his brother's criminal activities, resigned and moved away from Stanton. Miss Banner, too, had disappeared, and no move was made to find her since there was no proof that she had been involved in Santrock's crimes.

During the investigation of Loren Santrock, the authorities had discovered that he had been responsible for the embezzlement attributed to Dale Mallory. Even before that information became known, Dale and Linda had remarried in a private ceremony. They intended to buy Lance's house when he moved to Mountjoy.

Although Lance and Janice had wanted to be married as soon as Janice had escaped her captors, they delayed until Cecil could finish the renovation of Mountjoy. Lance insisted on paying for the work as his wedding gift to Janice. Their wedding reception had been held in the home that looked as it had when her ancestor had built it.

If she wasn't worried about her friend, Maddie, Janice's happiness would be complete. Maddie hadn't returned from Hawaii as scheduled. Her only letter indicated she was investigating the suspicious death of her father, and Janice sensed that her friend was baffled and afraid.

Lance sighed and turned in his sleep until he faced Janice, and she smiled at his disheveled appearance. His fair hair hung over his forehead and she blew a silent kiss in his direction. A year ago she'd never dreamed that she could be so happy.

Not only had she married a man that God must have ordained for her long before she'd ever met him, but she was reconciled with her parents. Leroy and Florence had exceeded her expectations in becoming good citizens and caring parents. She fully expected that in a few years, they could move out of their small apartment and into a home of their own. Now that they had aspirations to improve themselves, she and Lance were willing to help them. Brooke was a frequent visitor at their home, but she still wanted to live at Mountjoy.

Janice looked up to find Lance watching her. "How long have you been awake?" she asked.

"Long enough to realize what day this is and that our paradise is about to end."

Her dark eyes alight with love, in a husky voice filled with emotion, Janice said, "Oh, no! Our paradise is only beginning."

* * * * *

Look for Maddie's story in November 2006,
only from Love Inspired Suspense and Irene Brand!

Dear Reader,

Thanks very much for reading this book, and I pray that it has been a blessing to you.

Since I'm a "from-scratch" type of cook, I wanted to share one of the recipes I mentioned in the book.

PORK CHOPS AND RICE

5-6 boneless pork chops
3 cups boiling water
4 bouillon cubes
1 cup rice
½ cup chopped celery
¼ cup chopped onions
¼ tsp pepper

Brown chops and remove from pan. Add water and bouillon cubes to pan and stir until dissolved. Add rice, celery, onions and pepper and stir. Put chops on top and bake at 300°F for 1 ½ hours.

When you prepare this recipe for your family, I hope you think of me and pray for my writing ministry.

Irene B. Brand

Love Inspired
SUSPENSE
RIVETING INSPIRATIONAL ROMANCE

A Time To Protect

by **Lois Richer**

Nurse Chloe Tanner stopped a would-be assassin
from killing the mayor of Colorado Springs, and it is FBI
agent Brendan Montgomery's job to protect the single
mom. No one said anything about
protecting his own heart....

Faith at the Crossroads: Can faith and love sustain two
families against a diabolical enemy?

Don't miss this first book in the
Faith at the Crossroads series.

On sale January 2006

Available at your favorite retail outlet.

Steeple
Hill®

Love Inspired®

HOME TO YOU

BY

CHERYL WOLVERTON

He'd once pledged to be her friend forever, which was exactly what Meghan O'Halleran needed when a health crisis brought the now jobless woman home. Pastor Cody Ryder wasn't sure why Meghan was back, but he'd do all he could to help his beautiful childhood friend....

On sale January 2006

Available at your favorite retail outlet.

Steeple Hill®

www.SteepleHill.com   LIHTY

e♦HARLEQUIN.com

The Ultimate Destination for Women's Fiction

For **FREE online reading,** visit
www.eHarlequin.com now and enjoy:

Online Reads
Read **Daily** and **Weekly** chapters from
our Internet-exclusive stories by your
favorite authors.

Interactive Novels
Cast your vote to help decide how these
stories unfold...then stay tuned!

Quick Reads
For shorter romantic reads, try our
collection of Poems, Toasts, & More!

Online Read Library
Miss one of our online reads?
Come here to catch up!

Reading Groups
Discuss, share and rave with other
community members!

—— **For great reading online,** ——
visit www.eHarlequin.com today!

INTONL04R

LARGER PRINT BOOKS!

2 FREE LARGER PRINT NOVELS PLUS A FREE MYSTERY GIFT

Love Inspired

Larger print novels are now available...

YES! Please send me 2 FREE LARGER PRINT Love Inspired® novels and my FREE mystery gift. After receiving them, if I don't wish to receive any more books, I can return the shipping statement marked "cancel." If I don't cancel, I will receive 4 brand-new novels every month and be billed just $4.24 per book in the U.S., or $4.99 per book in Canada, plus 25¢ shipping and handling per book and applicable taxes, if any*. That's a savings of over 20% off the cover price! I understand that accepting the 2 free books and gift places me under no obligation to buy anything. I can always return a shipment and cancel at any time. Even if I never buy another book from Steeple Hill, the two free books and gift are mine to keep forever.

121 IDN D733   321 IDN D74F

Name _____ (PLEASE PRINT)

Address _____ Apt. ____

City _____ State/Prov. _____ Zip/Postal Code _____

Signature (if under 18, a parent or guardian must sign)

Order online at www.LoveInspiredBooks.com

Or mail to Steeple Hill Reader Service™:

IN U.S.A.
3010 Walden Ave.
P.O. Box 1867
Buffalo, NY 14240-1867

IN CANADA
P.O. Box 609
Fort Erie, Ontario
L2A 5X3

Are you a current Love Inspired subscriber and want to receive the larger print edition?

Call 1-800-221-5011 today!

* Terms and prices subject to change without notice. NY residents add applicable sales tax. Canadian residents will be charged applicable provincial taxes and GST. This offer is limited to one order per household. All orders subject to approval. Credit or debit balances in a customer's account(s) may be offset by any other outstanding balance owed by or to the customer.

LILPO05

Love Inspired
SUSPENSE
RIVETING INSPIRATIONAL ROMANCE

Even
in the
Darkness

by Shirlee McCoy

Called out of retirement for one final job, former DEA
agent Noah Stone was suspicious of Tori Riley—how
could a vet get tangled up with drug lords? But there
was no time for questions, because an unscrupulous
enemy was threatening Tori's little girl....

On sale January 2006

Available at your favorite retail outlet.

Steeple
Hill®

www.SteepleHill.com

LISED

Love Inspired SUSPENSE

TITLES AVAILABLE NEXT MONTH

Don't miss these two stories in January

A TIME TO PROTECT by Lois Richer
Faith at the Crossroads

When Chloe Tanner witnesses an attempt on Mayor Maxwell Vance's life, she becomes the next target. Agent Brendan Montgomery is assigned to find the mayor's would-be assassin and keep Chloe alive. He's drawn to the single mother, but with a dangerous man on the loose, he can't afford to be distracted.

EVEN IN THE DARKNESS by Shirlee McCoy
A LAKEVIEW novel

Tori Riley would do anything to keep the daughter she gave up for adoption safe from the men who were after her—even depend on former DEA agent Noah Stone. He didn't trust Tori's motives, but there was no time for questions, for every second brought an unscrupulous enemy closer to Tori's daughter....

LISCNM1205